Collisions

By the same author

Contact

Collisions

A Novel by
A. F. N. Clarke

Secker & Warburg
London

First published in England 1986 by
Martin Secker & Warburg Limited
54 Poland Street, London W1V 3DF

Copyright © A. F. N. Clarke 1986

British Library Cataloguing in Publication Data

Clarke, A. F. N.
  Collisions : a novel.
  I. Title
  823'.914[F]   PR6053.L32/

  ISBN 0–436–10015–0

Set in 11/13pt Bembo by
Hewer Text Composition Services, Edinburgh
Printed and bound in Great Britain by Biddles Ltd., Guildford

For my Father

Author's Note

I would like to mention those who, by saving my life, not only gave me a precious gift, but also provided the idea for this novel; the late Sir Alan Parks, his senior registrar Mr Peter Roberts, the surgical team and nursing staff of the London Hospital, Whitechapel, and also Mr R. J. Nicholls and the staff of St Mark's Hospital, City Road, London. My thanks and gratitude to all of them.

A. F. N. Clarke
London

'For in that sleep of death what dreams may come,
When we have shuffled off this mortal coil . . .'

Hamlet

One

SOMETIMES IT LAY DORMANT. Waiting. Watching. Always there. Sometimes it stirred restlessly, causing a moan of discomfort. Sometimes it bucked and kicked inside him, tearing at his inner self, thrashing about, making his frail body jerk and twist, wrenching weak screams from his blue lips.

His vision swam as the attack eased. Ceiling, walls, floor, other beds and white-coated figures drifted blurred and lazy across his weak eyes. A face above him; classical look of professional concern, a trace of pity maybe. Gone in an instant. He found his legs were tucked up under his chin in the foetal position. Thin, bony structures incapable of the use to which they were made. They moved slowly down the bed forcing apart the white sheets – once-white sheets, now stained.

The small, white group in the corner focused briefly into heads and odd-shaped bodies. Every now and then, they glanced in his direction as if looking at a struggling insect. A dangerous insect. A useless, wasted, disappearing body, that became more dangerous with each passing breath. One figure, short, bald and arrogant, adamantly shook its shiny head; it bobbed in and out of focus. The room moved around again. A window temporarily in vision showing dirty grey-green colours, impressionistic daubs on the unrelenting white wall. Two thin figures stood motionless. Elongated heads feeding, nourishing him through a thin proboscis. Every movement brought an exquisite painful sense of relief as the teeth moved inside his arm. The tube wriggled up to the head that wobbled nervously on its thin metal body. Again, the wall moved. A bed, long, shiny, strangely uncomfortable drifted past, and there it was: the unceasing blinking eye that told him he was still here. It sat looking at him unsteadily. He could make it blink to his command. He stared fixedly, and moved his body, and the blinks became erratic. Once, he seemed to remember hearing a strange sound. A long drawn-out vibrant wail from the thing. There had been a lot of noise. Many disconnected voices and hands. He'd been really dangerous to the small white-coated group then.

The scream shook his whole body. It leapt out of his mouth and bounced around the room. The spasm raced through his whole body, twisting it into impossible attitudes, throwing it around the bed like a rag doll. He was amazed by it. Appalled. When it passed, the blinking eye seemed to falter for an instant, then began its erratic tattoo again. Every time he opened his mouth, an incomprehensible sound fell out and lay meaningless on the stained sheets. It was really very simple. Just a relieving stream of fluid. A gentle cold river of relief. Why hold it back, he thought, when it does so much. Even to feel the little puncture and the cold fluid slowly work up his arm, even before the relief, it was nice to know it was on its way.

For a moment he thought the face was back. It could have been. Perhaps it was the shadow of a cloud. Now there's a thought. The second spasm, when it came, was slower than the first. They were like friends you love and hate at the same time. Like the lover who tears into your very lust and deliciously walks away leaving it unsatisfied. He wondered where these thoughts were coming from. Passing the time to the next relief.

There was a head. It was there now. He could make it out through the haze that surrounded it. It was the eyes that gave it away. Piercing blue, with clear whites. Level. Looking into him. The thin nose split the screen and sat on top of a sandy moustache. The mouth beneath was moving, but what was it saying? Where had the sound gone? He hadn't heard any sound for some time now. Why was that? He shook his head and the head nodded. It came closer. He could smell coffee and feel the warm puffs of breath on his face. Suddenly the sound was there jarringly clear.

'You're being transferred. Civilian hospital. They are going to operate.' A pause. The eyes shifted sideways. When they returned they weren't looking straight anymore. The mouth started to move again and he watched that. 'You'll be OK. Don't worry.' The mouth closed like a trap door and moved out of focus. Yes. He thought. Fine. But where is the relief? That's all I want.

Another face. The first face looking different. Happier. Smiling slightly. Then the cold rush up his arm. The tantalizing promise of liberation from the constraint of the spasms. The eyes could focus properly then. For a short while. Before sleep closed them. For a short while. It had reached the shoulder and was starting down into the rest of the system. Spreading now, warming through. Up the neck into the head. Down into the body. Calming. Controlling. The haze started to lift. The first object to leap suddenly into sharp focus blinked steadily, comfortingly at him. The green line, blipping happily away, almost smiling. Now the room stayed still. He could control them now. Choose where to look next. They were all familiar. The other three beds with their array of gadgetry securely, rigidly screwed to the wall. White walls. White ceiling. Grey and white floor. The window no longer impressionistic. Grey buildings against a grey sky. Foreground, a green park. They would be there again later. Much later. After the sleep and the next nightmare ride.

There seemed to be a lot of movement around and about him. It was difficult to concentrate because his eyes wanted to close. Waves of peaceful blackness kept sweeping in, blanking out the activity. It was annoying. Very annoying. Most other times he was glad of the respite of sleep. Most other times, there was little to see, little he wanted to see. He had given up wanting to watch things some time ago. How long? It didn't

3

matter. Perhaps . . . No, definitely, it didn't. Time had nothing to do with anything. Time was the space between waking and nightmare, before the relieving injection. He knew what it was now. He always knew what it was afterwards. Never before.

Now it was the movement he wanted to watch. It wasn't the morbid fascination of the brain-damaged cabbage who'd raged through his last days; nor was it like the burnt excuse for a human body that had whimpered and moaned into permanent oblivion. It was those things he had ceased to watch. Ceased to be moved by. No, this was different. This was something new and he didn't want to miss it. He didn't want to miss it because it was him they were moving. All the attention was directed at his bed. He just happened to be on it. But it was interesting to watch. And he didn't want to miss any of it. There seemed to be a lot of packing. A bit like moving house, but that was ridiculous because he had nothing. No possessions and few clothes. But then they were there in that funny little plastic carrier bag. Off-green with gold writing, strangely out of place here in this unreal world. He read the writing. Harrods. His eyes wanted to close but his brain wanted to laugh. The eyes flickered open again and watched as a brown cardboard box was placed on the end of his bed. It was strange that it didn't touch his feet. Then he found them in their usual place, up underneath his chin.

The box sat accusingly waiting for comment. Clear plastic containers full of blood peeked self-consciously over the top. A lid of the box trying to prevent them from seeing their new home. He stared at it. It stared back. A conversation without end. The sense of movement continued. It flowed, ebbed, swirled around him. It was intoxicating. There seemed to be no rational thought behind the movements. It was a chaotic, organized maelstrom. Centred around his bed. There was no discussion. No talk of any sort, just a concentration. Charts appeared and disappeared into large official-looking envelopes. They reappeared in someone else's hands and, with a shake of the head, guiltily vanished into another envelope that was

4

quickly rushed away. X-Ray pictures came and went, some looking vaguely over-exposed. He enjoyed watching all this from his place of privilege; the lone spectator in an auditorium full of empty seats.

He must have slept. He knew he must have slept because suddenly the nightmare was back and the scenery had changed. This time the scenery bucked and swayed and lurched, so that his body danced on the moving bed. The torturer was at work again deep in his bowels. Thumbscrews this time. Twisting, tightening, harder, more viciously. The screams were soundless and there in the haze of vision was a different face. A young quizzical face with big brown eyes and soft black hair that blurred at the edges. It swam out of sight with the next lurch-induced spasm. When it returned he could see the face staring down at an object on the bed. It was a blood bag. He knew it was. She picked it up slowly and placed it back on a hook, the tube tightening, twisting the needle in his arm. The eyes held no apology.

Because time held no value he couldn't tell, and indeed was oblivious to, the extent of the journey. It was only the sudden lack of movement that told him that a new set of sensations were on the way. The sensations were different, that was for sure. His vision now took on a strobe effect. A greatly interrupted strobe with large blank areas. The spasms ceased to be of any consequence. In fact they were an annoyance because they prevented him from filling in the blanks. The sounds were there now, but disjointed, as if somebody kept on pulling the plug. It was frustrating. Once he was travelling fast down what seemed to be a narrow tunnel, swaying round corners. He could see people blurring past, some staring, others walking slowly. Suddenly they stopped and an elderly face peered into his. It gave a toothless grin and then was gone as they moved off down another tunnel. Then he was in a large room. With curtains. Chintzy curtains. The walls were a creamy colour. He was being moved. Pushed. Rolled. The spasms were constant. Continuous.

A voice from the distance said very firmly and loudly. 'See you in the theatre in fifteen minutes.' He wanted to laugh. He didn't want to go to the theatre. He wanted to sleep. The movement no longer held any fascination. He felt tired. Very tired. Then it began all over again. Down more long tunnels. Dull lights drifted past silhouetting the two men pushing the bed. Men? Bed? He didn't know. He didn't really know. He just assumed. An assumption based on remembrance, a flickering image of what had been that slyly knelt at the back of his mind, refusing to come out into the light. Suddenly into a brightly-lit room. Figures bending over him. Murmuring. 'Sleep now. Just relax.' Yes please, he thought. Sleep. The cold fluid raced up his arm. Cold. It was ice cold, almost painful. It raced up into oblivion.

It was a voice from the distance. A strange singsong noise. A gentle murmur on the breeze. He wondered what it was saying. The sounds needed analysing, distilling down into their component forms and reconstructing. There was no picture. Just a white haze like a recently-emptied bottle of milk. The soft voice came from the centre of this creamy filter. He was reconstructing the sounds now, his mind working methodically. Slowly. Carefully. Just his mind.

'Come on my pretty. That's right. Grow for me. Be beautiful.'

He was beginning to locate the strange cadence in the voice now. It had a freshness. The smell of the open skies and sun. Of sea and music. An odd, driving, rhythmic music. Yes, it was there somewhere and he struggled to fathom it out. Gradually the creamy mist was beginning to clear. The water washing the inside of the bottle, slowly, gently swirling the opaque cloudiness away. There was a lot of light. Strong shafts of brilliant light. It lanced down onto him and the voice continued soft and rhythmic. He must have been noticed, because the voice suddenly seemed to be directed at him.

'Hello Captain.' The voice pronounced the last word

'Cupten'. Now it was easy to locate. Now he was beginning to see. He wasn't surprised when a black face came into view. It may have been that the face was silhouetted against the bright streaming light, but he knew it was black. A certain knowledge. Bright white teeth flashed a smile. The voice continued, soft and gentle, soothing.

'Come to join us now.' The face turned. 'Look my pretty, the Captain's come to see you.' The voice – it was female – seemed to grow arms and a body. It was shocking to see. He hadn't expected that. Quite what he had expected he didn't know, but it wasn't a normal body. He felt cheated, sold out, and the thought depressed him. He felt he was an unconnected mind watching an unconnected voice, and the realization that he too might have a body was loathsome. The initial impression had been so pleasant, so idyllic. Now with the certainty that he was still confined to his body he felt depressed. With the depression came the sensations. He was afraid at first, wondering if they would be the same as before. He didn't want that. The voice continued:

'The Captain's been away for a while but he's back now.' The plant pot she held seemed bored by the conversation. The geranium dropped a petal or two with the movement as it was replaced on the window sill. Window sill? Plant? Then the bright light has to be sun. Clever, he thought. Very clever.

'How are you Captain?' It was not really a question. He had no answer anyway. What did intrigue him was where had he been. And what had he been doing? It seemed pointless to have been somewhere and not remember it.

'I think sister's going to be pleased.' She giggled. An odd out-of-place sound. Not unpleasant, just odd. Then she was gone, out of his limited vision.

He couldn't see very much but what amazed him was that he could control the eye movements this time. Make a decision and the eyes moved across slowly to find another object. The next things to focus on were all too familiar. Tall metal bodies with the elongated heads. Three of them.

Standing silent sentinels behind him. It was comforting, like having a favourite teddy-bear in bed. Familiar and comforting. He noticed also that his body was semi-reclining. So he could see down the bed. It was a bed. Yes, this was very different from before. There were several things that were not pleasant, though. His throat felt enlarged and swallowing was a problem. It could have been the plastic tube that snaked up over the sheet and vanished from sight under his chin. That's got to go, he thought, and was surprised at the rationality of the thought. He hadn't had to try to think of that. Think? He hadn't actually thought for a long time. So this was something new. So was the tightness around his lower chest and abdomen. From his position he could just see a large white plastic covering the whole of his stomach area. It didn't seem to be part of him at all. Neither did the tubes that crept under the bandage and must have disappeared into him. Further exploration of his sensations revealed a disturbing fact. He couldn't actually move. Or he thought he couldn't. He could just. Only tiny insignificant movements. Twitches really, small flutterings on the surface of his skin. Impossible to detect without concentration.

Suddenly there was another figure beside the bed. He couldn't see it too clearly because it was to the right of his peripheral vision.

'Time for your blood pressure.' Another female voice. Not like the first. Caucasian this one. He thought. He was doing a lot of thinking all of a sudden. And that's OK too. Another thought. This was getting to be a habit. 'And temperature.' No, not there, he thought. 'Under your arm I think.' Thank God. Where did he come from? Too much thinking now. Becoming a nuisance, an intrusion on all the pleasant new sensations. Relax, he told himself, and tried to smile. His body already was. Then try the mind, what's left of it.

'That seems fine.' The voice tried to sound convincing. He didn't mind.

From behind his eyes the creeping blackness drifted up and around him. He didn't want it. He tried to keep it out. To stay

8

awake and enjoy the sensations. Explore the new experiences. But it crept through, unrelenting.

There were long moments between the darkness and the daylight. There were long moments of both. Everything seemed to take a long time. It was in complete contrast to the time before when time itself was unimportant. Gradually there was a frustration creeping in. An impatience. Several times since the time he thought of as the beginning of his 'borrowed' time, he'd had visitors. He knew that they were trying, and that it was difficult for them, but he felt they intruded. To say he wasn't glad to see his wife would be ungenerous, but basically true. The person he most looked forward to seeing was his surgeon. His own selfishly-regarded body mechanic.

The last visit was from his parents. Barely-concealed tears behind loving eyes. Tremble of the chin and faltering voice. He didn't want that. He was OK. Now. He knew it. The fact that he looked like something out of Belsen was inconsequential. He wanted to get on with the rebuilding programme. That was the prime concern. First to concentrate on basic movement. When the physiotherapist dragged him, reluctant and fearful, from his bed, he was terrified. He was completely incapable. A useless, stumbling object, trying desperately to make his limbs obey his commands. They didn't want to.

'What do you expect,' they had said. 'You haven't exactly had a head cold.' Well, that was true, but it didn't alter the fact that he felt undignified and useless. What about the other morning? He'd woken up to the thrill of his first erection for some time, firstly to experience the pain as his penis grew up the catheter and, secondly, to see the look of amused disbelief on the face of the young nurse. The pain as the erection rapidly disappeared was almost unbearable, the whole experience left him confused and depressed.

Sometimes he regarded his body with total revulsion. Looking down at the translucent skin showing the blue veins starkly against the thin bone of his arms and legs. The old scars, once proudly worn, became ugly smooth purple slashes, hairs were ridiculous foliage on a barren landscape. He looked at his skeletal face covered with stubble while the now irritating sound of the black girl's voice sang in his ear.

'First shave Captain. I do this one. You do it tomorrow.'

Christ was there no end? He stared into the mirror the whole time it took her to carefully remove every trace of beard, talking all the while. He didn't like the version afterwards either; the sunken face, cheekbones standing out as if they didn't belong, teeth seeming to force out his lips, unnaturally. A pulse throbbed at his temple. He tried to control it, but it continued, mocking him. The eyes were the things that really got to him. Piercing blue orbs with a tiny black dot in the centre showing nothing at all. Just staring back at him curiously, boring into him so that he had to look away.

He'd seen his wife look away too. She couldn't stand the sight of the creature either. She sat at the side of the bed, coyly almost, as if their conversation was so private that even the chance of being overheard was too much. He wondered idly what anybody else would make of it even if they bothered to listen. She sat picking nervously at a loose thread on her dress, Eyes downcast. They flickered nervously towards him.

'Your parents told me they would visit on Thursday.' He nodded. The voice still wasn't too strong and that provided the excuse to avoid any communication. He wondered what day it was today and decided pretty rapidly that it really didn't matter. One day was exactly the same as another. Sometimes the routine changed. Yes. Wednesdays, they were important. Not the fact that it followed Tuesday or came before Thursday. Not that it was any part of the seven-day cycle, just because Wednesday provided a spectacle. It was the day the crowds turned up to watch the Christians being thrown to the lions, so to speak. It was the day of the Operations. The preparations began the night before. Little hand-written notices appeared on the beds of the doomed. 'Nil by mouth.'

Short and to the point. Then on the day, the all important 'list'. The list determined the order of the sentencing. The chosen were dealt with expertly, cleaned, injected. And, when suitably incoherent, wrapped and wheeled away to the anonymous figure in the green gown and mask. The mood was always the same. Commiserations from the experienced to those about to suffer. It was a pleasing game played by everyone in the ward. Yes, Wednesdays were good.

What wasn't good was that he hadn't eaten for so long he'd forgotten what it was like. The thought struck him as he half-listened to his wife, whilst watching the woman by the bed opposite hand over a food parcel. The similarities to a prison were unbelievable sometimes. He watched as the man, half his head shaved for a minor brain operation, childishly opened the plastic container and guiltily took a bite of the large, fresh, ham roll. With mustard. It must be with mustard, he thought, watching the roll disappear rapidly into the vacuous face.

'David, are you listening? Am I tiring you? Do you want to sleep? Shall I go?'

He wrenched his eyes away from the feast and tried to smile lovingly. It didn't work. It probably came out as a grimace. He shook his head. He didn't want her to go. He didn't want her to go because he felt odd without anybody while the rest of the beds were swarming with people. Wait until the bell, he thought.

'I'll wait till the bell then. I just didn't want to tire you.'

She was attractive. Very attractive. Long blonde hair. Traditional English peaches-and-cream complexion with a Nordic line to her face, high cheekbones, strong jaw-line. He examined her body. Why he should bother he didn't know. He knew it intimately. Medium-sized firm breasts. Large aureoles and pleasing nipples. Her hips flowed outwards from the narrow waist separating into long well-proportioned legs. The space between them. Ah yes! The space between. Now that was another matter.

The man opposite had nearly finished a second roll. His wife watched him with obvious satisfaction. Like watching a dog perform a favourite trick. He grinned at her, some of the sandwich falling onto his chest. She leaned across and wiped it away. Smiling. Indulgent.

Jenny was talking again.

'I had to take the car in for servicing.' Pause. 'The dog's fine.'

He'd forgotten he had a dog – or a car, for that matter. Funny, the things that disappear into the back of the mind. Unimportant things. Well, perhaps he could have remembered the dog. He turned back to Jenny. She was crossing one leg over the other and he caught a glimpse of white, high up. He felt a stirring in his groin, a warm glow, an animal instinct too long suppressed. It was very nice, he thought. How much nicer to have the feeling transferred to action and satisfaction. If Jenny knew what he was thinking it didn't show. She was picking at another loose thread. She glanced up as the tea-trolley came around. The little old lady looked across at him and smiled.

'You going to have some?' He smiled and nodded. This was the signal that the bell was about to ring. End of which round?

'I'll be back on Monday.' Jenny, preparing herself to leave. He wondered if perhaps she felt the same way he did. That these visits were a trial, a bore. The sharp clanging broke in on his thoughts and he caught the imperceptible rise of her shoulders and brief sigh of relief. She obviously did think the same way. They really ought to stop the pretence, but he was relieved because he could settle down and get on with the business in hand.

Jenny leaned over and kissed him softly. He caught the faint smell of Chanel. It always was Chanel. Her hair brushed his face and the smell changed to the clean smell of shampoo. The ends tickled his nose. It was annoying. She straightened up and with a wave swayed elegantly between the beds and out of sight. He could see some of the other inmates staring appreciatively. He sipped his tea slowly. Swallowing was still a difficulty. That tube they had stuck up his nose and down his throat had done untold damage to the sensitive tissues. The tea was terrible as well, but he wasn't going to stop now. Make them believe he could handle it, make them step up the pace. He wanted, needed, food. That was the next milestone: to be fed. He looked back to the man opposite, who was alone now, lying back on the pillows looking a little lost. The crumbs were still on the stubble of his chin.

'Blood pressure again, Captain.' The young nurse standing beside his bed. This time he was going to say something. She bent to listen to his mumble and straightened again. She smiled. It was a nice smile, full of big straight white teeth. 'OK, I'll call you David from now on.' He listened to the sound of the little air bladder. It made a soft rude noise as she squeezed the rubber in the palm of her hand. There was something very sensual about the way she did it. She stopped pumping, looked at the gauge for a moment, then let the air slowly out, watching the gauge and listening through her stethoscope. How many times had he seen this exercise? It was unimportant, like the car, a daily ritual. The daily ritual. His daily ritual. The slow exhausting climb back to a sense of normality. At first it had been a game, once the shock of seeing himself had worn off. Now he was bored, angered and frustrated by it. The limits he set himself each day seemed petty and insignificant. A struggle to the end of the next bed amid applause from the other inmates yesterday; today, four steps further, then back to collapse into the chair beside the bed. Pathetic.

Then there were the nights. The long black nights while he listened to the night nurse sitting at a table at the end of his bed, listened to her flicking the pages of magazines. Tensing himself for each flick he knew was coming. When the flicking pages stopped, there was the scrape of the chair and the swish of starched apron as she moved around the ward like a jailer, rubber-soled shoes making a sharp low squeaking sound on the floor. Then back to the flicking pages. Sometimes, when the pages stopped, there was a silence and then soft snoring.

Other sounds broke the night up into sections. Groans and

13

moans. The odd cry of pain. The nights were long. There was also the fear that going to sleep would be the last one. And yet it was so pleasant, so very pleasant, to be able to close the eyes and drft away. Childlike. Eventually of course the body took over and just switched into autopilot. Down came the shutters and before he knew it somebody was shaking him, the curtains being dragged back, the light temporarily hurting his eyes. It was then, when he knew it was safe, that he really wanted to go to sleep. But they wouldn't let him. The daily ritual was always like this.

'Have you been sleeping well dear?' His mother's concern. The same question every time. Always answered by a nod of the head. His father always sat slightly embarrassed by the whole thing. He felt sorry for him having to be dragged here to sit next to an uncommunicative creature while Mother prattled away. That was the weekly ritual. God, how he hated rituals. Forced to accept it. Pinned to bed and force-fed doses of concern. Going down like castor oil – no, what was it they had had as children? Little pills shaped like rubber balls. Halibut oil. The trick at boarding-school was to make some poor idiot put it in his porridge on the pretext that it killed the taste. He could remember it happening to him. It had made him sick, right there at the breakfast table while everybody watched and laughed. The master in charge that morning had tried to make him eat it – the porridge, the pill and his vomit. His parents used to pay vast sums of money a year for him to have that privilege. From then on, he'd practised the deception himself. But he hadn't seen anybody else vomit at the table. They had all managed to make it out of the room. He'd felt that failure for years.

The stitches came out easily. Easily, that is, if you happened to be the person with the tweezers and scissors. Each one of the eighteen lengths of twine was snipped, grasped and pulled firmly through his skin, each one feeling like a sharp hot skewer. Maybe it would be a good idea to have someone who was experienced, he told himself. He looked at the girl, now

14

bent concentrating over the next stitch. Every time she removed one, she held it aloft in triumph.

'I've never done this before,' she'd told him as she settled the kidney dish on the side of the bed, her face flushed with anticipation and eagerness. He thought maybe her large bosom got in the way of her vision. It wobbled under the uniform, nipples standing out in excitement as she set to work. At first she'd moved the sheet down too far exposing part of his semi-erect penis. He'd been fantasizing. She coloured and the nipples became more evident. He thought he could smell her sex and then told himself he was imagining things now, hallucinating. During the last week, his erections had been frequent and almost painful. It was a sure sign of the return of his normality.

'There, all done now.' She dabbed at some spots of blood, counted all the stitches now resting in the kidney dish and contentedly smiled at him. He looked at her face for the first time and noticed the spots. Large white ones. Two on her chin. Her hair was somewhat like wire and eyes peered myopically at him through thick glasses. The erection had vanished with the first pull of the stitches and there was no chance of it surfacing again. Not just yet anyway.

The surgeon had been encouraging. First the drips, catheters and other various tubes had disappeared. Food had been allowed, on which he had gorged himself and suffered stomach ache for days after. Now the stitches. He himself was not satisfied. The trappings of illness, the props, had been removed but it still left the body. The emaciated corpse-like creature. A living Lowry, what about that? A couple of his visitors had been colleagues. All arrogance, strutting into the ward in uniform, to be struck dumb at their first sight of him. Good, he'd thought at the time. At least somebody else seemed to agree that he was a mess. Now it was time to get out.

Two

THE TERRAIN was a strange contrast to the Constable sky. Various shades of brown, dirty green and sandy colours. Gorse, poor heather and moorland scrub. On the tops of the flat-topped hills, spiky pine trees stood guardians. He dragged his feet up the stony sandy slope one after the other, breath coming in huge rasping pants that shuddered through his chest. Lungs grasping at the air, sucking it dry of oxygen, forcing it into the arteries and pumping it to the labouring legs. Not enough, never enough, they screamed back to his swimming head. Bollocks, he screamed back at them, and forced the legs to move up the slope and over the ridge at the top.

The pressure eased as the lungs sensed a temporary lull in effort. The oxygen moved around, catching up now. The dog stood at the top wondering what all the fuss was about, his ears pricked forward, tongue lolling sideways out of his mouth pink against his shiny black coat. He noted that they were not stopping and happily bounded away to find the next slope. He liked this game. It had been a long time since he had played it and this was great fun. He looked back at his playmate, watching the two legs struggling across the sand, thinking that four was better than two any day. That was just what the owner of the two legs was thinking. Wondering what the dog was thinking and thinking that he was probably thinking just this. Thinking was what made the effort easier. Forget about

16

the pain and discomfort, forget that with each stride every nerve and tissue screamed for relief. Think about anything. Think about the dog thinking of him.

He ran on, tripping sometimes on the uneven surface, nearly falling. Through the first pain barrier. It became a little easier then. A sort of numbness that spread through him. For a short time, before the second pain barrier. This was the worst. This, he told himself, was the testing time, the moment of absolute truth of endeavour, the time to stop. Cease. Desist. The time when the objective no longer seemed important. This was the crucial time and he steeled himself waiting for it.

'Why bother?' Jenny had said testily. 'Why go so hard? You don't give yourself a chance,' as he sat dripping, grey and exhausted in the kitchen, weak and light-headed. There was little point in answering. Unless you really understood the drive, the will to survive, the will to win, it was no good discussing it. He'd been through it many times before.

He thought of this as he struggled through the second pain barrier. Fought it. Controlled it. Beat it as the dog ran obliviously, happily, on.

'You'll kill yourself. You nearly died anyway and now you want to kill yourself.' Shut up, woman, he thought. He shouted the thought now, listening to it bouncing away over the hill and down into the valley beyond. He shouted it again and again. He shouted it into her face and watched as the shock hit her like a physical blow. He ran on, feeling the power suddenly surge through him. He ran on shouting, the dog cantering beside him barking in accompaniment. It was a wild excitement and it lasted until the next hill, the next exquisite torture. Then the shouting stopped and the gasping started again.

'If you want to expend energy, then mow the lawn.' That's the answer. Of course, why didn't he think of that. Stand behind the Flymo on a Saturday afternoon. After washing the car, of course. The gasping became harder. The thinking started to break up. No, don't let it, he told himself. Just this one and then back in. Just this one. This is one more than the day before yesterday. This one for today. And tomorrow. Force it. Push it. It's what you are used to. You've done it often enough. He grunted, gasped and moaned up the hill. Cursed. Groaned. Swore. The dog began to look concerned. At last the top. The blissful joy of the top of the hill and the gentle run back. Down all the way now, letting the wind drive into his face, flicking the sweat away.

'For Christ's sake look at you.' Jenny stating the obvious again, he thought. Don't answer. He climbed the stairs and lay soaking in the bath watching the muscles quiver from the exertion.

Later, much later, lying in bed, he could feel his heart getting to grips with the exertion. He lay feeling every portion of his internal body. He was getting to know it intimately now, getting to know every fluctuation in his heart-beat. In his breathing. In his defecatory functions. He listened to the gurgling of what was left of his intestines, just the small bowel, doing its best to cope, to do the job of two. He lay in bed feeling, cajoling, reassuring his body. Deceiving it slightly, maybe. Well, just a little. Not enough to do any harm. He hoped. It became an exciting game that he played every day. Pushing the extremities. Forcing the barriers. Extending the parameters until there were no boundaries. Only the boundaries of the mind. He firmly believed that, and he was going to prove it. There was no time to think of anything else except this.

He turned his head as Jenny came into the bedroom. She slowly took off her dressing gown and was naked beneath. She stood teasing him. He felt himself rising and watched as she bent over to pick up an item of discarded clothing. He noticed the piece of white string and felt an almost overpowering sense of anger. Jenny slipped into a pair of knickers and crept into bed beside him.

'It's just as well you are so tired from running.' She sounded smug. He wanted to rip the thing out and plunge his penis into her. Hurt her. Force her. Show her. He leaned over, kissed her and turned his back. He could feel her breasts and hard nipples against his back. A leg snaked over his and she pressed herself close into his body. He could feel her warmth and the soft fluttering of her breath against his skin.

The valley was closely forested. From where he stood he could make out the tell-tale movements. The girl beside him murmured softly, but he didn't understand what she said. His concentration was on the movement in the valley. He dropped the binoculars and hefted the M16 in his hand. The girl murmured something else and this time he looked down at her. She smiled and offered him a breast. He declined and turned back to watch the valley. It had moved closer. Much closer. The first few rounds smacked into the earth at his feet. He didn't move. From beside him came a short scream. He looked down and saw the girl clutching her stomach, trying to stop her entrails from falling out onto the road. She watched horrified as the blood pumped out from between her fingers, spewing upwards, covering her breasts, and downwards, disappearing into her mass of black pubic hair. He watched unmoved. Fascinated, slightly disappointed. He had been going to screw her after this. He shrugged and turned back as the first wave broke cover and charged. The first three he cut down with a single burst, the lead man's head vanishing in a cloud of red and grey tissue. Others charged. He cut them down. He was laughing now, an insane laughter, a maniacal laugh. It filled the air, cut through the gunfire, drowned out everything else. He kept firing, filling every living body he could see with copper-covered lead-filled rounds. Watching the blood and the gore with pleasure. Wallowing in it, bathing in it.

The scene changed suddenly, without warning. A brilliantly-lit bedroom. He was on the bed, naked. The same girl was next to him. She was smiling, pointing, giggling. He watched as she pushed her entrails back into the cavity that had been her abdomen. He wanted to throw up. She would let him. She took his hand and made him push the entrails in. He wanted to scream, but couldn't. She moved and sat on top of him

19

clutching handfuls of her own gut, making cooing sounds, moving upwards until her open vagina was above his face. A hand shot out and grabbed him by the throat. Suddenly there was no woman, no bedroom, no entrails. They had him. They had him stripped naked and were advancing, knives glistening in the sunlight. Next to him another man lay, his manhood cut off and sewn into his mouth. He screamed this time. He screamed and screamed.

The sheets were soaking and he was sitting up wild-eyed, screaming, terrified. Jenny stood at the far side of the room, crying, cowering. He heard the sound from a distance and watched the strange scene. The sound had dropped to a whimper and he found himself shaking uncontrollably. There was the smell of urine in the room. The smell was close by. It came from him. He was sitting in it. He was covered in it. The bed was covered in it.

He waited until the shaking had subsided and got out of bed. Jenny moved away from him crying and afraid. He passed her and went into the bathroom. He lay in the bath listening to the sounds of Jenny clearing up the mess. Later she came in and joined him. She had calmed down. She was smiling. Naked and smiling. She climbed into the bath. She felt for him under the water, found him and pressed and stroked him into a full erection. He felt himself almost bursting. She stood up and settled herself down on top of him. He opened his eyes. The bath was red with blood. He was covered by entrails. The girl sat on him laughing, letting her guts fall over his face, smothering him. She forced his penis into her, grinding, shouting in triumph now. He fought. Tried to fight. Tried to cry out. Suddenly the room was filled with the sound of gunfire. He was running, dodging, shouting for his men to take cover. The noise was deafening. The acrid smell of cordite and death hung close on the air, cloying and sickly. They weren't going to make it. He was sure now. And it angered him. He screamed in anger. Swore. Fought. Ran.

'It's OK darling. It's OK. It's only a dream. It's OK.'

What is? He wanted to know. He looked. The room was the same. He tested the smell. It was faintly like that of a pine forest. He looked at Jenny. She lay beside him propped up on one elbow, a concerned look on her sleepy face. Where was the other girl?

'I don't know what you're talking about darling.' Her voice was faintly mocking. 'You've been dreaming. That's all.'

A dream? It is impossible to dream like that, he thought. It can't be. What about . . . He felt down between his legs. The erection was still there and now a damp sticky area around his testicles and the top of his penis. It was everywhere. He shuddered momentarily and quickly turned over to hide the evidence.

'Are you OK now?' He nodded and settled down. Jenny lay back and was soon asleep, the gentle rhythmic sound of her breathing barely audible against the sounds of the night, the odd car on the road, the occasional aeroplane high overhead. He lay still, shaken by the clarity of the dream. He could replay it in his mind. Every detail fresh, stark. Frighteningly real. Sleep wouldn't come now. He knew it wouldn't. He would lie here until the dawn let the light in through the bedroom window. He would lie afraid of sleep. Afraid that they would come for him again and that this time it would be real. It was stupid, he had said to himself before. Really stupid. A ridiculous dream that had no basis in anything real. And yet it had been so real. Sometimes he looked across the room and saw the frightening shapes looming at him out of the darkness. It had required an effort of will to make himself face the objects, make himself realize they were only clothes hanging at odd angles behind the door, or maybe the tree outside casting an odd shadow when the moon happened to be in that particular quadrant.

Jenny lay sleeping, quietly, restfully. He was angry. Envious. Downstairs, the dog moved about the kitchen, his claws making clicking sounds on the floor. What does a dog dream? he thought by way of changing the dangerous mood. Where does he go in his doggy dreams? Maybe he'd like to

swop. Come and lie here. Unable to make love. Only to lie in
fear of sleep itself.

The wind outside stirred the tree and moved the shadows.
Strange different shapes appeared and disappeared. Ghouls,
goblins and ghosts played around the childlike remembrances
of his mind. Of his adult mind, he kept telling himself, his
adult mind.

He must have slept for a short while, because suddenly he was
aware of light in the room. At first the fear rose up and
threatened to choke him, then his eyes cleared and he saw the
room, the early morning light bringing all the old familiar
objects into perspective. Jenny lay half uncovered, sprawled
over the bed. He found himself screwed up against the wall,
his legs drawn up tight under his chin in a well-remembered
position. Slowly he unwound and stretched. His mouth tasted
of bad onions. There was the trace of sweat on his forehead
and he could smell it on the sheets. He looked over Jenny's
body. The night had been warm and she too smelt faintly of
sweat. Her arm was stretched up behind her head showing the
little black hairs in her armpit. Her breasts still stood firm, but
the nipples were wrinkled and flat.

She moved and sighed softly as he stretched out, relieving
the cramped muscles, stretching the scarred abdomen, feeling
the stitched-up flesh tighten against itself. He gently leaned
over and touched his fingers very lightly over the tip of her
nipple. She didn't stir. He felt the soft, puckered skin and
detected a slight firming of the surface. He took his hand away
and stared objectively at her. He moved the sheet down,
exposing her flat stomach, the smooth flesh. The promise that
lay beneath the white nylon. All this laid out waiting. All this
ready for the taking. Why didn't he? He didn't know. He
thought of the years they had been married. The years he'd
tried to awaken her sexually. The years of failure. The years of
frustration.

He threw back the bedclothes, climbed roughly over her
and went down to the kitchen. Jenny opened her eyes and

22

watched him go. He felt her gaze as he left the room. The dog greeted him like an old pal, then made straight for the door, waiting there tail wagging until it was opened and he could wander casually outside and greet the morning with his customary cocked leg.

The kettle whistled shrilly, dragging his gaze from the garden and the first rays of the late summer sun. Sitting down with the mug of hot sweet tea he continued to stare out, watching the dog.

'Thanks.' Jenny said, walking past and pouring herself a cup. He didn't reply. 'That was some dream you had last night.'

He got up and poured himself another mug, ignoring her. It was over and he didn't want any reminders. There were plenty of those without her interfering. The dog had finished his early-morning promenade and was standing whining outside. Jenny let him in and stood leaning against the back door. She did that very well – pose. He thought she should have considered a career as a model. But then models had to have something else going for them. A sense of cunning, or awareness. That was something Jenny didn't have.

'Aren't you going to say anything?' The tone was faintly challenging. Only faintly. She didn't have it in her to be aggressive. It was pathetic when she tried. A sort of soft whimper against the might of a typhoon. He ignored her and went to sit in the lounge amongst the lurid colours some fellow at the ministry thought was good taste. Cheap anyway. She followed him in and sat down opposite. The one thing she did know was that her body made him react. Not right now, he decided, staring dispassionately as she allowed a breast to be revealed, not now. Now he was bored with the charade.

The dog stood at the door questioningly. Looking from one to the other. He didn't have to bother with the complexities of everyday human existence. He just ate, slept, played, pissed and generally made himself available to be patted and stroked. Like now, as he sidled up to Jenny. She idly let a hand fall onto the dog's back then moved it up till she found an ear to play with. The dog sat contentedly, staring smugly across the room.

He decided he didn't really like dogs, especially when they behaved like this. The dog must have sensed the feeling, for he got up and sauntered over, crawling under his legs and lying down with a gentle growl. Jenny looked at them both, holding her mug in both hands, cupping it as if to warm them. That's silly, he thought. It's summer. Then considered the thought a little trite, if not petulant. She was still damn pretty, even at this hour of the morning. Yes, the dream had troubled him. It was a little unnerving.

'I thought so. You seemed very upset. Kept shouting take cover or something like that.' She seemed satisfied at his little concession. The atmosphere changed. Smoothed. Calmed. The pressure to explain removed.

They both sat staring at each other sipping their tea. Rather like boxers trying to gain a psychological advantage. He wasn't going to play this game either. The eyes defocused and he stared into the middle distance. It was dangerous here in no man's land. The reality of familiar objects vanished. A blurred background made way for imagined images to play upon the stage of his mind. He turned and stared out of the window at the tree. It looked very different from this angle. Very old and comforting. Its branches majestically protective, moving gently with the wind that rustled the leaves. Old. Wise. Unconcerned.

'What are you going to do? Apart from the fitness obsession.' She wasn't looking at him, just trying to provoke a reply. He didn't rise to the bait. Besides, he didn't know. Not yet. The important thing was the body. Call it an obsession but that was the primary concern. Without it he was nothing. The rest would come later. The remark angered him. It was unnecessary, flippant, he thought. He still had plenty of leave left. Christ, even he was beginning to think in an entirely defeated way. As if his entire life depended on what he was going to do tomorrow. Who the hell cared anyway?

He got up and walked outside into the garden. The sun was

24

breaking over the horizon now, casting long shadows that shortened dramatically. His Commanding Officer had been to see him in hospital only a few weeks ago. 'Don't worry. Take your time. There's no rush.' There was the answer. No rush.

The grass bent over as he walked, springing slowly back, hampered by the dew. He walked to the end of the garden, forcing his way through the long grass and the nettles, feeling the sting and the wetness, enjoying the sensations. He stood looking back at the house. The red brick box, designed by some bored civil servant with nothing better to occupy his time. He could see Jenny standing at the door making signs. Looking embarrassed. He didn't care. Why should he? He knew he didn't have a stitch on and it didn't bother him. It was his garden and he would do what the hell he liked in his own garden.

The dog joined him and snuffled through the long grass. The two of them crawled along, making narrow tunnels through the grass. Memories of childhood and the thrill of the imagined chase. Somewhere behind, the enemy, in the guise of his best friend, hunting, stalking him. The dog stopped in front of him, warning of a possible threat ahead. He stopped and watched while the dog sniffed and carefully put one paw in front of the other. The sensitive nose bored slowly ahead and then, the coast clear, the other paws followed in rapid succession. He followed the dog, trusting the nose, trying to keep as quiet as possible. The feet stopped him.

'What the hell do you think you're doing.' Indignant tone. 'Anybody could look out of the window and see you.' Social conscience. He rolled over and lay wet in the grass. Looking up at her. The dog suddenly barked. Jenny jumped and he leapt to his feet and ran laughing inside. Things to do! There are plenty of things to do!

'Sometimes I think you're insane.' Sometimes he thought he was insane too. But that was another matter. It actually didn't matter at all, not one bit. It didn't make any difference to anything. The course of the universe wasn't altered one bit by anything he did. Then or now.

'Maybe it doesn't matter to you, but what about other people? Don't you ever think about other people?' Not a lot. Not any more. What was the point? They didn't think about him. Who thought about anybody, when it came right down to it? A nice thought, this thinking about people. But did it work? Answer, probably not. A noble sentiment, but totally impractical.

She walked past him and up the stairs. He ignored her. The dog stood wagging his tail with total approval.

Three

SOME OF THE BOLTS were rusted tight. Locked solid by years of neglect. The surface turned a dull black shiny colour as he poured more oil into the joint. He watched as it dripped thickly onto the ground. Watched as the starved metal soaked up the remainder, the oil disappearing into tiny crevices between the bolt and the rusted metal of the chassis. He squirmed on his back and did the same to the next, and the next. It was satisfying work. Every now and then, he came across one that moved and spent the next few minutes painstakingly unscrewing it in the confined space between the ground and the chassis. Now and then the spanner slipped and his knuckles slid over a jagged piece of metal, smearing skin and blood onto the surface. A moment of pain, a curse, and on with the job. The front subassembly was nearly off, the four bolts almost free; then he could roll the front axle away, complete with wheels, suspension, steering arms. Once free of its old home it looked out of place and lonely. He ignored it and, standing, stretched his cramped muscles. Now this was doing something. He glanced over to the back of the garage and noted with excitement the dull bulk of the V8 engine. This was going to be some motor when he had finished. There was a childlike glow to his face.

'You're like a child with a new toy. Why don't you stop playing and do something constructive?' Stupid woman, he thought. What the hell is this. He crawled beneath the rear of the car.

27

A pair of legs walked past his eyeline. Long, well-proportioned, balanced legs that paused before moving on. He moved slightly to get a better look. He could hear the high-pitched murmur of Jenny's voice and the low seductive answer from the legs. They filled his whole vision, moving very slightly as the weight of the body was adjusted. Ankles turned outwards. He watched the small movement of the muscles and followed the smooth skin on upwards, noting the gentle swell of the thighs. The bottom of the car cut off further examination and he felt cheated. Suddenly annoyed. The legs moved out of vision completely leaving only the background of the brick wall to look at. He wrenched at the next bolt. The spanner slipped, added another cut to the knuckles, and he swore loudly.

Once, at a party some time ago, he had spent some time with the legs. They were both drunk. Not falling-over drunk, but enough to free the inhibitions for a few hours. He'd been OK then. Whole. In one piece. Confident. Arrogant like the rest of them. Then. The legs had sought him out, sitting on the lawn in the summer moonlight while the party raged inside the house. Jenny couldn't take drink and he'd packed her off to bed when she threw up over one of the guests. The legs had sought him out then. Looked for him through the house. He knew it and was confident in his arrogance. So he sat outside on the mowed lawn deep in the shade where now the grass grew long and tangled. The next bolt came out easily. Four left. She'd sat beside him, long hair ruffled, mouth slightly open and lips wet. Her tongue flicked out cobra-like and touched the corners of her smiling mouth. Her skirt was hitched-up high, exposing most of her thighs. He'd lain back against the stump of a tree and watched amused as she unfastened him and set to work with her mouth. He'd smiled up at the stars, drunk, listening to the soft sound of her mouth against him. The next bolt was much tougher, so he paused to squirt more oil into the join. He left it and wriggled further under the car to the next one. It came away quickly and easily. Sliding out without much effort. After the garden incident, he'd taken her once more. Unsatisfactorily, in bed. In the traditional sense. It hadn't worked, and since then they'd barely talked to one another. Jenny had no idea. Never would. He didn't feel guilty – maybe slightly about the second time. In the bed. In their bed, whilst Jenny was out shopping. Maybe then, but not the first time. The last bolt was the easiest of the lot. It unscrewed without effort. Now the rear of the old car was just resting on the sub-assembly. He crawled out from underneath and took the strain on the hoist, lifting the body just clear. He tied it tightly and gently manoeuvred the rear assembly out from beneath, moving it to one side. Now the task was to get the trailer under the old body and then off to the scrap yard with it.

The trailer bounced and jigged behind the Fiat. The dog watched it, his head out of the window, ears flapping and tongue lolling. His mind went back to the legs. It was today's obsession. That first time she'd been good. He wondered what she would be like now. It was interesting. Before, he'd never noticed the hard line of her mouth and the set of her jaw. Nor the eyes. He'd never bothered to look before. Ice cold. No trace of anything. Cunning. Devious. The dog pulled his head in and rested it on his shoulder, wet nose smearing against his cheek. The dog licked his lips and sent a fine spray of saliva across his face. He pushed the animal away, and it promptly went back to eyeing the trailer from the window.

'That was great,' she'd said, slurring the words. He could see a dribble from the corner of her mouth. It fascinated him. He watched as she flicked it away with her tongue. She rolled it around inside her mouth and then swallowed, eyes shut, head back.

His eyes snapped back to the road and the blare of an oncoming horn. The dog ducked his head in quickly, closed his mouth, and sat back on the seat looking somewhat confused. He accepted the apology and nervously looked at the window, wondering whether to chance it again.

They both watched as the crane dipped and swung,

bringing the grab down towards the body on the trailer. The dog sat in 'the car wondering. He stood outside, leaning against the door, watching with morbid curiosity. The crane driver deftly pulled the levers that sent the grab crashing into the body. He pulled another lever and the huge teeth punched into the metal, skewering it, tearing into it, crunching it into a painful caricature of its former self. It was like a dying animal, twisting in the grasp, crying out its own screeching tortured sound. The levers were pulled again and the shattered body was lifted up into the air, glass, dust and rust showering down.

The dog wagged its tail. The body was lifted higher and swung across the sky, dropping down again into the jaws of the waiting monster. The grab shook it loose to fall a short distance into the huge flat-sided mouth that suddenly howled and slowly clamped shut over the feebly protesting metal. The howling continued long after the body disappeared. Then the sound changed to a lower-pitched satisfied hum as the jaws opened once more to wait for the next victim. From the end of the monster appeared, almost gently, a shiny metal cube, a squared-off tangle of metal, plastic and glass, strangely sculptural. A large flat round object descended from the sky, attached itself to the cube and lifted it clear away to be stacked neatly with the rest.

He saluted mockingly, climbed back into the Fiat, and threaded his way past the waiting piles of rusted heaps, stacked amongst the mud, oil, grease and other rubbish.

His mind came back to the legs. Was it worth another crack? He decided not. Remember the second time, the feeling of frustration, the sense of uncleanliness. He had a bath afterwards and washed himself with Dettol. It was a ridiculous act, but he felt it was necessary. No it wasn't worth trying again. But the legs were good. And the mouth. Never forget the mouth. It was that that started it all. What about Jenny? Maybe she had already guessed. Or been told. Certainly the day after the first time she'd been very distant. He'd put it down to her guilt over throwing up all over that poor guy. Teased her about it. Mercilessly. 'And what did you do?' She'd thrown back at him. At the time he didn't relate it to anything. Maybe she set the whole thing up because of her own inadequacies. Maybe she'd watched the whole thing from the bedroom window.

Without the weight, the trailer bounced around the uneven surface of the road and he had to slow down to stop the snaking effect. On two occasions it nearly dropped a wheel into the ditch on the side of the narrow road. The other road-users were going to get pretty mad at him. The speedometer unwound and both he and the dog relaxed.

A past episode, he decided, driving slowly now, gently, enjoying the sun and the countryside. But the feeling when he saw those legs. Well! He wondered briefly what her husband thought – if he ever knew. She must have done this sort of thing before. He vaguely remembered hearing some mess gossip. He never listened to it normally, finding it petty, usually boring. But that piece of information had been interesting coming, as it did, after their brief encounter. The barrack bicycle, somebody had called her. They could possibly be right. Whatever, it didn't matter now.

He turned into the short drive and stopped. Reversed back out and then unhooked the trailer.

Trailer and car parked, he sat looking at the next stage of the construction. If he turned his head he could just see the legs watching him from her kitchen window. Everything was too close, he decided. He moved and again looked towards the parts laid out on the garage floor. The fibre glass body tub. The shiny black chassis. The new engine. The subassemblies he'd just removed, sitting there, greasy, dirty, in need of cleaning. Over in the corner the new alloy wheels complete with special tyres. Everything here ready to be put together.

There was a noise behind him. He knew what it was without looking. Now what the hell was her name. He couldn't keep referring to her as the legs. Amanda.

'Hello David.' She moved round into his eyeline. Her eyes seemed to be devouring him. Her voice low. 'John and I were wondering whether you and Jenny would come round for supper tonight.' Why not ask Jenny? 'I'm asking you.' The voice was mocking. The eyes teasing. She looked over at the pile of car parts. 'Collecting spare parts?' She didn't mean for cars. Her gaze transferred itself to his stomach region. 'Didn't take too much away, did they?' God she was obvious. He got up and moved past her out into the sunlight. Jenny came in answer to his call.

'Yes, Amanda asked me earlier. It's OK with you isn't it?' He suddenly felt very alone. Cut off in the middle of enemy territory with no way of escape. They had him hemmed in on all sides with no sign of escape. Both sets of eyes mocked him. Both sets of eyes challenged him. Both sets of eyes were trying to destroy him.

'Well?' Jenny forced the point home. He shrugged and smiled. He hoped it looked convincing – it felt like a grimace of hatred and anger. 'Good.' Turning to Amanda and smiling, their little game at his expense.

He screamed, lunged and drove his fist into her face, feeling the bone shatter and splinter beneath his knuckles. Feeling the blood start and spread over her face. He turned and kicked hard at the other woman's gut, his foot burying itself in the soft flesh, driving the wind out of her, turning her face purple with pain, the eyes starting out of the face. He kicked them both there on the ground, writhing in agony, crying through shattered teeth. Their heads rolled around with each kick, blood splattering the drive.

'Tonight then.' Amanda smiled secretly in his direction. Jenny smiling at Amanda. He stood watching them smiling. He was not smiling. Jenny turned and went back inside. Amanda started towards her house then stopped and turned, looking at him intensely once more. He noticed for the first time how old she was. The thought made him smile. She couldn't get to him anymore. She was an old hag. As he smiled at her, her face grew older. He noticed the lines around her mouth and neck, the crows' feet at her eyes and the vertical lines on her upper lip. He laughed, a short harsh sound. Her smile disappeared and for the first time she looked off-balance. He allowed his gaze to wander slowly over her body now. She still had a good body. Well used, but good. He took his time, she standing uncertain, slightly afraid at this change. Her breasts were starting to sag, the weight dragging them ever closer to her waist.

He turned quickly and went back into the garage.

'Bastard.' It was hissed rather than spoken. Like you darling. Like you. We make a pair. Made a pair, but not anymore. Not now. Go find some other young fool.

John sat back puffing on his pipe. It looked strangely uncomfortable in his mouth. It didn't belong, although he was expert in the mechanics of smoking it. Filling the bowl with a detached concentration, tamping the tobacco down with his index finger, carefully wrapping the pouch up, and then, the ritual of the matches. It took a few, over several minutes, to get the thing lit properly. Clouds of smoke drifted slowly up to the once-white ceiling. It was possible to see exactly the concentration of smoke on the ceiling. It was darker in some parts than others. John always sat in the same seat, his own special chair. Just above this chair was the darkest spot. There was another over by the drinks cabinet. He liked to stand taking his time pouring the after-dinner liqueurs, all the time talking in his pedantic way and puffing on the pipe. The talk was always boring, always predictable, always safe. He had his audience pinned to their seats and he knew it. They were waiting for the drinks, waiting until the ritual was over. He hated rituals and John's were the worst.

He looked across at Jenny and Amanda. They were ignoring the pantomime, talking to each other. Amanda had positioned herself so that she could just lift her eyes and see him.

'I blame the Government myself. Should never have happened in the first place.' Of course. What shouldn't have happened? What the hell was he talking about? No wonder Amanda shopped around. Was he like this in bed?

He nodded in agreement. Anything to hasten the arrival of the brandy. Thank God this man wasn't in his regiment.

'Amanda and I both agree.' Said with a sense of satisfaction, a condescending tone. He caught Amanda's look and nearly laughed. He caught the second look of quickening interest and turned away, eyes veiled. The house itself was a testament to John's character. It was full of mementoes that would have been better off in a military museum. Little plaques of Regimental Arms that were best placed on the walls of local pubs, statuettes of soldiers in various uniforms, silver cigarette boxes with sickening inscriptions from people dying to see the last of him. And the ever-present 'me' photos. The record-player thumped out some march or other and still the brandy stayed in the bottle. He stood up and walked over to join John at the drinks cabinet. End of ritual. Time to drink up and get out. He took the bottle from John's hand and poured three brandies. He took one over to Amanda and settled back in his chair with another. The third stood on the cabinet beside John's surprised figure. He raised the glass to John and drank deeply. At least the brandy was good. He saw John glance at the bottle and blanch. The measures had sent the level plummeting. Jenny looked suitably shocked, Amanda amused.

'Serve you right John. You should stop talking and get on with it.' How many times had she had to say that to him, he wondered. He winked at her, a calculated gesture, and was pleased to see her colour, the advantage no longer in her court. He could determine the state of play now, because he didn't feel anything for any of them. He could mess around with them any which way he cared. It was a comfortable feeling of power.

'Sorry if I was taking too long.' Well stop talking next time. You're so boring anyway. 'Sorry. I didn't realize.' But then again the last thing you said was very interesting.

John was confused now. He couldn't even remember what that was. Amanda looked from John to him, her eyes watchful. Jenny just stared at him angrily and then smiled apologetically at John.

This was more like it. This was more enjoyable. He let the

silence roll on. Nobody wished to say anything for fear of being wrong. This was very good. No small talk now, no more useless prattle. How about telling John about his wife's penchant for other men's services? He looked slyly across at Amanda. She knew what he was thinking and there was a look that implored him to stop.

The rest of the brandy drifted, burning, down his throat. The atmosphere was tense.

He stood up, Formally thanked both of them for the meal and walked out of the house. Jenny followed rapidly on his heels. She wasn't talking to him. He didn't care. He was bored now. Bored with the game. It was time to find another game.

Max would understand. Max would know what was going on.

'Well go and see Max then.' He was surprised that she heard. She lay on the far side of the bed. The duvet pulled up over her head. She'd been crying. Not from unhappiness, merely from embarrassment. Well that was OK as well.

He got out of bed, dressed and went out into the garage. The parts lay in exactly the places they had been. He shouldn't have been surprised by this, but he was. From the corner he took a large can of Jizer and a bucket. Then he pushed the front axle assembly out onto the drive by the drain. He propped it to prevent it from rolling away and settled down next to it. The light from the garage and from the back door was enough to see by, the joint pools of yellow falling exactly onto the area of the axle. He opened the can and poured a quarter into the bucket. He went back into the garage and found a two-inch paint brush. He unrolled the garden hose, connected it to the tap just inside the garden, and led the hose back to the drain, allowing the water to fall gently down the hole.

He sat down, dipped the brush into the bucket, and began to clean the muck and grease off the axle. The night was warm and still. The moon gradually climbing up the sky. Long shadows strolled across the gardens and houses as the clouds drifted slowly past. He worked steadily, every now and then pausing to pick up the hose and wash away the sediment left by the cleaner. Slowly the axle changed colour and form, its rounded anatomical shapes becoming more obvious. The knuckle-joints, cleared of the accumulated mud and grease, glinted dully in the light. The squared shape of the shock absorber units sat atop the springs, coiled in anticipation. It was absorbing work. He didn't see Jenny come into the kitchen and watch him. She left and went back to bed.

'Will it go fast?' A child's voice full of glee. His voice at ten years old. 'Will it?' He looked up and nodded, noting the sparkle in the eyes, the misty wonder. 'How fast?' Very fast. Very very fast. Faster than anything else on the road. Faster than anything else in the universe. 'Cor. Did you hear that?' Turning to his mates. 'Wish I could have something like that some day.' Mind suddenly made up with a grim and determined set of the juvenile jaw. 'I *will* have something like that someday.'

The little figure disappeared into the shadows. The water trickled over the surface of the metal. He put the hose down and brushed away some more dirt.

'Why did he have to die? Why?' The child's voice was tremulous. The words coming out from between body and shaking sobs. 'Why can't he drive again?' The burning wreckage shone in the reflection of his tear-filled eyes. Slowly the image receded. He sat thoughtful, looking at the now cleaned axle.

The explosion ripped through the patrol. Blew down the garage and showered him with wreckage and bits of body. He jumped up shocked and dazed.

'Hey what's going on? Steady, I didn't mean to startle you.'

He turned and saw her standing just outside the pool of light. The garage remained intact and the hose sprayed water onto his leg. He moved it quickly away and dropped it back into the drain. When he turned back she was sitting on the low wall, knees drawn up to her chin, looking at the axle. She looked up at him as he picked up the bucket, moved it to one side, and rolled the axle back into the garage. He wheeled the

36

rear assembly out and into the same position over the drain. He sat down and, dipping the brush into the cleaning liquid, started on the differential casing. She watched him.

'Isn't it a little strange to be doing this at two o'clock in the morning?' He didn't think so. It was quiet, and normally there was nobody around to bother with. Anyway what would a married woman be doing at two o'clock in the morning, dressed in nothing but a short nightdress, talking to another man?

'Just that. Talking.' She paused, moved her hair away from her eyes, and shifted her position on the wall. It was a natural movement, not suggestive. He was glad. A few drops of water splashed onto her feet as he lifted the hose and carefully washed the casing. She didn't move. Seemed not to notice.

'It was good, you know. It could be better. Much much better.' Her voice was husky and he could see her nipples standing out against the thin material of her nightdress. She was still staring down at his hands moving slowly backwards and forwards with the brush and the hose. The water turned the cleaning fluid a milky colour as it mingled and then ran off down the drain. He wasn't going to answer. Let's see just what this is all about. Maybe with the next passing shadow of the clouds she wouldn't be there anymore. A cloud passed and he looked up. She was still there staring fixedly at his hands.

'I really want you. Need you.' No darling. Not me. You need a man. Any man. Anybody who can screw you all day and all night. Not me. He watched her face. There was a hint of tears. Just a hint and then it was gone. He wanted her to cry. He'd feel good if she cried. He'd feel happy if she cried.

More water and the back axle was clean. The leaf springs shook as he ground the brush into the crevices, forcing the fluid between the strips of flat sprung steel. The shackles rattled gently against the springs. He wished she'd crawl back into bed with her boring husband and leave him alone. He'd been perfectly happy out here preparing the axles. It meant that in the morning he could get on with the assembly of the new chassis. That's what interested him most.

37

'Anybody else would jump at the chance. Anybody normal that is.' Not good enough. She would have to do better than that. He continued unconcerned.

She stood up and slowly removed her nightdress. She stood, legs slightly apart. He looked up and the empty drive stared back at him, the garage light unblinkingly shining down onto the axle. He thought he heard a faint sound in the distance, but it was gone before he could grasp it.

'Don't turn the light off Mummy.' His own child's voice.

He shook his head, then scooped up a handful of water from the hose and doused his face. It was refreshing. He did it again and felt the cold water run down his neck and drip through onto his chest. He looked round again and saw that he was alone. He sighed with relief and continued with the job.

He finished it quickly and then walked over and turned the water off. He rolled the hose up, returned the remains of the cleaning fluid to the large can, and washed out the bucket under the tap. The axles back in the garage, he manoeuvred the chassis into position and placed the rear over the corresponding positions on the rear axle. They mated perfectly. He slid the twelve bolts into position. The new bolts. Then stood back looking at the handiwork. The front fell into position just as perfectly, the four bolts for the front subassembly sliding in just as easily. There it was. The chassis and its suspension was now ready to be tightened up. He thought of doing it now, but decided the pleasure could wait until the morning.

He turned off the garage light and shut the doors, then watched as the dawn chased away the child-figure and Amanda's naked pleading body.

Four

THE PUB WAS DARK, crowded and noisy. Full of students from the nearby College of Art. The air thick with the sound of argument and sweet smell of marijuana. The bar itself was a dull glowing island in the midst of hazy faces moving blurredly past his vision. Tired and bored bar staff endured the noise and the constant battle for orders. In various odd corners, tables were tucked away, small scarred tables in little dark wood alcoves, hiding behind stout wooden pillars.

Max was at one of these. He sat relaxed, drinking a pint of real ale. He insisted upon real ale.

'The other stuff's water by comparison,' taking a long draught from the straight glass. When he put the glass back on the table, there was foam sticking to the end of his moustache. He casually wiped it away and looked over at him. The blue eyes looked right into him. Saw right through him, dug deep into his soul. Max sat back against the hard straight wood of the bench, brushing his long hair away from his face. There was silence between them for some time, Max watching him thoughtfully, he sat drinking slowly, tasting the strong bitter beer, not sure whether he liked it or not. He knew that it would go straight through the gut: it always did.

His gaze wandered, watching the girls in the bar in the gloom. They were young, mostly good-looking and very self-assured. He wondered how many were virgins, and

39

decided very few. A couple held his gaze challengingly. He looked away quickly and was aware of their sniggers.

'Don't know why you bother,' Max lazily observed. He'd shifted position so that he could see as well. One of the girls came over and sat beside him. Max gently kissed her and let a hand move slowly up and over her breast. Nobody else in the bar seemed to notice, and if they did they didn't care. The girl got up as Max waved her away and went back to join her friend. Max turned back to him.

'The secret is not to bother. Take it as it comes.'

He sat watching Max like a student watching a revered master. Away in the corner of the bar a guitarist started to play. The melody sweet and soft. 'Lay lady lay. Lay across my big brass bed.' Bob Dylan's lyrics from another age floating across the room. They were both quiet, listening to the music. He watching Max looking at nothing. He wanted to talk but didn't want to spoil the peace. Wanted to explain but didn't want the answers. Wanted to question, but didn't want the truth.

The second pint was easier than the first, the bitter taste not quite so pronounced. It seemed smoother, seemed solid in his mouth and down his throat.

Max sat, eyes closed, listening to the music. Sometimes a girl would pass, stop, lean over, and touch his face. He didn't move. Occasionally a man would do the same. It was strange and frightening and yet somehow comforting. Max suddenly opened his eyes and stared right at him.

'Don't think you are any different from thousands of others. It's everywhere. It's amongst every one of us who've been there. Every single naïve asshole who decided to do it. You're no different.' Yes but. Max held up his hand to silence him. Eyes locked. But. The hand remained, commanding silence. Getting it.

He couldn't agree with Max. It troubled him. He didn't like to disagree with Max. Not that it made any difference to Max. Nothing annoyed or angered Max. It was just accepted, with a wry smile maybe, or a stare that meant that he knew better.

But he still couldn't agree with Max. He, David Trowse, was different. Not like those thousands of others. 'No you're not. You may feel, may think you are, but you're not. Don't kid yourself.' The eyes moved off him now. There was nothing more to say.

The music had stopped and the bar was empty. David hadn't noticed anyone leave. Didn't care. The bored bar staff slowly cleaned up. Glasses, some half-full, with cigarette ends floating about. Most empty, some broken. The litter of an evening. The litter of entertainment.

Later, much later, they sat on low cushions in a small room listening to Mozart sonatas, passing around marijuana joints. Max sat back, a girl either side of him nestled into the crook of his arms. David smoked, drawing the fumes deep into his lungs, feeling the heat at the back of his throat. The sounds of the piano crept in and bounced around inside his head. Sometimes his head would swim and a tingling sensation creep up his legs and spread throughout his body, taking his breath away. It was then the music seemed to fill every part of him, echoing inside him. Max grinned. Smiled. He grinned back idiotically. A lopsided leer. The girls paid no attention.

'We should take off somewhere. You and I.' Max talking through the dope and the music. 'Just take off.' He motioned with his hand, palm downwards, fingers pointed, moving up and away like an aeroplane. He nodded, then shook his head confused. He couldn't take off. Couldn't go. There was something to do. The car? Jenny?

'All excuses, temporary things. Not reasons. Of course you can.' Max paused and motioned to the girls beside him. 'Look. You, me, these two here. We can take off. Go.'

Suddenly he was afraid. Very afraid. He wanted to be out of this room. Didn't want to hear Max's insistent tones. Didn't want to see the mocking eyes of the girls. Away.

He stood up, knocking aside the Japanese floor lamp. He looked at it lying there accusingly on its side. He ran out of the room and down the stairs, hearing the sounds of laughter. He turned once and saw Max at the top of the stairs looking at him reproachfully. He ran outside into the street and stood letting the large drops of summer rain splash down over him. It was warm but he was shaking. Soon he was soaked, the rain running off his hair and down his face. He walked. Fast at first, sometimes darting across a road without looking, catching the glare of headlights and the blare of a horn, imagining the shouted obscenities. There was no direction to his walking. It didn't seem to matter. Just get away, that's what really mattered. Get away. Run. Find a hole. Crawl in and wait until the dope wore off.

He slowed. His body couldn't run anymore. He sucked the rain into his lungs with great gasps, then threw his head back letting the fresh water run into his mouth, filling it. He swallowed choked and spilled a lot down his chin. The rest tasted good. He tried again and succeeded in drinking a mouthful. The shaking had stopped now and he found himself beside the car.

The sound of his panting echoed inside the Fiat. The rain ran solidly down the windows, the sound interrupted only by another car splashing slowly past. Some, their stereos turned up, went past as if on their own. Darkened windows showing no sign of passengers. After a while, the rasping panting eased. His body slowly returned to normal respiration. The rain eased with it until only a few drops fell from the laden branches of the trees.

He got out of the car and retraced his steps to the flat. His feet made funny sounds inside the wet shoes, leaving dark marks on the floor. One of the girls was lying on the cushions, listening to the music still. She pointed to the other room. He stood by the door and watched as Max plunged and writhed on top of the other girl. She lay twitching, jerking, her mouth open emitting groans and moans, her legs moving either side of his body, knees drawn up. They were oblivious to his presence. He turned and went into the bathroom, stripped, and climbed into the hot steamy water, allowing the heat to relax him. The other girl came in and gently washed his back, a slow gentle motion that almost had him asleep. She shook him and held the towel out, beckoning him to step into it. He let her dry him, too exhausted and doped to resist. She led him to the cushions, laid him down and covered him with blankets, then lay beside him.

'Are you going to lie there all day. I know it was late when you crawled in but half the day has gone.' Jenny's voice sliced through his sleep. Jarred him awake.

His mouth felt terrible and there was a dull ache behind his eyes. It was raining outside. Jenny stood looking at him, waiting for an answer, an explanation.

'Max again. I'd like to meet Max.' She sounded angry, left out: she was. She had no part in his friendship with Max. He shrugged, crawled out of bed, and slopped water over his face. It stared back at him from the mirror, unshaven, hollow-eyed. How long had he been gone? 'Two days. Without a word. Nothing.' Really? As long as that? It surprised him.

'You could have phoned. Anything.' Her voice was irritating. Why didn't she go downstairs?

The door slammed and he buried his head once more in the water. It was pleasant. Not at all like last night. Was it last night, or the night before? He looked at himself again in the mirror. Max was a bastard sometimes. A real bastard. He tried smiling at himself, and noticed that it didn't reach his eyes.

'And how the hell did your clothes get into this state?' The voice shouted through the closed door. He had no idea, no idea at all. What state anyway?

'Filthy and wet. Soaking.' Must have been last night then, not the night before. Must have been. He shrugged again, trying not to let the voice get to him, trying to shut it out, make it disappear into the background.

His mother stood in front of him shaking her head.

'Really you should try. Don't treat her like that. After all the support she's given you.' Yes mother. Of course, mother. Shut up, mother. Her image faded from the mirror. She was right, but he didn't need to be told. He knew anyway, but there was always a but. He shook the thoughts away and went to dress. Clean clothes. Clean T-shirt. Clean jeans, now starting to fit as he filled out, his body no longer as emaciated as it was.

He passed Jenny on the stairs, scooping up a mug of coffee from her hands with a hurried thanks. She stared after him, a mixture of sadness and confusion.

'Bill rang. He'd like to see you in the office tomorrow.' He nodded without turning. He wondered what Bill wanted. There was still plenty of leave left. He didn't have to be back yet. Christ, there was a medical board to attend yet. They would decide when he would be fit for duty, fit to be cannon-fodder again.

Was that a good idea, he wondered? Still, the fact that Bill wanted to see him was irritating. Everything was irritating today.

He went outside into the garage, running to avoid the rain. It was all there. The chassis with the body tub in position, the engine nestling perfectly in place. Not much more to do. He moved closer, his excitement quickening his pulse and bringing a slight flush to his face. He ran his hand along the lines of the body. Almost a replica of the Aston Martin Ulster. Same boat-tail, long bonnet, cycle wings on the front. It was going to be great.

The mass of wires and instruments lying inside the car waited patiently for their turn to be positioned and then permanently secured; walnut dashboard staring vacantly, full of holes, waiting for its face. He picked up the wood-rimmed steering-wheel and ran his fingers over the surface, feeling the indentations where his fingers would rest comfortably. There was a movement at the door. He turned and saw Jenny standing, leaning against the wall, arms crossed, one hand holding a steaming cup.

'When will it be ready?' She sounded interested. That was a question. He turned back. That was a question. Perhaps he really wanted it to continue for ever, the building, the creating. Then sometimes he was eager for it to be finished.

44

Somehow it would find its own time, its own birth. Maybe it wouldn't be long. It was difficult to tell. Take the wiring for instance. All those individual little wires looking like confused multi-coloured spaghetti lying in the bottom of the car, all those wires had a purpose. All those wires had to be followed, connected, tucked away, hidden from view. All those wires were like nerves in the body carrying the messages. Hundreds of feet of wire that, after hours of exasperating work, would suddenly be finished and out of sight. Then, with a hope and a prayer, it would all work. If it didn't, then out they all came, and the process would begin again.

She nodded, listening. He was surprised.

'It's beautiful. It seems a shame that it's a car.' He looked at her trying to find the mockery. There was none; he wasn't sure. She moved away from the wall and walked round the car, running her hand as he had done over the smooth lines. She made it sensual, sexy, feminine. For a moment she became Amanda. For a moment naked Amanda, teasing. Then she was Jenny.

'I wonder what Bill wanted?' The moment was lost. Gone. The veil dropped over his eyes. He wasn't going to say, treating the question as rhetorical. Jenny looked at him expecting an answer, saw there was none and, tightening her jaw, snatched her hand away from the car as if it was hot. She stood back against the wall. Tense, annoyed, staring jealously at the car. He ignored her and bent down to continue the painstaking process of wiring. She watched him and gradually relaxed. He could sense her every move as he carefully pared the plastic coating away from the wire and, using the crimping tool, attached the connectors. He worked steadily, methodically, until every wire had a male or female connector.

He straightened, feeling the ache in the small of his back and the stomach muscles protest from being bent over for so long. He hid the pain, but it showed in his eyes. He kept them averted, away from Jenny's gaze. He wished she would go away and leave him.

'What did you and Max get up to?' He sat back, rubbed his hands across his eyes, and stared at her. It was none of her business. If she wanted to know, they'd had an orgy for two days. Loads of booze and women. He could see from her expression that she didn't believe a word of it.

'Probably sat exchanging war stories, more like.' Fine, he thought, think what you will. She fell silent, still leaning against the wall looking at him.

He tucked the wiring loom away, along the side of the body and the floor, using little ties to fix it in place. He fed the end through to the rear and connected the rear lights and indicators, referring back to the diagram he'd roughed out before starting the job. Once finished, he moved to the dashboard. Each small switch had to be screwed into place. He took great care not to scratch the surface of the wood. It shone at him, the grain seeming to move as he stared at it. He had to lie on his back inside the car to secure the instruments. Jenny moved to another position where she could see. She was just in his eyeline. Once he looked up, and she smiled at him. He ducked back under the dashboard, wishing she would go. She was intruding. This was his private sanctuary, no one allowed. He felt she knew that and was deliberately challenging him. Getting her own back for spending time with Max.

He pulled hard on one of the wires and the connector came away, leaving the frayed copper threads looking forlornly at him. He took a deep breath and reached for another connector and the crimper. At this rate it was going to take a long time before the car was anywhere near ready. Jenny leaned unconcernedly against the body, watching, bored now.

'Cup of tea?' He nodded and breathed a sigh of relief as she sauntered away to the kitchen. He sat up and watched her go. Watched the firm flesh tightly held by the blue jeans, watched as it swayed out of sight. 'She's got a good figure, son,' his father had said appreciatively and by way of making conversation. 'You could do worse. She's a nice girl too,' by way of an afterthought. Paternal ramblings on the day of his wedding.

46

He never did have much to say to his father anyway. But perhaps he'd been more right than he knew. His father. That was all there was. Something good to look at.

'Well there it is. That's what they've decided.' Bill paused, sitting back in his chair, avoiding his eyes. 'I don't think it's that bad.' He shrugged meaninglessly. 'Could be a lot worse.' That was all he had to say? Could be worse. All the training. All the experience. All that he'd been through and they were going to put him out to grass like some horse. Give him a desk, a salary, a pat on the back, and make sure nobody knew he existed. Stuffed away in some dark corner to fester for the rest of his life until they could legitimately retire him with a modest pension and a liver about to pack up from years of boozing away the memories in the mess.

'Steady on a minute, David. It's not quite like that. You know it isn't. It's just . . . Well . . .' Precisely. It's just precisely like that and Bill knew it. He could sit there, Major's crowns on his shoulders, and say that. He who had nowhere to go anyway. Came from nowhere. 'That's a little strong. I know you're upset . . .' Too damn right. Too fucking right. Too shitting pissing right.

Bill sat looking at him, slightly unnerved by the outburst. Unsure. Not knowing whether to summon somebody. The muscles stood out on his neck as he looked at Bill. Stared him out, ground him into a small pile behind the desk. Well, if that was the case, then he'd take the money and sod the lot. Piss on everyone. A slight hiccup in his life wasn't going to stop him. It hadn't stopped Max. It wasn't going to stop him.

'Take some time to consider the proposal.' Stuff your proposal. He turned and strode out of the office, slamming the door behind him. The two soldiers standing in the corridor looked uncertain, then snapped to attention and saluted. He ignored them, Ignored everybody who passed him. They didn't exist.

He stopped by the parade ground and watched a squad of recruits being drilled. He saw himself, face tensed in concentration, tying to remember the movements. Right turn. About turn. In T L V left right. Left form. Mark time. He was good. Knew the moves. Had it all there in the brain. The rhythm, the precise steps, everything. Now ten years slogging, fighting, enduring, was washed away. Not by a sniper's bullet or a terrorist bomb, but by a crawling insidious creeping thing that destroyed slowly from the inside. That started with ground glass in the tea during a long wet summer and ended with the surgeon's knife. Fuck them! The sound echoed across the parade square causing the squad to falter only momentarily.

Lou Reed screamed, cajoled, and terrorized through the Fiat's cassette stereo, full volume while he screamed out of key with him. Hurling the saloon impossibly into the corners, getting light over the dips in the road, tyres screeching for an end. The faster he drove, the narrower the road became. Pushing in, forcing the trees and hedgerows unwilling towards the maniacal metal beast. He jammed his foot down hard, trying to push it through the floor, feeling the rear wheels slide out of line round the corners, adjusting with the front, secure in the knowledge that he wouldn't crash, that it wouldn't end this way on this road. No, there was no easy solution. No chance of avoiding the failure. The failure of his body. He suddenly stamped on the brake. The hatchback protested violently across the road before coming to a halt, leaving a line of black marks and a cloud of blue smoke, now disappearing in the wind. Dispersing among the relieved trees.

He sat cold. Emotionless. Calculating. Scheming. Thinking. Resolving. He'd take his training, his eight years, and use them elsewhere, where they would be recognized. Where the state of his defecatory functions would not be a hindrance, where nobody need know. He didn't need Bill or the system. He didn't need the Army, the administration, the red tape. He would take his experience where it would be prized and nurtured. Rewarded.

He started the engine, waved two fingers at a gesticulating

48

motorist, and continued on slowly. Revelling in his newly-found power, his new hardening resolve. Eager for his new life, wondering what Jenny would make of all this.

'Jesus,' she said and sat down with a thud. The dog looked up from his bed beside the boiler, questioningly. 'Jesus,' she said again. The blood had drained from her face. She sat immobile, eyes staring fixedly ahead, focused on nothing. He shrugged and took a beer from the fridge. He was feeling good, feeling ready to take on all-comers, Bill included. Anybody. The beer tasted good. Cold and satisfying. The bubbles boiling up his throat, exploding out of his mouth in a loud comforting belch. Jenny, normally keen to reprove, sat quietly. He walked outside and watched as John arrived back and carefully parked the car. He shouted cheery obscenities to him. John smiled back, a little confused, then went into his house. He laughed. A bark, more than laugh, that had the dog jumping up from his bed and racing into the garden to see what intruders there might be.

He heard Jenny step quietly up behind him. He turned and noted the look of near-panic on her face.

'No don't do it son. Don't hurt her.' His father's voice lay uncomfortably on his shoulder. Why Dad?

'Are you sure it's the right thing?' Her voice was trembling slightly. Unsure. Frightened. 'Have you thought it through? Right through?'

He looked at her curiously, wondering why she should be so concerned. They didn't have any children, only a scatty dog. No responsibilities to tie them down. It was his life and, if somebody else had decided to piss on him, he was going to take his experience elsewhere.

'It's a nice thought, but is it practical. What are you going to do? You're still not fully fit yet. We don't know what the long-term effects of the operation are.'

He walked off out into the garden to shut off the stream of noise. It was making him angry and right now he didn't want to be angry. He was enjoying himself. He knew what he was going to do, and, anyway, the ten thousand pounds they were

49

going to pay him should cushion any difficulties. And Max would have some ideas.

'You worry me sometimes. Really worry me.' She was very close to tears now. He wanted to see those tears. She should worry about herself. He didn't need anybody's worry. He'd had a bellyful of worry and concern.

Jenny turned and ran back into the house. He felt cheated that he hadn't seen the tears. He felt uncomfortable, no longer happy as he had been not long ago. He felt a sudden rage, an overpowering urge to destroy. The beer can presented no obstacle and he left it wrinkled and torn on the grass.

Five

THE CAR sat nearly complete. Its body a deep blue, sitting on wide squat tyres, silver side pipes glinting in the light. He carefully attached the cycle wing to the supporting struts, passing the bolts through the holes and slowly tightening them. Now the project was nearly finished, he wanted to slow the process right down, enjoy every last nut and bolt, every last throat-catching spray of paint. He wanted to polish and shine the car, give it an identity all its own. Make it live, not just to be another car on the road, but different. Alive. To embody his life.

'It's just an inanimate object.' Jenny had scoffed to Amanda as they stood, entrenched in their positions. Hostile towards him. Jenny for what she could see as a mistake of judgement that she didn't like or want. Amanda for being continually snubbed. Neither aware of the other's reasons. He watched them, hating them.

The car was more than they could possibly imagine. The car had helped him forget the shredded body he had to live with, forget the hatred and bitterness that had caused it. No, the car was something very special to him. Not an inanimate object.

He moved round to the other side, carefully lifting the nearside wing and placing it in position. Once that was on, he turned to the aero screens. Small semi-circular shapes of glass, complete in their chromed half-frames. He fingered the butterfly screws that would enable them to fold flat against the bonnet. They fitted perfectly into the pre-drilled holes. He reached under the scuttle and blindly concentrated his effort into the nerves at the ends of his fingers, allowing them to be his eyes. He felt for the threaded ends of the holding bolts, carefully fiddled the Nyloc nut onto the end, and gently turned, feeling for the tell-tale solidity that told him the nut was on the thread. He completed the same thing three more times then, reaching under once more, tightened the nuts with a ring spanner.

'Boy, Mister, that looks really super. Cor! Look at that.' The young David walked around the car, eyes wide and sparkling. He reached out a hand to touch the shiny surface and then, looking guiltily up, withdrew it quickly. It's OK. The boy smiled.

'Can I have a look at the engine Mister?' He opened up the bonnet and the boy savoured, open-mouthed, the sight of the big V8. He smiled down at the small figure.

The boy turned, abruptly, looking harassed and suddenly old for his age, his face troubled, eyes close to tears.

'I have to go now Mister. They want me. I don't want to go, but they want me.' He headed for the garage door, socks falling down bare, muddy legs that looked thin and bony in the baggy shorts. He turned and looked up at him.

'Can I have a ride in it someday Mister?' Then he was gone. Jenny stood at the door, watching him.

'What were you thinking?' He turned back to the car, closing the bonnet. 'I heard you talking. But there's nobody here.' That was obvious. Of course there was nobody. Jenny shrugged and walked over to Amanda's house. She looked tired, he thought. An idle thought with no feeling, an objective observation. It had been the same last night. 'Make love to me,' she'd said, somewhat shyly. Embarrassed at having to ask. He had. Short sharp and unsatisfying. Objective lovemaking. No feeling, no emotion, a pure animal function, a function totally without point. Not for procreation, neither for pleasure, simply a habit, a ritual for married couples. Another ritual, completed in the dark, in the

52

fumbling blind dark. He'd come quickly, feeling the physical release. Feeling the mental prison closing in, suffocating.

'That was good,' she said unconvincingly. He wanted to shout and scream at her, tell her she was the lousiest screw he'd ever had. He kissed her gently, turned over, and went to sleep.

He picked up the beige carpet roughly and threw it into the car then, noticing what he was doing, carefully straightened it. He pulled his mind away from thoughts of Jenny and pushed the carpet into the corners of the body and floor. The underlay, already in position, felt coarse and springy under his fingers. As he bent down his face brushed close to the leather trim covering the side of the car. He breathed the smell deep into the lungs, enjoying the fresh tanned-leather smell. He ran his hand over the grained surface, feeling its softness, then tucked the carpet away, flattening the surface around the contours of the propshaft tunnel, cutting the edges around the seat runners until it was done. The seats took no time at all to fit, and he stepped into the car and tried it out for size. A few adjustments of the seat were required and then everything fell to hand; the pedals comfortably within reach, the steering wheel close to the gearstick, both of which could be reached without stretching. The seat fitted close around his body. He threw himself sideways against it and was pleased that it was firm and unyielding.

It was nearly there. Nearly finished. Just minor adjustments then tax, insurance, and it would be on the road. His feeling of elation looking at the car evaporated slowly to one of anticlimax. He sat on the floor of the garage staring at the blue machine sitting quietly, waiting.

'Mister. It's the best car I ever saw. Ever. Ever.' The little boy was standing close to his shoulder resting a small grubby hand on his knee. Staring again. 'What you going to call it Mister?' Call it? Does it have to have a name? 'No. But it would be good wouldn't it? What about . . .' He screwed his young face up in thought then suddenly it cleared in a blaze of inspiration. 'Blue Flash.' He stood hands on hips in triumph. Blue Flash. Well, it's a thought! The boy strutted around the car repeating the name in different tones. In different situations.

'Blue Flash, winner of the Tourist Trophy, driven by David Trowse. Blue Flash, driven by David Trowse, winner of the Mille Miglia, beating Stirling Moss and Denis Jenkinson into second place.' It was heady exciting stuff. The boy was full of it.

'Looks nice. Is it finished?' Jenny, standing in the doorway again. Nearly finished. It's nearly finished, can't you see it's nearly finished? She shrugged and went back inside the house. He turned back to the boy. The blank wall stared back at him.

The faces peered into him, screaming, pointing, thrusting towards him. The high-pitched howl came and went in waves, sometimes trying to crush him with the weight of noise alone. Objects fell about him, out of the sky, some bright and burning, others jagged, feeling for his yielding soft flesh. He felt the wall hard up against his back, could smell the stink of a thousand breaths wafting up and over him, jamming in his nose, sticking in his throat, trying to throttle him. There was no obvious escape route. No way out except to drive forward, forwards into the heaving mass, brushing aside the peering faces, throwing the grasping hands away from his neck, feeling the blood start from the gash on his cheek. He sat up, suddenly, hand feeling the scar. It was quiet and dark. Jenny was asleep. He didn't trust anything. Suspiciously looking about him, calming now. There was nothing dangerous here. He got out of bed and stood by the window. The full moon made the small Army housing estate look very white, the shadows very black. He could still hear the sounds of the crowd. The baying of their voices. The screams fading away through the trees.

He put on his track suit, went downstairs, collected the dog and quietly let himself out of the house. It was a warm night. The dog, unused to nightly adventures, stayed close as he jogged slowly down the road, his running-shoes making a soft patter on the road. He moved off the road and into the woods, running across the dead leaves of the previous autumn; the sound now muted to a swishing rustling. The dog padded alongside him, every now and then looking up to make sure he was still there. The trees reflected the moonlight through the branches and onto the track, lighting the way up towards the hill.

His breath was labouring a little now and he imperceptibly slowed. The dog looked grateful. The woods gave way to the coarse-tufted grass and heather, the woody track to the sand of the open moorland. The hill stood begging him. He stopped and looked up to the top, breathing hard. Max stood there, hands on hips, beckoning him up. He hesitated and then turned to his right and ran along the base of the hill. He was conscious of Max tracking, keeping pace. The dog was unaware, risking a dive into the undergrowth when he could no longer resist the smell of something unaccountably exciting.

He stopped again and looked once more to the top. Max was there, breathing hard, turning towards him. Again he turned and ran on, continuing around the base of the hill. When he stopped for the third time, he found that Max was closer. He could see him smiling, his face framed by his long hair and the hint of a beard to join the moustache. He looked classical. Arms outstretched. Biblical. He was beckoning again.

'The offer's still open.' The voice drifted down to him. He shook his head. He wasn't ready yet. Might never be ready. 'It's up to you. You'll be doing yourself a favour.' Maybe. What the hell did he want to do himself a favour for anyway? Again he shook his head, then turned once more and continued running, driving harder this time, catching the dog unawares. Running, running. Feeling the sweat starting to come, to pour down the side of his chest from his armpits. He felt the salt in his eyes, blurring the sight. He wiped it away. Finally he made the top of the hill without being aware of having been climbing. He looked around for Max, but saw only footprints, scuffed into the sand, next to where he was standing.

The dog stood beside him panting and wondering whether there were any more stunts like that one. They both sat on the top of the hill looking out over the moonlit landscape, resting, letting the lungs breathe and the blood recirculate.

Far in the distance, once, he thought he saw a figure running. Floating over the rough ground, then it was gone. He blinked and looked again, but the horizon was bare and quiet. Nothing moved. The glow of the town away to the right, and high overhead a jet blinking its way to some foreign destination. Nothing else.

He sat back, rested his hand on the dog's neck, and listened to the gentle thump of the tail against the sand.

'Supervisory Clerk is what your rank equates to.' He could see the man now. The rodent-featured little man behind his desk with his big book. He noticed that the man enjoyed imparting the information. Then with even more satisfaction, 'No jobs available for that particular calling.' A pause for effect. 'Phasing them out, you might say. Obsolete.' It was then that he'd leant across the desk and wrapped his fingers round the scrawny throat. The rodent's eyes bulged, terrified. He could smell the urine and see the dark stain getting bigger at the man's crutch. There was a stunned silence in the room, nobody rushing to the rodent's aid. A few of the clients waiting their turns sniggered with glee. He tightened his hold, watching the face turn purple, then threw the man coughing and retching back onto his chair. How about that for qualification then? The rodent sat, tears in his eyes, trying to cover the stain. Some of the girls, realizing the danger was over, giggled nervously, backing away as he strode out of the office, knocking aside the manager who'd ventured out to see what the fuss was all about. He sat on the sand, hugging his knees, smiling at the memory. The wind ruffled the dog's ears and cooled the sweat, making him cold. He ignored it. What did that little idiot know? Never been out into the world at all. Just safe behind his desk, trying to tell others what to do. Classify them. Pigeonhole them. Dehumanize them. Not him. 'Oh Jesus!' Was all Jenny could say. 'Oh Jesus!' Well,

56

that's a great help! Perhaps he should go with Max. Get away for a while, away from the nonsense. Away from the nagging and moaning. Away from . . .

He lay, clean after a bath, listening to the soft sounds of the dawn. Jenny stirred, once or twice, restlessly beside him. He got up and stood by the window, watching the early-morning mist cling stubbornly, gently, to the trees. It was the best time of the day, the time when nothing moved that didn't belong. A time when most human beings were still, sweating in bed, or staggering from sleep, unaware of their surroundings, unseeingly moving from room to room. He watched as the odd light flickered on in the houses opposite.

He watched as an Army patrol, led by himself, moved slowly down the road, using the gardens for cover, moving cautiously, distrustfully, even in their home territory. His face scowled as he noticed the odd mistake. The patrol leader, himself, looked up and smiled, acknowledging his presence. He watched them move out of sight.

The road was empty again. A car crawled past, smoke coming from the exhaust, the engine spluttering in the dawn, starved of oxygen. He watched it all. The lonely jogger, thinking himself too early for prying eyes, struggled past. Garish track suit, clean new running-shoes, multi-coloured sweatband. Pot-belly wobbling to the disturbed rhythm of his legs. He looked quickly around then, satisfied, stopped running and sat down on a tree stump at the edge of the road. The sound of a car made him rise wearily to his feet and bravely continue.

Once again the road was empty. The sound of the birds louder and the sun rising once more.

He dressed and went out to the car. The little boy was there waiting for him.

'I thought you weren't coming, Mister. It is finished yet?' Concerned eager face. Nearly. Just these studs to fit for the tonneau cover and then it can go down to the garage for the test and then to the tax office.

'Can I come for a ride, Mister? Please.' He nodded and watched with pleasure as the boy climbed into the passenger seat and sat patiently waiting.

He worked steadily, glancing up now and then to watch the boy as he imagined himself at the wheel. The car sat patiently waiting. It gleamed nobly, waiting to feel the tarmac under its wheels and the wind along the long straight bonnet.

'Can we go to Silverstone, Mister? Can I drive? Can we race?' The questions tumbling out, falling all over him. He turned smiling and walked out of the garage into the sunlight, the job finished.

Amanda stood in front of him on the drive. She smiled nervously. He noticed she wasn't wearing a brassière. The breasts moved beneath the T-shirt as she breathed, nipples peaking the material.

'Morning, David.' She spoke quietly. Shyly. Unlike her, he thought, very unlike her. He watched her suspiciously. She looked over his shoulder.

'It looks really good. You've done a good job.' She was silent. What do you want Amanda? What is it this time? Hardly a cup of sugar. He thought he saw a hint of tears in her eyes and was surprised.

'Just enjoying the morning. Thought I'd have a coffee with Jenny.' At this time in the morning? She shrugged. He sat on the wall dividing the two houses. She stood looking into the garage. At one point she frowned as if seeing something else, then her expression cleared. He glanced at the car. It was empty. No sign of the boy. He was sad, yet a little relieved.

Amanda stepped over the low wall close to him. He could smell her perfume and the fresh scent of a recent bath in fragrant soap. He breathed it in involuntarily, enjoying it, then watched as she walked across to the back door. Jenny was watching from the kitchen window. He went back into the garage, climbed into the car, inserted the key, turned it and pressed the starter button. There was a moment of anxiety as the engine turned over before firing and throbbing into life. He climbed out, opened the bonnet and adjusted the tickover, then stood back and listened with satisfaction to the smooth, solid, balanced sound of the engine.

He climbed back in, selected reverse and carefully backed it out of the garage. The clutch was smooth and light, the brakes firm. No servo to help on this car. He backed out into the road, adjusted his seat belt, waited until the boy was strapped in and then, selecting first gear, moved off, gently at first. The speed gradually built up as he felt the car, nursed it along, listening to every sound, feeling every bump, testing the self-centring of the steering. Maybe a touch more castor required. The gearbox was a little stiff and notchy, but that was to be expected. The brakes needed getting used to but, when pressed hard, brought the car to a halt very quickly and with no tendency to wander off line.

The basic functions working, he pressed the accelerator to the floor and thrilled to the sound of the exhausts and the feeling of being pressed hard back into the seat.

'Wow! Fantastic!' The little boy was laughing beside him. He laughed too and threw the car into the corners hard, feeling the grip, testing the oversteer. The car enjoyed it, lunging into the corners, greedy for more speed, secure in its capabilities. The engine responded instantly to every slight change on the accelerator, the 170 horsepower sending the light car hurtling down the road. The fat tyres gripped the surface tenaciously, leechlike, unwilling to give even the slightest, except when centrifugal force demanded.

It was exhilarating stuff.

'Why can't you find some other hobby, David? Something like stamp collecting?' Stamp collecting, mother? She had some funny ideas. 'Well something other than fast cars, dear. Surely there must be something else that interests you?' Girls, mother? She'd smiled shyly at that. 'Now, you know what I mean. Don't be silly. It's just that you could get hurt.' I'm in the Army, mother. Soldiers get killed with regularity. 'It's not the same.' No, it's safer driving fast cars.

The speedometer flickered around the hundred mark before he eased off back down to a pedestrian sixty. The wind noise died from a banshee howl to a gentle roar, sweeping his hair backwards and forwards in the slipstream. He slowed to a halt and turned around in a gateway.

'Do we have to go back, Mister?' Disappointment on the face. Afraid so. Just one of those things.

'Wouldn't it be nice to just keep on going.' The voice sounded older. He looked across and the boy watched him, troubled. The car rumbled impatiently. He slipped it into gear and let it go off down the road. Slowly now, the car enjoying its arrogance. Other passing cars seemed to slow in deference, the drivers glancing enviously at the car then at him. How many would love to trade places just for a short time? Just to feel the wind in their faces and the thrill of the power and speed? He relaxed and enjoyed the drive back, parking the car in the drive and sitting listening to the cooling tick of the hot engine. He turned in his seat, but the boy had gone. Jenny and Amanda stood in the garden watching him.

Six

MAX STOOD LEANING against the car. The beard had grown and he looked like an out-of-date hippy. He tried to ignore him. Max kept within his eyeline, not saying anything, waiting until he finally succumbed and acknowledged his presence. Eventually of course he had to, coming face to face with smiling Max as he moved round the car, checking everything was tight and as it should be after the test drive.

Max didn't move. Just stood there smiling at him. He wanted to get to the spot that was directly behind Max's left leg. He sighed, shrugged, and looked directly into Max's eyes.

'Ah, you do know I'm here. For a moment I thought you had gone blind or something.'

He didn't answer, just watched Max, who moved out of the way, allowing him to check the rear right wheel. He noticed Max had his jeep-type vehicle on the road. Huge tyres, roll bar and 'roo bar, the seats high-backed with full racing harness. It was painted an Army green and had several spotlights, the lenses covered with wire mesh. It was an interesting machine. Max saw the interest.

'Have a go, if you like.' Max tossed him the keys. He looked at them and threw them back with a shake of the head. Max shrugged, still smiling.

'Well? How about it? You coming with me?'

There was a long silence. No. He wasn't going. He'd had enough of Max. The time before last he'd been picked up drunk and naked by the police five miles away at two in the morning, after a distressed woman had rung in hysterically claiming that she was attacked. The police found him incapable of standing, let alone sexually attacking the woman. They'd brought him home. He shook his head. Max was still smiling. An annoying, knowing smile.

'If you change your mind you know where I'll be.'

He stood up as Max sauntered over to the Jeep and drove away, the engine sounding threateningly loud.

'Was that Max?' Jenny standing right behind him, making him start and turn suddenly. Defensive. Tense. 'Hey, it's only me. You know, your wife.' Her eyes were mocking his reaction. He slowly straightened, feeling foolish. Feeling angry at her making him feel foolish. He nodded and bent back to examining the car.

'He looks pretty dishy to me.' Teasing, trying to goad a reaction. 'Bet he doesn't have a problem with women.' He stood up and pushed her roughly to one side and leant inside the car. Why didn't she go and polish her nails? She laughed without humour at his discomfort. His next push sent her off-balance, staggering before recovering, and looking at him frightened now. 'Hey, I could have fallen. There's no need for that. Can't you take a joke?' He ignored her, checking for any play in the steering. She sidled up to him and ran a hand down his back, round his buttocks and down between his legs, then back up again feeling for him. She leant forward and gently bit his ear. He pushed her off. This time she fell against the wall, raising a blue and purple mark almost immediately on her thigh. He looked at her dispassionately and turned once more to the car. He felt the blow as an irritation against the back of his neck. For a moment his eyes swam. There was no pain, just momentary disorientation.

He heard a sob and the sound of running. He didn't bother to look. His head cleared and he felt a dull ache where the small fist had landed. It was a small annoyance, starting to grow in stature. Leave it be, he told himself. Let it go. Calm down.

'Had an argument?' Amanda leaning against her back door.

He looked for mockery and found none, found no trace of expression. She stood for a moment and then went back inside leaving the door open. For a moment he was tempted. For a long moment, he considered the possibilities. For a short moment he felt a strong desire for her body.

'That was a great drive wasn't it. Fantastic.' The boy's voice brought him back to the car and away from the dangerous thoughts. Away from the delicious thoughts. Away from certain satisfaction. He sighed and looked down at the smiling face. He ruffled the boy's hair and noticed the frown appear. It disappeared when he took his hand away.

'Me Mum's always doing that. Makes me feel like a dog sometimes.' The small freckled face was serious for a moment until he looked back to the car. Sorry. Adults don't think sometimes, just like to touch. Silly thing, touching.

'It's OK. I don't mind really. Well, sometimes. But you can do it, 'cos we're mates.' He stopped, looking uncertain, doubtful about this last request. He smiled and the boy smiled too. Yes, mates. Together they finished the rest of the meticulous check of all the mechanicals.

'My Mum doesn't like cars. She thinks they're dangerous.' He paused and putting his hands on his hips continued. 'Mums don't know very much sometimes, do they?' Satisfied that he'd solved the problem of Mothers, he bent down again and avidly watched as the checking continued.

They worked side by side, he showing the little boy what to do. How to check the bearings. How to check the brakes. How to check for leaks in the oil system. It was totally absorbing. When they had finally finished, they stood up with aching backs, stretching their tired muscles. Amanda was leaning once more against the back door. Again expression-less. Again she went back inside, leaving the door open. She reappeared again this time with a pint of beer and wordlessly gave it to him, watching him drink. He didn't realize how thirsty he was until the liquid slid down his throat. After the first mouthful, he gulped half down without stopping then, pausing for breath, he looked round for the little boy. There was no sign. He hadn't even waited to say goodbye. He put the glass to his lips once more and greedily drank. He could feel the liquid pouring into his dehydrated body, feel the tissues soaking it up, fighting to grab every last ounce of it. The shrivelled cells swelling again with water content, accepting the alcohol and the other impurities just for the water. The life-giving water.

Amanda lay on the bed, naked. Waiting. Waiting as she'd always been waiting. He stood in the doorway letting the sight of her spill over him. Seeing and not touching. The agony of suspense becoming an enjoyable pain. Feeling himself grow and lust and yet waiting. She lay expressionless as she'd been before. Slowly she moved on the bed. A sensual move designed to will him over and he saw it. Recognized it for what it was, but still enjoyed it. Still thrilled to the movement. He was no longer concerned with the rights and wrongs, with his ego. Only his body. Only the lust that welled in him, the lust that seemed to take over all senses, all priorities.

At last her expression changed. An excitement gleamed in her eyes as she writhed on the bed waiting for him. Still he stood in the doorway enjoying the picture. The fantasy.

He moved over slowly, removing his clothes. He was thinking now, thinking how to make her. How to be the best she'd ever had. How to make her really want him, beg him, yearn for him. He was thinking, scheming, plotting, figuring all the different ways, deciding upon a plan that would have her body leaping with desire. He wanted her to break and acknowledge her total commitment to his body. Her complete want. She watched him approach, her breathing becoming shorter, in tune with his.

Her body was better than he remembered. The nipples responded to his touch as if by magic. She groaned and he felt the power in him to control her. Now she was his to control as he wished. Every time he touched her she moaned and he felt stronger. His fingers ran down her soft skin, feeling the tiny soft downy hairs and the quivers of her flesh. Down and

64

down he moved finding the velvet triangle, parting gently and finding the silky wetness. She closed her eyes, arching her back slightly, an expression now, one almost of pain as he pressed the buttons, like a computer game, he thought. He, judging the right moves, she reacting to every stimulus. Her breathing became shorter, soft whimpering sounds finding their way from her throat. Her nipples grew and changed to a darker colour, a flush appearing on the skin of her breasts, moving up her neck slightly.

The room seemed to grow, to expand into a hall, into a vast arena, into an emptiness so that nothing else existed. Not the bed, not the dressing-table, nothing. Not even the rest of Amanda. He was completely entranced by her femininity, by her feel and smell. By her womanhood. Somewhere there was the sound of his own voice. His own dismembered voice uttering primeval noises, deep dark sounds from another age, from the prehistory of all remembered sounds. A guttural, animal rutting snuffling sound unlike anything he'd heard. It thrilled and scared him, goaded him on. Mixed with his voice was Amanda's soft whimpering, urging, the desire for procreation driving her unbidden, uncaring, onwards. He felt her hands on him, sometimes softly tickling, sometimes hard, almost painful. He could feel himself throbbing, the blood pulsing, forcing its way into the veins and capillaries. The uncontrollable urge was beginning to overpower him. He moved and entered her, forcing his way. Driving without heed. She cried out loudly this time, but there was a different tone to her voice. She cried out in triumph, wrapping her legs around him, keeping him locked inside her as she writhed and jerked, raking his back with her nails. Laughing now as she forced him deeper into her. She was in control now. She had conned him, fooled him, duped him with her body. Now he would pay the price. He would pay with his very essence.

Jenny stood in the doorway watching transfixed, the blood draining slowly from her face. She watched as they rolled, plunged, fought each other, until they lunged for the last time and lay still, sweating and panting. He rolled off Amanda and looked straight into Jenny's eyes. He smiled. The smile broadened and he laughed. Jenny was carrying a jug. She threw it complete with contents. He raised his arm and the jug smashed, slicing the skin. The blood welled and dripped onto Amanda. She screamed, cut short by his slap. Jenny stood looking at them both, then turned and walked calmly away.

Amanda lay sobbing quietly, the marks of his fingers red on her cheek, eyes puffy with the tears. Whore! She felt the word like a lash and cried out in anguish. He hit her again and again, her head flopping from side to side with the blows. Her nose started to bleed. She looked at him and then smiled through the tears and blood.

He got up, dressed and left.

Jenny was throwing everything out of the window. It was landing in a heap on the drive, some things just missing the car. He ran up the stairs and caught her from behind, turning her face to his. She was pale and calm. A terrifying calmness. He let her arms go and she hit him, her fist balled perfectly, the punch catching him on the side of the eye, making him fall back in surprise and pain. She hit him again. This time he caught hold of her arm. She fought now, like a cornered cat. Spitting, hissing. Legs, arms, nails, everything she had. He grabbed at her, missed, caught her dress and ripped it from neck to waist, leaving long scratchmarks down her breasts and belly. She ignored it and threw herself at him again. This time he caught her and held her, staring into her eyes, now alive with hatred and fury. She bent her head and buried her teeth into his shoulders. He could feel the blood run warmly down his arm. Feel the pain flash up his neck.

She lifted her head, smiling in triumph, blood around her mouth staining her teeth, a smear on her chin. He threw her back onto the bed, ripping her clothes off this time, leaping after her before she had time to move. He raped her. There on the bed amidst the blood and the wreckage of the room he raped her repeatedly until neither had the strength to carry on or to resist.

'You animal.' She was gasping for breath. 'You unfeeling

animal. That's all you are. All you ever were. All you'll ever be. Destroyer. Destroyer.' He didn't have the strength to retaliate. She lay back exhausted, her legs still spread, scratchmarks across her breasts, belly and thighs, the blood on her face now caked and cracking, flakes falling onto the stained sheets.

'Are you satisfied now you've had two women one after the other? Or do you want a whole harem?' She looked across at his expressionless face. 'You disgust me.'

He got shakily to his feet and went to the bathroom. Waves of nausea flooded through him and he vomited, then, taking the hand-shower unit, sat with his head bowed letting the ice-cold water run over his hair and down around his face and neck. He could feel the swellings from her blows starting to consolidate into tender lumps. Gradually his breathing eased and his head began to clear. From the bedroom, he could hear Jenny moving around. The noise suddenly appeared close and with a start he dropped the shower unit. She was standing next to him, dressing-gown pulled tight around her, hair back off her face. Her face was unmarked, just the swollen eyelids from recent crying and the flush of the struggle. She walked over to the cabinet and took out a bottle of Dettol, making up a solution in a small bowl. She came across, sat down beside him, and bathed the wounds on his arm and shoulder. The antiseptic stung. The wound on his arm was deep, that on the shoulder superficial. She dried his arm and, turning to the first-aid box, took out a packet of adhesive stitches. She sat back examining her handiwork, got up and put the things back in the cabinet. She went back to the bedroom. He bent his head under the cold water once more.

He stayed there until she returned with a cup of tea, placing it within reach. His face remained expressionless, watching her move out of vision again. He turned the shower off, dried, and drank the tea sitting looking at himself. The mirror seemed to put him a long way from himself. He knew the dimensions of the bathroom and it was smaller than it appeared, ergo the picture was a false one. That wasn't him in the mirror, but an image of some wasted, scarred soul. Not him though. But it was. He moved his arm and the figure moved his, but the opposite. Mirrored.

'You should take care of women son.' His father sitting beside the man in the mirror, uttering truths he thought he knew. Puffing on his evil-smelling pipe, nodding wisely.

'Your father's right.' His mother, staunchly supportive, even if she didn't believe any of it. She looked down at him maternally. His father smiled up at her, nodding.

Downstairs he could hear voices. Thought he heard voices. Thought he could hear Amanda and Jenny talking. It struck him as funny. He laughed, the figure in the mirror grimaced. He wondered why he didn't feel anything. A sense of excitement perhaps, but that was all. No regret, remorse, sorrow, anger. Nothing. It worried him for a brief moment. The only certain feeling was the throbbing of the wounds, but that would pass. The voices ceased and it was silent again. A tangible, stretching silence he could almost taste.

They sat opposite each other. Across a short distance. Across a desert a million miles wide, scarred with ravines, rapids and staggering snow-capped peaks. They coud see each other across the divide. Could hear each other across the divide. Could reach out and touch each other across the divide. He studied her face abstractly, separating each part into its own space. The eyes became two individual almond-shaped framed orbs, blinking. The nose straight, slightly turned up at the end, nostrils flaring. The mouth, now looking like a scar, opening to allow the pink tongue to moisten the cracking surface. The hair hung lank and lifeless, with fraying ends. The chin, rounded, soft, dropping fractionally with the movement of the mouth, or so he supposed. The neck was long and slim, Adam's apple clearly defined and twitching a little. Swallowing perhaps? That was what he saw. A dismembered living face, divided into its own individual pieces, its own unemotional practical pieces, there to perform a particular function and nothing more. He didn't want to see the ugliness of the whole. If it could have appeared statue-like, then maybe. But he didn't want the whole thing to stare at him in expression of anger or hatred or love if it could remain a mask.

He wondered about his own mask. Had it moved? Was it separate, individual, like hers? For an instant, he thought he saw it mirrored in her eyes, but it wasn't a mask. It was the face of a gargoyle. A trick of the light perhaps? It was gone before he had a chance to see it again, gone as the eyes suddenly blanked off, became opaque. Who had said the eyes were the mirror of the soul? It didn't matter, but whoever it was wasn't looking into these. They had closed just as effectively as the doors of a bank vault. Shut off.

He felt himself stand up and walk away. He could feel the accusation burning his back. He didn't care, just walked away.

Seven

THE MOUNTAIN AIR smelt fresh and invigorating, the peaks standing stark against the cloudless sky. He slowed the car and pulled off the narrow road onto a broad stretch of flat grass that rapidly became coarse and gave way to the first slope of the mountain. The dog sensed excitement and leapt out almost before he'd stopped, bounding away up the slope and disappearing in the heather. He looked around for signs of sheep or cattle, saw none and, relieved, sat back, letting his gaze wander down the valley to the lake, shimmering, away in the distance.

'We could make a good camp just up there in the rocks,' the boy said, moving around the car, pointing to the advantageous spot. 'Look, just up there.' It was good, certainly, but he wanted to move on further before stopping. He saw Jenny's face against the bare rock. Still accusing. Standing hating him as he drove away. He wanted to be well away from that face. With the distance the image was getting fainter. He wanted it gone for good.

'I could make it very good. Nobody could get us up there,' the boy, insistent. He resisted and saw the downcast look. He resisted that too, although it was difficult. There would be other, better, places. Bigger rocks. A running stream maybe, perhaps a rocky pool to swim in. Yes, there would be better places.

'I hope you're right.' With a last longing look. 'This is a real good place for a camp. We could stay here forever. There must be plenty of rabbits and things.' The boy climbed into the car, followed by the dog, which had reappeared.

As he drove he glanced sideways and saw the boy staring longingly back at what could have been his defensible camp site. They rounded the next bend and the boy swivelled in his seat, eyes back on the road. The dog adjusted himself to the movement and sat panting, ears flapping in the wind.

'Nobody could have attacked us.' The boy waved his right arm holding an imaginary sword. The dog ignored the arm flailing inches in front of his nose. They drove along the narrow, winding, lonely road. Twisting through the numerous blind bends, slowing to skirt the rock-falls, the car sure-footed through the potholed stone-scattered stretches. Tight and satisfied on the smooth tarmac straights. As he drove, the wind seemed to penetrate every pore in his body, filling his body, making the skin tingle, electric. He had the urge to scream, shout, let the wind carry the sound. It filled his lungs and came out in a rush. A howling high-pitched tearing sound, whipped away and left behind, followed instantaneously by the next decibel. And the next. And the next.

The straights joined the corners ever more rapidly, until there seemed to be one continuous meandering corner, the car flying controlled, barely, from one side of the road to the other. The apex of the corners rushing to meet the front tyres, first the left, then the right, then the right again. A mesmerizing stream of tarmac.

The scream lay in the wake of the car, tumbled over and over, bouncing away across the valley to rebound from the mountains and hurtle back at the car, until it seemed that it was one continuous sound. An ever-existing noise and he was the centre of it, the very existence of it. The source, the soul, the essence. It was the essence of him, he, the essence of it. It was a wild exhilarating ride. A ride that he wanted to last for ever. The mountains challenged him and he was up to it. He could handle whatever they chose to put in his way. He and the car could do it. He felt all-powerful. There was nothing that they

71

couldn't do between them. The car seemed to sense, seemed to know. Already knew. A common consciousness between them, requiring no thought.

'You should stay. There's a lot you could learn.' Amanda leaning in her customary position. He could see her framed against the aero screens, with the mountains as backdrop. She turned and watched the road. 'I'm better than this.' She turned back to him with a slow smile. 'You know I'm better than this.' He laughed and tossed her aside with the next flick of the wheel.

Jenny stood on the corner. He drove straight at her, turning to look as she spun into the ditch like a rag doll. He laughed again, glancing in the rear-view mirror to see the damage. The road was empty. There was another sound to replace the scream – his maniacal laughter. It startled him momentarily and the sound stopped, only to echo back at him a moment later. It sounded harsh in the temporary silence, then was gone.

Suddenly the thrill was gone and he slowed the car. Gone like the snuff of a candle flame. Its time was gone, its place changing. Changing. The mountains gave way to rolling hills and stark, jagged, individual peaks such as he had never seen. Dolomite peaks on a desert landscape. Yet not desert. Deserted.

He drove carefully, letting his eyes wander now, letting the car find the way down the road. He let go of the steering wheel and took his feet off the pedals. The car continued soundlessly now, and yet the vibration was there. He just didn't hear. Wasn't aware. Didn't care. Driving in a vacuum while he looked, looked as the green gave way to the scree slopes of the severe mountain peaks. The pillars that rose suddenly, without warning, from the flat land. He turned slowly and wondered where the other mountains had gone, where the twisted road had gone. There was no sign. No answer.

The boy sat quietly playing with the dog's ears. They were both oblivious to any change. He looked at them in sudden panic.

'I told you it would have made a great camp.' The boy didn't look at him. He turned back to the landscape. The ravine loomed without so much as a hint. He felt his gut turn and heart falter. The car seemed oblivious. He wrenched the wheel and brought it to a shuddering halt, wheels parallel to the edge. Stones tumbled and fell away down the sheer face, down into a bottomless void. He sat shaking.

'There's a place over there. It's better than the other one.' The boy stood watching him. He sat in the car still trembling. The boy shrugged and moved away. The dog followed him. Still he sat, his fingers held out in front like shivering talons, long, thin, shaking bone. He watched them. As he watched, he calmed. They entranced him. They were from another time, another dimension, and yet so obviously attached to him, attached to the arms, pale, strange-looking things. He calmed.
Away, in the distance, a voice carried over to him.
'Come on. It's got what you said. Bigger rocks. Running stream and a rocky pool. You were right. Come on.' The voice was persuasive. Bored. Excited. Young. He lifted his head, slowly, wearily, looking across in the direction of the voice. The car sat on the edge of the road, wheels on the lip of a shallow ditch. Over to the right he could see the boulders, some as tall as a two-storey house, some squat and menacing, all massive blocks of cracked granite, grey in the sunlight. The dog appeared briefly, skittering across between the boulders. He could hear the boy's laughter carried easily by the perfect acoustically-constructed rocks.
He stopped the engine and climbed stiffly out of the car. Removed the rucksack and sleeping-bag from behind the seat and walked over the rough ground. The boulders became bigger as he approached. They barred his way, unwilling to let him through. Stopping the trespasser, preventing passage. He could hear the boy singing close by, Singing made-up nonsense songs. Hear the sound of small feet kicking up the dirt and stones, the splash of a pebble being thrown into the water. The patter of a flat one skipping over the surface.

Which way through? There was no entry.

'Yes there is. Go to your right. There's a passage. It's very narrow. Come on. It's great.' He hunted, feeling along the rough-smooth surface of the boulders, suddenly seeing the passage hidden in the shadow of two interlocking sculptural blocks. He felt his way in, sliding between the rounded unyielding rock. He could feel the bruises rising on his knees as he climbed over an obstruction, feel the skin smear off his elbow, then he was through, standing breathing heavily on the grass.

It was a naturally fortified hollow in amongst sheer granite walls. A clear stream, running from a cleft in the rocks on the north side and into a rocky pool, nestled against the far southern boundary of the hollow. The grass was soft and springy beneath his feet. He took his shoes off, curling his toes into the earth, feeling it move, tickling. The sun sparkled off the water, warming the hollows.

'You were right, weren't you.' The boy stood stripped to the waist, his muscleless chest pushed out. 'Just as you said it would be.' The dog seemed to agree, standing panting beside him, then flopping to the ground with a satisfied grunt.

The boy ran off, disappearing into the rock face. He was confused. A moment later, the boy reappeared.

'There's a place I've found where you can put the car.' He followed the impatient little figure towards the rock. There was another well-disguised passage, wider than the first, that wound round two complete hairpin corners, opening into an area just wide enough for the car. He looked for the exit and found it without difficulty, walking through and back out to where the car stood waiting in disgust.

He parked it in the 'garage' and went back to the hollow where the boy had already laid out the sleeping-bags and was busy arranging them in a natural cave, not so much a cave as a hole in the granite wall that went in ten feet before branching to the left for a further ten feet. At the widest it was no more than twelve feet but high enough for him to stand without stooping.

74

Having laid the sleeping-bags, the boy ran out and dived into the pool, leaving the dog barking excitedly on the edge, darting at the water then backing away, distrusting the wetness, the shimmering mystery of what was below the surface.

He lay back on the grass and all sound slowly faded. The sky stretched out blue, framed by the tops of the gentle cliffs that seemed to narrow in then open out as if breathing in time to his heartbeat. He was aware of the rest of the hollow within his peripheral vision. The empty hollow, resting in the sunlight. He closed his eyes, letting his body feel the earth pressing up against him. He knew that if he opened his eyes, the earth would want to throw him off. He could feel the force building up, so much so that he had to grasp handfuls of grass to prevent himself from falling. His legs felt as if they were lifting. Weightless. He opened his eyes and sat. The hollow spun a couple of times, steadied and stopped.

He smiled and lay back again, this time enjoying the sensations, not grasping the ground, just letting the floating sensation persist until he wasn't aware of any feeling at all. Total non-existence. Complete non-entity. Everything all at once and nothing at all. Part of the surroundings. Not a stranger, not an intruder. He was as solid as the granite, as yielding as the grass, as fluid as the stream, as unfathomable as the pool. It was all here and he was part of it.

Thought ceased as the moment became the present, became the past, became the future, became nothing. Became the basic sound of the air rushing into his lungs, into every single cavity. Became the squeezing thump of his heart, the gurgle of dissolving fluids of his internal organs. Became the internal body, externally filling the hollow. Closed eyes seeing the hollow, mouth wordlessly soundlessly filling the space with noiseless songs.

He sat up again. Back to the same position, unchanged from before. He could see his mother over by the pool. She turned and waved to him smiling and continued to paddle her feet at the water's edge. She faded.

'I'll go and find some rabbits to eat. Maybe some apples and stuff.' The boy's voice startled him and he looked round to see the little figure strut confidently away. How was he going to catch rabbits? 'With these.' Holding up a handful of snares. 'My Uncle showed me. He's a poacher at weekends.' He watched until the figure disappeared through the cleft in the rock, then lay back again. His mother sat once again by the poolside.

The fire flickered its yellow-red light over the rock, lighting the immediate surfaces, enhancing the already existing shadows. Tiny puffs of wind played with the flames, pushing them this way, pulling them back and over to one side. The rabbit hissed and spat as he turned it over the fire. He could see the boy busy, stretching the skin over a makeshift frame, scraping the inside surface and rubbing salt into it, pulling the skin tight over the wood until when flicked with a finger it sounded like a high-pitched drum. When he was satisfied, it was leant up against the side of the cave. The dog sniffed at it and stepped back reluctantly at a word of warning from the boy.

He picked up a piece of wood and carefully removed the potatoes from the glowing embers. The skins were black charcoal. He passed one across to the boy who tossed it in his hand before splitting it open and placing it on the wooden platter. The white flesh steamed, soft and fluffy in the light. The boy took half the offered rabbit and, pulling a leg off, bit enjoyably into the meat. Some of the juice ran down his chin and what couldn't be licked off was hastily wiped away with the back of a grubby hand. He watched with amusement, slowly eating. The meat was tender and tasty, the potato as he'd always liked. The crisp burnt smoky taste of the skin with the light soft interior. There seemed no better banquet, no better setting. No better company.

Sometimes, in the distance, he thought he heard the sound of other cars passing. Thought he heard, but couldn't be sure. There seemed at times to be the distant glow of lights reflecting off the sky to the west. Other times he looked, there was nothing. He finished eating and sat back against the rough wall of the cave, looking out across the hollow now lying in flickering shadow, dancing, moving shadows that teased, scarcely hiding whatever lay in the darkness. Sometimes the light would nearly reveal all but, just in time, the shadows would jump back again, laughing silently at the onlooker. The stream gurgled, its detached hidden melody louder in the darkness.

He relaxed, watching the fire. The boy and the dog left him happily alone. Content. Secure. Warmed by the fire, safe behind the granite fortress.

'I loved the sea at night.' His father's voice heard clearly. 'The only sound, that of the ship and the water rushing past and the wind. I shall always remember the sound of the wind.' The silence was only interrupted by his father's lips making a soft popping sound as he smoked his pipe. 'The eerie screeching of the wind. Sometimes it tore right through. It was terrifying sometimes, there in the North Atlantic.' He listened to the voice telling the well-remembered tales. Comforting tales that enhanced the security. Was the security. 'Sometimes, in the Pacific, you could hear the silence stretching over hundreds of miles, then, at others, in the same Pacific, there was the horror of the revolving storms. Calm in the centre, so calm and peaceful, a boiling frenzied hell on the outside.' Again the silence. Just the fire crackling gently. The voice carried away on one of the gentle puffs of wind, becoming a sigh in the distance. A well-known sigh. A sigh that filled the entire hollow and then was gone, leaving a warm glow.

The spit, burnt through, fell, dropping the remains of the rabbit into the fire. He leaned over quickly trying to rescue it, burning his fingers in the process, but managed to salvage the carcass. He sucked the ends of his fingers, already feeling the blisters begin to form. He got up and walked over to the pool, dipping his hands into the cool water. It gently soothed the skin, calming the damaged nerves. He watched as the firelight caught the ripples, strobe-like.

He stood up and stripped, dropping his clothes at the

water's edge. He stood feeling the freedom of his nakedness. Feeling the eroticism of his nakedness. Feeling himself grow. He slowly let himself into the pool, allowing the cool water to flow over his body, enjoying the way it found every crack and crevice, the way it moved between his legs, around his penis, feeling the weight suddenly lift from his testicles. Feeling them floating cool. Feeling them contract tight into the sac. Feeling the water close over his head, taking his hair and spreading it around so that every individual follicle was surrounded. He swam underwater in the darkness, blindly sensing direction. Sensing the far end of the pool before he arrived, reaching out his hand to feel the roughness of the wet rock. Sliding up to the surface again, to the light flickering across the disturbed water. He was alone. Completely, totally alone.

He lay on his back in the water allowing the feeling of weightlessness to penetrate every part of him. He could feel himself grow in the darkness. Feel the blood pulsate, pump, swell, making him throb. He lay back and enjoyed the freedom to feel. The freedom to lie unashamedly male, unashamedly aroused. Nobody to cast doubts. This was his place, here amongst the grey walls, here where nobody could reach him. He laughed underwater, the bubbles wobbling up to burst with the sound on the surface. He listened to the sound underneath, watched the bubbles catch the refracted light here just below the surface. He laughed again then giggled as a bubble tickled his nose. He burst to the bank spluttering, eyes filled with water, climbed out and lay gasping on the damp grass, feeling the soft texture on his aware, alive, aroused skin. Later he would sleep. Peaceful.

Eight

THE VILLAGE looked deserted. Grey stone cottages with an air of dilapidation and neglect. The atmosphere cold, unwelcoming. He drove slowly down the street between the little houses. A supermarket stared garishly out at him. Its doors were open, but there was no sign of life. In the gardens of some of the houses, washing still remained, flapping in the breeze. It looked fresh. He pulled up beside the supermarket, got out of the car and, after a cursory glance down the road, went in.

The shelves. Anybody here? The shop yelled silence. Nothing moved. He walked down past the shelves collecting what he needed. There were no prices on the goods, no date stamps, but it all seemed fresh, new. All the shelves arranged in typical commercial order, moving him past the rows, tempting him as he went. They stretched endlessly. Brightly-coloured lines, uneven, like some futuristic apartment blocks on a massive scale, the aisles – the roads, the ceiling – the city cover. He walked down the rows. The check-out desks lay empty, forgotten islands, forlornly isolated, without use.

He pushed the trolley back out into the deserted street to the car and loaded the goods into the passenger seat.

'Got what you want David?'

He spun round at the sound of the voice, heart speeding, crouching slightly. Max stood beside his Jeep, the well-remembered smile playing over his face. In the Jeep, the two women, watching him without expression.

79

'I knew you'd finally come.' Max walked over. Where the hell did he spring from, without sound?

'This is my domain. My land. My territory.' Max waved his hands expansively. There were people now on the streets. Just a few, walking along the pavement. A horse and cart trotted past. He was surprised. An old woman came out of the supermarket and pushed past him impatiently.

'You're in my country now, David. This is where I wanted to bring you before.' Max paused. 'A pity you have come here out of desperation. To escape.' Escape? He'd never considered that was what he was doing. Well, maybe, in a sense, he was. He'd had enough of Jenny and Amanda. 'Oh is that what it was? You'd just had enough? I stupidly thought that you may have had a conscience about raping Jenny. Silly of me.' Max's face seemed to grow and the eyes bored into him. Conscience? Rape? What the hell did that matter to anybody? Anyway as far as he was concerned it was an act of retaliation.

'Excuses, my boy. Excuses.' Max turned and went back to the Jeep. He spoke without looking back. 'Follow me, I'll show you something.' No! An emphatic no! Take your girls and go, Max. He didn't need the confusion of Max and his entourage. Didn't need to feel the insignificant. The poor relation. Didn't want to be the next boost for Max's ego. He finished putting the things back in the car and climbed in. Max pulled alongside.

'I'll pick you up later.' If you know where. 'I know where. You forget, this is my beat. I know everything that goes on here.'

He drove off with the wheels spinning, screeching on the tarmac, making the horse rear, leaving the carriage driver angry. He saw Max start after him and pressed the accelerator flat to the floor, feeling the V8's power transfer to the road and push the car ever faster.

He took chances on the road, throwing the car into the bends at frightening, impossible speeds, flicking the steering wheel into opposite lock to control the slide. He glanced in the mirror and saw that he was losing Max. He didn't want Max to find the entrance to the hollow. Didn't want anybody to find their way in. It was his sanctuary.

'I like driving fast. It's great.' The boy shouted above the engine noise, face gleaming with excitement and pleasure. 'Can we go faster?' Jesus, this was fast enough. As fast as the car could go. As fast as the protesting tyres could possibly hold onto the road. The engine wanted more, but there was a limit. There was always a limit. He didn't know if he could drive it any faster, didn't know just where his limit was. Wasn't prepared to find out right at this moment. There was still no sign of Max in the rear-view mirror. It was disappointing.

'What are you looking for?' A Jeep that was following. 'Like that one there?' His eyes snapped back to the road and there, ahead, just turning from a side road onto his, was Max's Jeep. He braked hard, the car slewing sideways as one tyre lost grip on the stony surface at the side of the road. Max stopped beside him.

'I told you, this is my country. I know it like the back of my hand. Or yours for that matter. Now how about following me? And leave the kid.' Max drove off slowly down the road. He looked over to the boy and saw him walking back up the road, hands in pockets, shoulders hunched.

He started the car and slowly followed the Jeep.

They drove back into the small town. It was deserted again, as the first time he'd seen it. Max drove through and turned sharply through massive iron gates and up a tree-lined drive. Cedar trees, rhododendrons, and vast areas of lawn. The drive winding through the grounds. He was aware of the presence of the house before it came into view. Could feel the vibrancy of the place before getting near. Knew what it looked like before he saw it.

It was a modern medieval castle. Round towers, crenellations, massive doors studded with iron. Slit windows and the modern concession of glass. Somehow, it seemed to work. A folly on a grand scale. Max parked the Jeep to the side of the main door and got out, walked to a small door let into the base of one of the round towers. The girls followed, flowing behind him. He stopped the car beside the Jeep, switched off and sat for a moment looking up at the yellowy block-stone of the castle. The door was open and he went in, blinking and squinting in the darkness of the little hallway. There was a light ahead and he made his way slowly towards it.

'Come in. Sit down. One of the girls will get you a drink. Anything you want.' The room was large. Very large. A minstrels' gallery stretched the entire length of one wall, tapestries covered the other two walls and half of the third. The remaining bare wall had a door at the base and a coat of arms above it. It was too dark to make it out. A huge fireplace glowed with a couple of burning half trees and two Irish Wolfhounds lay peacefully in front of it. Max sat in a comfortable settee, two more of which formed the other two sides. A huge low oak table covered the area between the settees. One of the girls lay curled up on Max's lap, the other poured a large glass of claret, handed it to him, then sat down by the dogs, picked a magazine off the table and idly flicked the pages.

'Welcome to my home.' Max, smiling as always, watching for a reaction. He tried to force his face to remain expressionless. He wasn't going to give anything away to Max. Nothing. Max with all this affluence. No wonder the girls hung around him like adoring pets. They looked sharply up at him.

'Now, now. That's no way to think about my guests.' Max shook his head reprovingly, the long hair swinging across his face catching the light from the fire, shining golden. What the hell! He shrugged a form of apology and the girls relaxed back to their former positions. He sipped his claret, not wanting even to think now. Just letting his brain cease to function, letting the senses take over. Listen to the sound of the music. Music? He'd suddenly become aware of the music filling the room. Loud enough to be insistent but not offensive. Dire Straits in full flight in the 'Tunnel of Love'. The piano sounds resonated around the high-ceilinged room, and he let the sound flow over him. It penetrated deep into his head, swirling around, sometimes the pounding almost unbearable, then seeming to awaken all the nerves, setting them alive. Involuntary movement of his body as he swayed to the rhythms. Intoxicating. He allowed it to seep drug-like into his soul, wiping out thought.

He felt a hand on his thigh and opening his eyes saw one of the girls kneeling in front of him, eyes closed, running her hands gently up and down his legs. He watched her detached then looked across to Max. There was no expression. Max watching without expression. Without reaction. Without seeing.

He ate steadily, watching her all the time. She was aware of his look, glancing every now and then in his direction, meeting his eyes and then turning to laugh at someone's joke. Her blue eyes sparkled in the light of the thousand candles. Her honey-blonde hair hanging in hundreds of ringlets, a mass of dancing lights. He let his gaze fall to her breasts, full, firm, proudly jutting forward in the confines of the tight shirt. She laughed again and turned towards him and he saw her cat's eyes flash with mischief, saw the flash of her even white teeth.

'You like the look of her?' Max whispering quietly in his ear. 'I can see you do. A word of warning. Be careful of that one. Look around, there are plenty of others.' He let his gaze wander reluctantly off the girl, noticing briefly the petulance of her annoyance. Max was right. The hall was full of other beauties. Girls of all types and descriptions, shapes, sizes. What the hell did he want with all this anyway? He just wanted to be left alone now. No more. Never. He'd had enough with Jenny and Amanda.

'Maybe. But are you sure? You still can't keep your eyes off that one.'

Max was right. His gaze was back on the honey-haired blonde. Suddenly her expression changed. She became cat-like, hissing and spitting, then slashed long talons down the side of the face next to her. He sat back, shocked, blinked, and saw her smiling innocently directly at him. He looked for the torn face and saw nothing.

A girl swayed up to the table in front of him and slowly stripped. Then she disappeared at his annoyance. The blonde girl was gone. Vanished. Where? He felt cheated, frustrated.

'You'll have to find out. If you can really be bothered.' Max knew. He could see that Max knew, but Max wasn't telling. 'No, I'm not. This is your game not mine. If you want to play it, play it on your own. There's no help from me.' Bastard. Max smiled cheerfully.

'Don't bother son. Think first.' His father standing in front of him, barring the way. Get out of the way. He vanished. Just the last syllable hanging in the air.

He stood up, pushed the chair back from the table, and left the hall. Left the sounds of the banquet. One of Max's girls stood in front of him, blocking his path. She let the robe fall from her shoulders, exposing her perfect breasts. Suddenly they became hands that leapt at him, leapt for his throat, her face a hideous screaming mask. He struck out, driving his fist into the screaming face, feeling the blood burst over him warm against his face. Then she was gone. A groan in the shadows. He stood panting, wildly looking around. Over in the corner of the hallway he thought he saw a movement and ran across. A curtain covering a door mockingly swayed. He opened the door and ran through to stand in the courtyard. Car lights disappeared through the gate and down the drive. He ran to his car, jumped in and sat in frustration without the keys. Slowly he walked back to the castle.

Max joined him in the galleried room, poured two large brandies and sat down in the same place as before. The girls were not with him. He watched Max, waiting for comment. There was none. Why not? Max shrugged. The smile was gone. The look now serious, penetrating. Still no comment. He felt he preferred Max to talk. To needle. To annoy. The silence was unnatural and alarming. He didn't like it one bit. Max sat back, eyes closed.

Suddenly he felt very tired. Drained, feeling he didn't care any more about anything. He longed for the hollow, the safety and the sanctuary, the hollow where nobody else would go. There he could ignore whatever lay outside. He didn't want what Max had to offer. Didn't want the booze, the drugs, the women. Didn't want the strange surroundings or the pace. Just wanted the peace and the silence.

'Why are you here then?' Max, still with closed eyes. What was the answer? He thought he knew, once. Thought he might have known, once. Back when he'd decided to move away, leave everything behind. That seemed so long ago. Seemed an age, aeons ago, Centuries past.

Jenny had watched him pack. At first there wasn't any recrimination. Then the look appeared and stayed until he drove out of sight. He felt the anger start to rise again, boil up inside him. Max was watching from the other side of the room. Watching him pace up and down the room. 'Feeling guilty?' Guilty? What for? 'Why the pacing? Why the anger?' You're the one who seems to know. You supply the answers. Max lifted his shoulders and shook his head. 'The answers, if there are any, are not so readily available, my friend.' Of course, the perfect answer from one who had no answers. What was the question? That's the problem. Find the question and the answer will be readily available. Maybe the honey-blonde is the answer. Max laughed, a short harsh sound that spun around the room and battered his ears.

'That's it, is it? Dip your dick and pull the answer out on the end, complete with question. You're worse off than I thought.' So what help are you in this bizarre place? Question. Now where's the answer? He looked round at Max but he was gone.

A noise from the minstrels' gallery made him look up. Max stood spotlit as if on a raised stage. He held his hands out. 'What is the answer to the question? What is the question? The question is what is the question? Therefore the answer lies in the question itself. Ergo, there is no answer for there cannot be a question.' He looked down accusing, pointing his finger, his voice booming from the gallery. 'Now you supply the question that does not require a question for an answer?' You are deliberately confusing the issue for no apparent reason. 'The question must therefore be why? The answer being the question why not?'

He walked away from the gallery to rearrange his thoughts. What had this to do with anything? Another question. He answered it before Max had a chance, playing Max's game now. What has what to do with what?

Max's laugh boomed out from the gallery. 'You're learning. Learning that the question is unimportant. Because it doesn't matter. Doesn't mean anything. The answer doesn't resolve itself, because if it did, there would be no question. Therefore no answer. The circle completes itself. The answer is already there with the question. Both together. Your question and answer need not necessarily be mine or anybody else's.' He leaned forward grasping the gallery rail. 'Now what was the question?' Max's eyes mocked him. Stared down at him, pinning him to the floor. Laughing at him. Playing with him. He smiled back without flinching, wanting to reduce Max. Wanting equal terms, trying to understand the riddles.

'There are no riddles. What you have to understand is that there is no mystery. No question. No answer. Existence is all that there is. Your existence, my existence. The existence of this.' Suddenly a tiger leapt from the gallery straight at him. He dived to the floor to see it disappear into thin air. 'Or this.' A Zulu warrior stood in front of him, assegai ready, the soft ululating sound growing louder. The Zulu lunged and again he dived to the floor, rolling over and back up onto his feet to crouch, watching the Zulu disappear like the tiger to be replaced by a huge breaking sea bearing down on him. He knew he couldn't escape. It vanished just as suddenly as it appeared. Max walked down from the gallery and sat down, picking up the brandy glass. 'Simple electronics. Holograms. Enhanced, magnified. Real. They existed for you. For those seconds they existed for you. There was no

86

question, therefore no answer. Existence. The question of existence is no question. Existence is.'

He stood on the battlements looking over the night landscape, lifting his head to stare at the bright sky filled with the sparkling brilliance of the stars. A breeze, warm, blew into his face, carrying with it the scent of the distant pine trees and the new-mown grass strong in his nostrils, pungent odours. The sound of Max's voice was still fading in his head. The breeze was clearing the confusion. He let the air chase the thoughts away.

The lights of the small town flickered. There was a movement beside him. He half expected it. Wasn't alarmed by it. The honey-blonde moved beside him, staring out over the land, not looking at him. They stood silently side by side. He noticed her nose was slightly hooked. Not unpleasantly so, just a feature on the otherwise flawless face. Her bone structure was fine and light. High cheekbones. Her full heavy breasts should have been out of place, but her flaring hips complemented them. The honey-blonde fine hair streamed back away from her head in the breeze. She let him study her without affectation. Without embarrassment.

'I got bored with the small talk. You're David. I'm Lisa.' Her voice was low and huskily sexual. He felt a sudden thrill. An electric charge ran through his body, raced through shaking him so that he shivered involuntarily. She didn't seem to notice. Just stared straight ahead. He felt strange. An unknown feeling creeping through his body. A new and mistrustful feeling. He felt unable to talk, afraid of spoiling the moment with his own inarticulate mutterings.

'You been playing the Max game. I know.' She was silent for a moment remembering. 'I used to come up here after a session too. Just to clear my head.' Again the silence, this time lasting. He turned to stare back out over the landscape. He thought for a long moment that she had turned to examine him. He was too afraid to look. Too afraid to catch her look, to see into her eyes, afraid of what he might see reflected there.

'Isn't it beautiful.' He nodded. Now he was beginning to feel numb. Not to feel. Trying to drive out feeling. The unwanted surge, wanted to keep everything at bay, didn't want and yet yearned for the feeling. 'You don't have an ounce of feeling in your entire body.' Jenny said, hands on hips, standing above the tree-line. 'Nothing. Not a thing. You don't even know what the word means.' He watched her move away across the sky, fading.

'Peaceful here. But sometimes you can still hear Max's voice.' Lisa still standing quietly beside him. Still watching the cloudless night and the darkened earth.

He ceased to feel the stone walkway of the battlements. As if he were weightless again as he had been in the hollow. This time his eyes were open and he felt he was an inch or so above the stone. He looked down to check but his feet were lost in the shadow. If he was floating a few inches then she must be too. Their relative positions hadn't altered. She still just up to his chin. The castle seemed to move, to revolve around its own axis leaving the two of them vertical, side by side, looking ahead, seeing everything from the same place but without the backdrop. He thought he would fall and put out a hand to steady himself. She noticed the movement and he felt foolish, changing the move into a further extended exaggerated movement to lean on the battlements.

The castle reverted to its normal place with his touch and the weight back on his feet. So immediate was the realization that his feet for a moment almost couldn't take the weight. He held on tight. Lisa adjusted her balance and swayed close to him. He could smell the freshness of her hair as it brushed his face lightly. There was a stirring sensation deep within him. He had the urge to reach out and crush her to him, an urge he didn't understand, an urge so powerful it was alarming. He wanted to feel her body against his. Feel her lips pressed close to his, smell her skin, her hair, absorb her into his very being. He wondered at this strange dominant feeling. This alien form that had risen from a murky uncharted depth.

One thing was suddenly and blindingly clear. He wanted

this woman. Wanted her as no other before. He fought the rising obsession and knew he couldn't win. Knew it would envelope him. Welcomed the invasion. Tried to throw it off. Invited it closer.

'Are you sure you know what you're doing David?' His mother's tremulous voice just before the wedding. He never knew what he was doing. Never thought. Just acted. Instinctive. No point in thinking, Mother, never did any good before. Won't now. Trust the instincts, trust the lust. That's all there is, nothing more: lust. Sex. Animal instincts. Procreative drive. The need to continue the species. That's all Mother. Nothing more.

Lisa shivered. He wondered if she was cold.

'Just a little. This breeze isn't as warm now as it was. I think I'll go inside.' He followed her off the battlements and down the spiral stone staircase back to the galleried room. Max sat in the same place as before. He seemed not to acknowledge their presence, sat stroking the head of one of his girls whilst the other lay asleep at his feet. Lisa turned and smiled at him. The smile was her whole face. She paused, then slowly turned and continued to the door, opened it and disappeared from sight. He stood watching the empty space. The disturbed air still held the smell of her. He inhaled deeply, holding his breath until his head began to swim, then slowly let it out with hardly a sound. The image of her smile lingered in front of his eyes. Shimmering.

Nine

'NOW WHAT you going to do?' Max had said. He'd driven back to the hollow, back to safety. He sat staring into the water. He saw her smile from the depths of the dark pool. Saw the unfathomable look, wondered if it meant what he'd not dared hope.

'Well. You wanted her. There she is. What's the problem?' Max scoffing. 'Existence. She exists. You exist. The time exists.'

He'd walked out on Max then. Left him to his girls and his dogs. To his hologram toys. To his fairytale castle. Max could stuff himself. Could shove his word games, his manipulations. He wasn't having any of it. Questions and answers. Answers and questions. Crapulous nonsense, and he didn't want to hear any more of Max's mental mix-ups. He shouted across the pool at the granite. It refused to shout back, kept the sound, held it tight, so that he had to shout again to be heard. This time the sound came back twofold, swamping him with his own insanity. He felt better for it, the tension eased although it left his throat sore.

He got up and walked slowly around the boundary of the hollow, running his hand along the rock, feeling the rough smoothness, walking past the hidden clefts and little passageways, loving the very security of his home. His fortress, his castle. Max might have toys but Max didn't have this. He couldn't penetrate this place. There was no way in. He'd checked first thing as soon as he returned.

The climb from the outside had been rough as far as he could go. Only once had he been able to conquer the granite cliff, but once on top had been unable to find the hollow. Once he thought he spotted it but there was no way round to it. He climbed for hours. Checking and re-checking, ensuring there was no way for a surprise attack. No chance of anybody sneaking in unannounced.

'Told you it was a good place. No problem here,' the boy had said when he returned tired and dirty. 'Nobody can find their way in here except you and me.' He was right. It was an impenetrable fortress. The only possibility was for somebody to follow the car and he'd been very careful not to be seen.

He continued walking round the walls. Even though he'd checked there was still the doubt. The sneaking, unbidden, treacherous doubt lurked behind the shadows, creeping out at night to threaten, to scare, to catch the unwary and destroy the self-built confidence. He wanted to bury the doubt, ensure that this was indeed his sanctuary. The very womb of his existence.

'Frightened are you? Unsure? Something you can't handle?' He could cheerfully have killed Max then, see his blood and brain mingle with the pale tapestries, watched the dogs finish off the rest. The thought had excited him.

Here Max couldn't get to him. Wasn't going to. He'd keep him out. Climb the cliff if you can. Find the passages if you can. He shouted backwards and forwards across the hollow, running now, racing across to touch the walls, swimming across the pool. Pushing, pushing, forcing the legs and arms to work, forcing the pace until he dropped exhausted by the entrance to the cave, sweat pouring off his naked body, his legs trembling with the exertion. Eyes wide and unseeing, mouth a gash across his face, saliva dripping from the corner to fall down his cheek and across his neck.

'I love you when you sweat. Love to see the muscles tense and bulging. They tell me it's the best time then. The blood pressure's high.' Amanda with piranha eyes, salivating at the thought. She liked to watch him return from the runs. Sometimes he thought he could see her hand moving between her legs. He'd always brushed her aside. Like now. Wiping the image off the rock face.

Slowly his breathing returned to normal. Normal? He wondered what normal was. What was it? Was this normal? To lie here naked in the sun, alone, sweating, thinking of the past, watching the parade of images from the past saunter past at will. At their will, not his.

Where was Lisa? He wanted that vision of the previous day. Wanted to know whether or not she was one of Max's hologram figures. Afraid that she might be a passing figment of Max's imagination.

If Max had done this to him, then Max would suffer.

No, Max couldn't have done that. Surely not? That was the one image that he knew to be real, knew it with an aching certainty. Saw her now, standing on the battlements, her hair streaming away in the breeze. Felt the relaxation of her presence, the tension of her presence. He yearned for the confused thoughts and emotions. Yes, emotions. He wasn't sure he knew what the word meant, but it seemed to fit, seemed to sound right, to roll off the tongue. He could live with the expression at the moment. Maybe later he would consider the total sexual lust aspect to drown out the word. Maybe that's what it was anyway. Maybe.

Hypothetical meanderings across the grass and away into the sky. Meaningless mouthings. Sightless thoughts. No images, no pictures, nothing. His head ached with the jumbled, jarred, deranged, dyspeptic nonsense. He rummaged amongst the goods he'd taken from the supermarket and hadn't paid for. Found the bottle of Armagnac and, stripping the lead cover, pulled the cork. The cognac tasted good. Very good. So good he choked, spluttered and nearly lost half the first mouthful. The second mouthful drifted easily down his throat. Soon he'd be mercifully drunk, oblivious to the slight sounds that would make him jump in the dark, to lie awake straining to hear in the night. Listening for the tell-tale sounds that would warn him of approaching enemy. Not tonight. Tonight he would lie without fear, without concern, without hearing. When the bullet came, he wouldn't feel it. Not tonight.

'Grenade!' The cry was shot and screamed with the intensity of the firefight. He rolled to one side seeing the smoking, rolling, bouncing object career towards him. The explosion was long, slow and hot. He felt the blast and the pieces of flesh and blood splatter against him. Saw the face minus one eye make one brief plea and then fade sightlessly away. The rounds sang, buzzed and cracked around him. He saw Atkins get to his feet, angry frantic expression, rifle firing from the hip. Shouted a warning and watched as a burst of machine-gun fire cut through his abdomen. Could see the chunks fly from his back. Saw the body fold, jerk and fall backwards with the impact.

He crawled through the mud and entrails. Ducking, crying, digging into the earth at the sound of the shells that whistled a short brief moment before exploding with ground-jarring, ear-shattering precision metres from him. Still he moved forward, slowly, feeling the blood drip from his torn sto-mach, the flesh hanging loose from his face. Not caring now. Knowing the whimpering terrified sounds were him, but not paying any attention. All objectivity was on the enemy bunker ahead. All his entire training was focused on the flame-spitting slit in the ground. All his life distilled into this one moment. As he crawled he pulled the grenades from his pouch. Held the small round objects lovingly. Tenderly. Crawled forward. Closer until he was deafened by the clatter of the machine-gun. Could hear the frightened breathing of the men in the trench. Could smell the cordite, faeces and urine. Could taste the stale blood on the ground as he crawled over the corpses littering the battered earth. Closer. Closer. Don't look now! Please don't look now! For God's sake don't look now. The pins came out of the grenades smoothly and he tossed them perfectly into the trench, rolling back down the hill. He stopped, lying on his back, and looked up at the bayonet.

He screamed as the steel plunged down. Screamed and screamed. Woke up screaming. Woke up crying, shouting, screaming, the smell of faeces and urine strong in his nose. Mucus running from his nose mixing with the tears and the sobs with the pain. He crawled into the cave and lay curled in the corner. He could hear them hunting him, hear them calling him. He crawled forward as the sounds died away. Crawled forward to the entrance to the cave. If he could make it to the car, he could escape. If he could make it.

There was nothing outside only the wind songs sighing against the rock. The firing had died away. Over in the distance a flare lit the night sky and then fizzled out. He ran for the passage then. Ran stumbling, sobbing for the passage, tripping on the potholed, cratered ground. Sometimes his face buried into the stinking rotting gut of a corpse as he fell. The smell stayed with him, the sickly cloying smell of rotting death. Worm-ridden decaying bodies. He screamed again. Screamed and screamed as another salvo rocketed in from nowhere, exploding all around him. His screams mingling with those of the wounded and dying. There in front of him, a legless man holding his arms out in supplication, tears of pain on his surprised face, blood staining the ground as he wriggled towards him. He ran on, crashing into the rock wall, stumbling round it trying to find the passage.

He thought his head would explode. Thought that he'd never find it and behind coming closer and closer was the terrible sound of the voices of his death, laughing now as they knew they had him cornered. Laughing, revelling in the excitement of a kill. The knowledge that the end of the hunt was near. That soon his life would be pouring, writhing, screaming, sobbing, gurgling in front of them while they bathed in his blood. Nearby he could hear the insistent roamings of a rock guitar rising and falling on the beat. Organ music and synthesized sound mixing with the crack, thump ear-splitting explosions of the battle. A bizarre prelude to the final black curtain of oblivion.

Still he ran fumbling in the dark. Hysterical mad clawing fingernails against the rocks. He could feel them splinter and rip, feel the nerves exposed on the raw skin, see the white bone scrabbling at the granite. Until finally he fell through. Fell flat into the opening, and falling, tripping, belly-crawled his way towards the car. Round the corners he knew. There it was suddenly, lit by the brightest flare close overhead. He still in the shadows, frozen. White eyes staring wildly, still in the blackness waiting eternally for the light to die. Go! Go! Go, damn you!

The darkness returned. The car fading into an unrecognizable lump hiding against the rocky walls. He moved forward quickly now, reaching with his bloodied bone-revealed fingers for the comfortingly smooth body. His hands touched the sharp, razor-sharp edge of the knife and he felt himself being clutched from behind. Dragged back. Felt the cool hot slice and the warm slow stream.

He passed out. Dying on the ground inches from the car. Passed into the comforting, frightening gloom. And then: nothing.

When he woke, he was lying beside the car. It stood, slightly dusty in the early morning light, but still shining. Quiet and confident. Totally secure. He ached all over. His scar hurt. Felt pummelled, as if somebody had tried to open it again. He looked down and saw scratchmarks. His fingernails held the evidence of skin and traces of blood. He was naked. Next to his leg lay the remains of the bottle.

He looked around suddenly afraid. Looking for the enemy, looking for the corpses, looking for the reality. It wasn't there. Slowly he stood, shakily. The faeces had stained his legs. He felt ashamed and embarrassed. Felt small and dirty. Gently he touched the car. The reality. The only stable solid object. Then he turned and unsteadily went back into the hollow.

The boy sat by the fire and he could smell bacon frying over

95

the hot coals. The boy didn't look at him. He went over to the pool and slowly slipped into the water, dipped underneath, washed his hair and face and cleaned the rest of his body. Then swam quickly backwards and forwards two or three times.

He hauled himself out onto the grass and noticed the towel and clothes lying within easy reach. The boy was still at the fire. He dried and dressed, then self-consciously went over to the fire.

'Thought we'd have a good fry-up this morning. I love breakfast like this. Don't you?' Looking at him without accusation. Without prying. He was glad. Suddenly the boy seemed older than his ten years. Seemed to change from moment to moment. Sometimes young and naïve. Others, old and innocent. Never clever or wise. Never accusing. Always just accepting. He nodded and sat down close to the fire, feeling the heat begin to burn through the jeans.

'Got some sausages as well. And some eggs. But I'm not very good at doing eggs.' What he didn't understand was where all this had come from. He didn't get it from the supermarket. 'The woman brought the stuff. Put your clothes out, tidied up.' The boy looked resignedly resentful. Where was the girl then? He looked around for her. 'She left a few minutes ago. Not long.' He ran to the car, and stared back down the road. There was no sign. He went to the cliff face and began climbing the way he'd found before. At the top, the horizon stretched away. There was no sign of anybody. He returned to the cave in the hollow. The boy handed him the wooden platter with the bacon, eggs and sausage.

'She said she'd come back. Some time. Didn't say when. Said you'd know where she was anyway.' The boy turned to his own breakfast and ate with obvious relish, bolting the food down, wiping the yellow egg from his chin. The dog sat expectantly beside him, watching as the food was transferred from platter to mouth. Watching every move. Only a few paces away was his own bowl of dogfood. Every now and then he glanced towards it, licking his lips, and then looked back panting at the platter just inches from his nose. The boy finished the meal except for a piece of bacon and a sausage. He looked at the dog, he glanced quickly from face to platter, to face, to platter. The boy put the platter down and watched with pleasure as the dog devoured the two pieces and then ran over to his bowl.

He was thinking about her. Was it her? Was it his blonde-haired fantasy?

'Yes she was blonde. Sort of nice-looking.' The boy screwed up his face, trying to be grown up. 'I suppose she was beautiful. For a girl. I suppose.' Then it must have been Lisa. It had never occured to him until now how she managed to find her way in. When it did, it frightened him. If she could find her way in, Max could too.

'I don't like the sound of this bloke Max. Don't want to meet him.' The boy sat pouting, chin on his knees, drawn up. Held tight, rocking to and fro very slightly. 'I wouldn't like to know him.' Mind made up and confident. 'He won't get in here. I promise. He won't find his way in. I'll let the girl in, but not him.' The boy stood with a hand on his shoulder. Protective. The self-appointed guardian of the hollow.

'Fallen in love, have you?' Jenny's mocking face appeared briefly. He pushed it away.

'She won't be as good as me. No chance.' Amanda's smile from the jaws of madness itself. She disappeared, as had Jenny. He was content now. Now that he could banish them at will, block them out as soon as they appeared at the stroke of a thought. It was pleasing to be able to do it. Pleasing. Gratifying. Rewarding. Summon their images and then throw them away. Watch them fade, surprised, angry. Summon and dismiss. Power. Power to control, power to disregard, power to do nothing. His mind came back to Lisa. Back to now, back to the strange sensations. Back to what? To something he knew nothing about. Perhaps now was the time to find out. To analyse in the cold light of the summer morning. Analyse what? There was nothing to analyse. He was attracted to a girl. To a member of the opposite sex. A natural, normal, essentially practical arrangement. devised over the centuries for the express purpose of the continuation of the species. Why should he wonder at the simple fact that he wanted her. Wanted to bed her. Wanted the most basic thing any human being wanted. Wanted to discharge his seed into her. Feel the process begin. Feel the thrill of that fact.

'What does this bloke Max want?'

A question from the now. From the mouth of the boy. What was the answer? Did he really want to get into that again? What did Max want? Maybe Max didn't want anything. Maybe Max just liked playing games. Maybe. A lot of maybes. He decided it didn't matter anyway. Whatever Max wanted was whatever Max wanted and that was nothing to do with him. He just wanted Lisa. That's what he wanted.

'Are you going to try and find her?'

The questions. There were a lot of questions all of a sudden. Questions about questions. Questions he didn't know the answer to. Questions he didn't know the question to. He stood and walked to the car. The boy faded away into the background. He knew that the young face would be sad, but it was unimportant. Lisa was out there somewhere. Lisa had given him the come-on. Now like a knight in shining armour he was going to find her, bring her back to his castle, care for her, boost his own ego, feel himself swell with the male vanity and arrogance.

He reached inside the car for the duster and the polish. The car seemed slightly offended at being cleaned. The dirt marks stubbornly resisted his efforts until finally fading into the paintwork; slight pitting in the aluminium scorned his polish, his vanity, not wanting to be a part of it. He stood back and looked at the car. It shone in the sunlight, Shone like a schoolboy being shown off to adults after a prize giving. Shone uncomfortably.

'Can I come?' No. 'I won't get in the way. Promise.' There's no room. He didn't want the boy there. Didn't want the complication. 'I won't get in the way.' The young repetitious face insistently naïve and innocent. 'Please.'

98

He tried to ignore the plea, turning back to the car and checking the oil, water, tyre pressures. Constantly aware of the boy's presence. There, just behind him, at every step. Didn't want him. Didn't want to hurt him. . . . Well maybe just for the ride. A short way. Provided he wasn't in the way.

'Great. Really great.' The face alight with joy. The dog jumped about barking in the excitement. It was catching and he smiled as well, enjoying the pleasure he'd just given.

Ten

VAN MORRISON BLUES from the tape player, booming out
over the landscape, exhorting the caravan. He, singing to the
words, tunelessly in the breeze, wildly happy in the sliding,
vibrating speed hit of the car. The drug coursing through his
brain in blurred enjoyment and balanced mania. The boy
sitting, laughing, shouting, howling to the elements as they
drove. Both high as the skipping clouds below the sun. Both
living vital moments vividly on the summer's day. He,
careless in the ecstasy of his mindless joy, the boy caught up
paralleling his mood.

They drove, seeing the entire countryside with their
vibrantly attuned senses. Seeing. Feeling. Touching the wind.
Drugged by their total happiness.

'There's nothing in the whole world like this!' The boy,
joyously bellowing over the wind. 'Nothing anywhere.'

He barrelled into the next bend, power-sliding through,
hearing the boy squeal with delight and fear, mixed emotions
combined to heighten the thrill.

The wheel felt live, slippery and solid beneath his hands. He
watched, fascinated, as the hands blurred with the speed of
the opposite-lock flick, dazzled, as his feet danced from pedal
to pedal. Heel, toe, braking, accelerating, declutching, the
engine singing to his conducting, hitting the right notes in the
right places. The exhaust pipes echoing the poisonous sound,
rolling it over down the road, a lead-stained memory on the

tarmac. Tyres, hot, soft and bending into the corners, flexing, breathing, sighing over the bumps. The dashboard needles flickering tell-tale indications of satisfaction, sometimes to spin alarmingly over the dials in frantic loss of control, to be saved and gently returned to the safe area.

The car seemed almost to have a self-destruct mechanism, the screaming urge to go harder, faster, beyond the limits. A couple of times he knew he'd just caught the runaway. The boy laughed and squealed in delight, thought it was skilful control. At those times he felt his heart falter then crash around inside his chest, adrenalin shaking his body with deliciously excited, frightened tremors. The car barrelled on, oblivious to the emotions rising and falling on its back.

'Stirling Moss doesn't stand a chance.' High-pitched, wildly-shouted, ecstatic nonsense from the boy that made him smile and relax, allowing the car to go faster. The dog panted, ears streaming, head swinging from side to side annoyed at not being allowed time to see the passing countryside.

'Slow down or I'll be sick. Slow down.' Jenny, pale and frightened, angry and uncomfortable. He wasn't going very fast, just liked to place the car with precision into the corners. Feel the balance. Enjoy the judgement. She was spoiling it. Spoiling the enjoyment. 'Do it on your own if you want to kill yourself, not with me.'

'This is fantastic. Fantastic.' The boy's shouts broke through. 'My Mum wouldn't like it. Dad wouldn't either. I do.' Shouted to the wind, to anything, anybody that cared to hear. It didn't matter. The mood was infectious and he relaxed once more. Just drove. He slowed at the entry to the town. Threaded growling engine sounds past the few people in the street, then out, away from the buildings, back on to the open road. A different road. Not so open. Winding through pine forest, up and down short hills, the sun streaking through the disciplined fire-breaks placed with military precision.

Amanda had been waiting. Sitting on a log. Waiting as he came sweating, gasping, the dog bounding before. She

101

stepped out and nearly tripped him. Sweat in his eyes, stinging, salt like little needles on his skin. She was in her running shorts. Pulled up tight, her crutch obvious. Painfully obvious. T-shirt stretched tight. Hair held away from her face with a multi-coloured headband. Very chic. Pure crap. Staged nonsense, even down to the slight signs of perspiration on her upper lip and forehead. He'd wondered where she managed to find the water out here. Probably had a little bottle.

'Hello David.' Slightly breathless. Just enough. Not too much. 'I didn't know you came this way.' Like hell. There was a hint of derision in her eyes. Just a hint? She fell into step beside him, making sure he could see her breasts bouncing rhythmically. He drove hard into the next corner, banishing her from his sight. The car slewed sideways through the corner, throwing the boy and the dog hard against the side of the car. He glanced quickly at the young, suddenly-scared expression, and slowed. Eased his grip on the wheel. Breathing out slowly, letting the tension seep away. The dog seemed happier now being able to catch the myriad of differing smells, mouth dropping open again, tongue dangling from the side.

'That was quite a slide.' Shakily. Colour returning to the boy's cheeks. 'It's a good car.' Enthusiasm returning. 'Very good.'

The shot was perfect. The bird seemed to stop, fold, and spiral out of the sky, to land with a still thud among the coarse grass. The sound echoed away across the moorland. Two more were brought down very quickly. One was messy, the bird obviously wing-shot and struggling on the ground. The only sound was the flutter of its bloody feathers against the soft grass. It tried to stand but the shattered legs refused to move and the bird fell onto its beak, head bent back, confused, desperate survival in its eyes. The man walked up casually, bent down, and broke its neck with a practised move. The bird's eyes glazed and stared unblinkingly, no longer concerned. The man slipped a noose over its head and hung the body from his belt. It dangled obscenely from his side.

'My Dad taught me to shoot. Used to go with him quite often. Bit cold in the winter. Especially with the ducks. I didn't like that.' The boy, leaning back in the seat, holding onto the struggling dog. He wasn't listening, just nodded absently and continued to stare at Lisa walking along beside Max. He wanted to turn around and drive away. Had wanted to when the men had stopped him while the drive crossed the road. Knew that Max was around when he saw the Jeep parked. But Lisa kept him there. His entire concentration was focused on her. He knew she knew it, but didn't seem put off by it. Max was grinning as they walked over.

'Well, David, you remembered the shoot.' He hadn't. Didn't remember it ever being mentioned. It didn't matter. He was here now. He nodded absently and continued to stare at Lisa. She smiled back at him. Teasing perhaps? Max leaned against the car. 'One of the men will fix you up with a gun. Anything you like. From Armalite to shotgun, four, ten, or twelve bore. Pump-action or single-shot. Side-by-side or over-and-under. And a choice of magazines for the Armalites. One rule on the use of the rifles: single shot only. No spraying the poor bloody prey with thirty-odd rounds. That could be considered over-kill.' Max laughed, relaxed and easy. Lisa smiled. He got out of the car catching the boy's eye. Lisa took the boy's hand. Uncomfortable young eyes, small feet that scuffed the ground. Max looked at the boy. 'You could have left him. Still, no matter. Lisa will look after him. Come walk.' Max moved off. Lisa nodded slightly to him, urging him to follow Max. Reluctantly he did, taking the offered shotgun. 'Come on then. Let's have some fun eh?' Anything you say Max, he thought, his mind still firmly on Lisa. 'A truce, yes? No more stupidity from either of us. What's the point.' More questions Max? 'Purely rhetorical this time.' A short laugh. He didn't reply. Still wary of Max, not knowing what was coming next. Wary or jealous? Which? No, not jealous, envious maybe. Envious of the seeming wealth, health and happiness that Max undoubtedly had. Had what he wanted. Some of what he wanted. 'What do you say, David? Forget the other night? Clean slate. Fun time. What do you say?' He nodded and it seemed to satisfy Max. 'The shooting is good here. Plenty of game and no silly laws about seasons. All game shot are for the pot. There are quite a few people that rely upon the estate for a livelihood. The town, for instance, is technically part of the estate. Goes way back in history.' Max stopped, cocked an ear, and raised his shotgun as the pheasant broke screeching into the air. Max lowered the gun. 'Yours.' He rapidly raised and fired. Instinctive. The bird fell. Clean. Max grinned, the boy shouted with glee, and Lisa cheered. Max clapped a hand on his shoulder. 'Alternate shots. How about a little wager. Nothing ridiculous.' Another game. Yet another of Max's games. He should have known. 'No, nothing big. Let's say you buy the drinks if you lose, if I lose I treat you to dinner.' Sounded reasonable, but there was still the worry in the background. Not worry. Caution.

'Go on, I dare you.' Roger his best friend goading from the safety of the ground. He stood on the top branch and looked over at the other tree. It was a good ten feet to the other branch, and now he wondered why he'd bothered to brag he could jump across like Tarzan in the film they'd just seen. Easy, he'd said, nothing to it, his childish pride unable to back down from Roger's taunts.

'You can't do it. If you do it, I'll do it.' It was that last taunt that had sent him up the tree in the first place. Now his nerve was failing rapidly. He looked down the thirty feet to where Roger stood looking up, secure in the knowledge that he wouldn't do it. Roger's expression began to change, become uncertain. He felt the power then, felt it spread through his body for the first time. Felt the uncertainty and fear lift, just felt the elation of victory, the sure knowledge that he'd won before he did it. Roger was panicking. He laughed. A cruel strange sound from the young body.

'Don't I was only joking. Don't. I don't want to. I can't.' He enjoyed Roger squirming like this. Loved the power. He stopped laughing, looked across at the far branch, braced himself and leapt across the gap. Half-way across he knew he wasn't going to make it. Knew it with a sickening certainty. The end of the branch tore out of his grasp and he fell crashing through the lower boughs. Curiously detached. His fist caught a branch. Fingers instinctively curled around the rough surface and he felt the muscle wrench in his shoulder as his full bodyweight was brought up short to hang, dangling, by one arm. He could see Roger below him crying, staring up, frightened, terrified. The pain in his shoulder faded. Your turn Roger, and watched as the little figure turned and ran crying through the wood.

'Are you as good as Max?' Lisa's mischievous smile. The boy looked at her crossly.

'Of course he is. He's better. Much better. He's the best.' Pouting, pulling his hand away. Lisa giggled.

'If you're not, it's going to cost you a lot. If I know Max.' She was probably right, but Max wasn't going to win. Concentration time. The next bird rose, Max hitting it clean. The dog bounded off and retrieved the bird. Was disappointed when nothing was offered as a reward. Lay down disgusted, panting. The boy fondled the long ears.

'Clean shots count as one point. Anything else a half. OK?' Max, secure in his confidence. Sounded fair. He wondered if the prey thought it was fair.

'How did you hurt your shoulder?' Mother, concernedly inquisitive. 'Why was Roger crying?' Said he didn't know, and hoped the questions would cease so that he could go to his room and cry with pain. Away from the prying eyes. Didn't want anybody else to see that he wasn't as strong as Tarzan. 'Have you been climbing trees in your good shorts again?' There was no answer to that. Pain came in many forms. At that moment his pain was simply physical. At least he could take comfort that Roger's was deeper. If only he'd understood at the time, he'd have enjoyed the bluff more and not suffered the pain of the proof. Roger's pain would have been more enduring then. Always there to be resurrected. But all he had

105

was a painful shoulder and the knowledge that Tarzan was far better.

The bird tried to fly as it fell. Max grinned savagely. He was angry at the missed shot.

'Only half a point David. The lead is mine. I don't miss.' Lisa shrugged apologetically and the boy turned away, hiding his disappointment. Tears in his eyes.

She was five years old with big brown eyes, red hair and freckles. And he was was totally enraptured. He wiped away the snot the handkerchief never seemed able to capture, then absently rubbed the back of his hand down the side of his shorts. Mouth open, eyes wide and funny things happening inside his chest, he couldn't explain. When she smiled at him he scratched his head in embarrassment. She held her mother's hand, clutching a rag doll in the other. He was in disgrace again. Roger and he had been fighting, hence the torn shirt and shorts and the bruise on the side of his face. None of that seemed to matter. He was in love and he knew this was the only girl in the world.

He dug into his pocket, found a Liquorice Allsort and handed it over to her. She looked at the dusty fluff-covered object as if it was the crown jewels, and would have put it in her mouth if her mother hadn't knocked it away. He picked up the plate and passed the smoked salmon across to Lisa. Max talking again.

'Can't understand how I winged that last bird. Wasn't that far.' He shrugged, dismissing Max's comments, eyes on Lisa.

'He seemed to move at the last moment. Jink out of the way. Just bad luck Max. That's all.' He felt a little annoyed that she should provide Max with an excuse.

'Just a bad shot if you ask me.' The boy, still disgruntled at having to be behind the action instead of at his side, sitting cross-legged tearing the flesh off the chicken bone with his teeth. Lisa scolded him softly, stroking his hair, the boy moved his head away annoyed.

'Come now. Be a little generous. It wasn't that bad, now

was it. Anyway it's not a serious competition.' Max's turn to laugh. 'If it was, we both would be shooting better. Eh, David?' He didn't agree but raised his glass. Of course they both could shoot better. But then there was no competition was there? He watched the red-haired girl walk away with her mother, then bent and retrieved the even-dirtier Liquorice Allsort. The now holy relic, to be treasured because she had touched it. He put it carefully in his pocket trying not to squash it, walked home beside his mother glowing with pleasure, oblivious to all the lectures he was getting over the fight.

The next day his dreams fell in ruins as he saw the red-haired girl walking hand-in-hand with the boy opposite. He couldn't understand how she could like someone with buck teeth and glasses. The Liquorice Allsort disappeared down a drain, no doubt a tasty morsel for a hungry rat.

'Listen David, why don't you come and stay up at the castle? Plenty of room, it's big enough so you can be on your own if you want. How about it? Instead of camping out. Can't be very comfortable.' Max lifted his glass and one of the women filled it to the brim. Eyes looking straight into him waiting for a reply. No, was the reply. The hollow was independent and, besides, he rather liked it. Had grown attached to it. The boy was looking mistrustfully at Max and sighed with relief.

'The hollow's great. We've got everything there. Everything we need. Don't need a house. This is a holiday.' Emphatically spoken. Little jaw thrust forward aggressively. Stubbornly. Max shrugged.

'Well, the offer's there if you want to take it up. I just thought it would be good. We could spend a lot more time together. All of us.' Lisa looked enquiringly at him. But he wasn't going to change his mind. Wasn't going to get into Max's grip like those other hangers-on. These hangers-on that were serving them here. The 'gun-bearers', the 'maid-servants', it was all positively feudal. No. He would stay where he was.

What he wanted most of all was to get Lisa on her own. His

107

wanting was fast becoming an obsession, a passion to possess. He wanted her, a simple straight-forward gut-wrenching demand that was going beyond any logical reasoning. He just wanted to be with her but, although the castle would provide the obvious means, he wasn't going to risk it unless all else failed.

'This place of yours sounds intriguing.' He was confused. Hadn't she been there to bring food and clear up? Wasn't that what the boy had told him? The boy looked puzzled. Liza shook her head quickly at both of them whilst Max was checking one of the Armalites.

'You should go and have a look then, Lisa.' Max, right on cue. All a little too convenient he thought, his suspicious mind trying to figure out Max's devious ways. This time there didn't seem to be. Just coincidence perhaps? Doubtful. Max would know what was going on. That was guaranteed. 'Here.' He caught the Armalite, checked the magazine was off, and cocked the weapon, looking inside the breech. An automatic set of actions done without thought. Satisfied the weapon was safe he looked across at Max. Three, full, thirty-round magazines were placed by his side. Max held his gaze. 'Rough shooting at targets with the rifles. Any distance from thirty metres to two hundred. Hits against you register by laser. Two lanes, we both go together. First to the end with the least number of hits against them and, of course, the most on target, the winner. Same bet as before. OK?' It seemed to be. How the idle rich play.

He was completely absorbed. The wooden sword flashed in his small hand. The Black Knight despatched here, the dragon moaning and groaning in death-throes there. He carefully wiped the blood off and winced as a small splinter sneaked its way under his skin. He poked it out without finesse leaving a red bloody hole. Hunting, he found the sandpaper and, pretending to sharpen the sword, smoothed the handle and the blade, the sanded wood covering his hand like a fine pale-yellow powder. He blew it away and watched the dust spiral

108

into the shafts of sunlight streaming into the garage door. He slid the now-smooth sword into his belt and, hitching his shorts up, squared his shoulders and prepared to do battle.

The target swung up and he instinctively dropped, rolled, and fired two rounds. The laser struck the ground beside him as his rounds tore two holes in the target. He smiled and crawled off to one side, staying within his lane. Off to his right, he heard the sound of Max firing. Even, so far, with four targets to go. Even, with a perfect score each.

'You can do it. Go on. He's bound to miss.' Lisa held the boy back out of the way. Two observers, supposedly impartial in this competition. He raised himself to his knees and searched the ground ahead for possible positions.

'Come on, you haven't got all day. Move. Get going.' The instructor sent three rounds from his SMG into the ground at his feet. He shakily, exhaustedly, raised himself, pushing the steel helmet back on his head, feeling the band tighten as his head swelled with the exertion. Another target appeared and he threw himself into the mud, crawled and fired.

'Crawl. Two rounds and crawl. Move your position. Do you want to die?' He saw Max out of the corner of his eye. They were level. Max looked over and grinned happily. In answer, he rose and sprinted forward, zigzagging. The target came up as expected thirty metres ahead. He put two rounds into it and dived off the the right as the expected laser lanced towards him. He crawled behind a rock, took the empty magazine off, reloaded and cocked, crawled left out of cover and leopard-crawled another twenty metres on into a ditch, and lay there gasping for breath. The next two targets came up rapidly, both despatched quickly and efficiently. The mistake came on the last. The laser caught him full on the torso. He stood up angry.

'Hard luck. Nearly a perfect score. Still, Max had the same problem so you're still even.' Convenient. Max, playing games. Definitely playing games. He wondered how long this was going to last.

'All square. Let's leave it at that David. We're both pretty tired. There's some beer back at the vehicles.' Max didn't look tired. It upped the annoyance factor another notch. Lisa smiled at him. He unloaded the rifle, tucked it under his arm easily and slid the magazine inside his shirt. Max turned suddenly and emptied his rifle into a target that suddenly appeared off to his right.

'The boys like to see if they can catch me off guard.' Grinning. 'They haven't yet. Not likely to either.' It was a nice demonstration of his skill with the weapon. Max handed it to the man next to him. Nobody moved to carry his weapon so it remained cradled in his arm. Just the unwanted guest, the interloper in this way of life.

He fell into step beside Lisa. The boy moved around and walked beside him. Max went on ahead talking earnestly with his armourer.

'You did very well. I've never seen Max lose.' Still hasn't. 'To Max, drawing is as good as losing.' She was silent for a moment. The boy snorted in disgust.

'If you ask me, he cheats. He knows the course so he can't lose. You're much better than he is. Can we go soon? I'm bored with this.' No, not yet. He didn't want to go and leave Lisa. Didn't know how to stay or ask her to come with him.

The other guests watched him mistrustfully. He thought. Thought their looks were disapproving. Felt uncomfortable, the starched detachable collar of fashionable cut-away design, cutting into his neck, the stud pressing hard into his Adam's apple, making talking difficult. His girlfriend sat opposite, between her father and her uncle. She seemed to be enjoying his discomfort. Safe within her home.

'Tell me, David, what sort of things you get up to at home. Do you hunt? Shoot? Fly-fish perhaps?' No. No. No. All answers in the negative.

'Oh! Well, I'm sure you must do something.' What can you do spending holidays working on a local farm to earn pocket money? Sometimes he visited his parents in Singapore where they were stationed at the moment. But that was once a year. 'I'm sure Katherine will invite you to one of our shoots. You could join the beaters.' Everyone laughed. He wondered what a beater was. Maybe one of those strange practises the rich got up to. One of those things rather like an orgy he heard about from other boys at school. He smiled politely and watched as the butler cleared away, wishing he was miles away and yet wanting to stay with Katherine. Uncomfortable agony. Unbearable discomfort. He hoped it would be worth it.

'Beer? Or something else?' Max passed him the full pint of ice-cold lager. It tasted very good after the exertion. 'Nothing like a beer. Nothing at all.' Max's platitudes and too light conversation. 'How about some light relief?' Here we go, another game. 'No competition, just some off-road fun with the Jeeps.' Max turned and wandered over to his Jeep. He watched, then went to the car and put the Armalite and magazines behind the seats. Nobody seemed to notice. He walked over to where Lisa was pouring a drink for the boy.

'Come on, let's go. I've had enough.' The boy was sullen and whiney. Unlike him. Lisa shrugged at him pulling the corners of her mouth down.

'Come on, David. Just a quick spin. Let me show you what this thing can do.' Go ahead Max. Observer this time. Max climbed into the Jeep, started the engine, and, wheels spinning, screamed away across the rough terrain leaving clouds of dust spinning up into the air. They watched as the Jeep bounced, leapt, careered over the ground. He turned back to Lisa. She walked over to the car and sat down on the ground, leaning back against the tyre, sipping delicately from her glass. He joined her. The boy watched and sulkily walked away, kicking the dirt, the dog ambling along by his side, also casting a disgusted look in his direction.

'He doesn't seem very happy in our company does he? Not with Max anyway. I think we understand each other a little better.' Yes, agreeing without being interested. Just liked the sound of her voice. The Jeep came roaring back throwing up a spume of dirt over them. He stood angrily. Max was laughing wildly in the Jeep. Strapped tight into his seat. The Jeep and Max disappeared from view flying over a hump. The sound of the engine muted once more. Lisa was laughing softly. 'He's a boy with lots of toys to play with. That's all.' Games. 'If you like.' And what about Lisa? What did Lisa like? She looked over to where the boy was standing, throwing stones at one of the empty beer cans. She didn't answer. The sound of the Jeep grew louder. Suddenly she stiffened. He tensed and followed her gaze. The shout was too late. The Jeep flew over the ridge and landed, ploughing into the boy and the dog. Max's wild laughter ripped through the screams and the whimpering howl of the dog. Max veered off onto the road and away.

He was running, stumbling, Lisa beside him crying. The boy lay, a bloody mangled heap, blood staining the ground around him, eyes open and puzzled. He knelt down beside the little boy and gently wiped the dirt off his face.

'What happened? Is the dog OK? Can we go now? I don't want to play anymore.' The eyes glazed and the faintest puff of breath floated away into the air. Lisa buried her head. He went over to where the dog lay whimpering. Its one good eye watched him as he gently stroked the shattered body. He walked over to the car, took out the Armalite, and put one round through the dog's head.

'Oh, God. Oh God.' Lisa, imploring some mythical deity. Max was going to die for this.

Eleven

HE STOOD ALONE, stripped to the waist, by the two small mounds in the earth. Looked away into the distance but could see only Max's maniacal wild look as the Jeep plunged down into the helpless boy and dog. Felt the hatred rise up inside him.

'It was an accident. He couldn't have known they were there. He couldn't have. It was an accident.' Lisa, covering up for Max. Maybe it was, but they were dead because Max was playing games. Max killed them as surely as if he'd shot them. 'No. He didn't. It was an accident.' Then where the hell was Max now? Hit-and-run is what it was. 'Maybe he doesn't know. Maybe he just didn't see them and doesn't know.' Not a chance. Max knows everything that goes on. He had watched as Lisa walked away to the car. Had stood looking down at the two small graves. There were no tears, no emotion other than hate.

He picked up the rifle and went back to the car. Checked the other magazine. Ten in one, the other full. Not many rounds, but then he only needed one for Max.

'Please not that. That's not the way to settle anything.' She was getting to him. He felt her quiet insisting, creeping into his mind. Felt himself beginning to relent. Wasn't going to, he owed the boy something. 'I'm sure it was an accident. Max would never have done it on purpose.' There's one way to find out. 'If you just talk to him. Tell him what happened, I'm sure you'll see I'm right.' We'll see. He busied himself stowing the rifle, then climbed into the car beside Lisa. She laid a hand gently on his, an imploring look in her eyes. He smelt her perfume, her skin. Felt the strange crawling, tickling sensations in his belly. Almost relenting. Pulling his resolve back from capitulation. He started the car. Talk to Max was what he would do. Find out. She was right, but if Max was guilty then he'd kill him. Lisa relaxed with an audible sigh. 'You'll see I'm right, after you've talked to him. It was an accident.' Her repetition was beginning to annoy him now. He wondered why. Probably because she was siding with Max. He felt jealous. Couldn't understand why.

The car was glad to be on the move again. Tired with sitting, a silent observer to the boring play, it wanted the open spaces and the speed. He gave it that. Gave it the thing it needed. Opened the fuel valve. Could feel the injectors spraying the vapourized petrol into the cylinders. See the pistons rushing up, forcing the compacted air, and then see, feel the spark and the resonating, flashing explosion. Eight times every micro-second. Blurring into continuous staccato sound that turned into speed. That converted into thrill. That destroyed time. Time that didn't exist anymore. The only existence was his desire for Lisa and his obsession to find Max and confront him. Now, after the boy. Max would regret that. Accident or not, Max would regret it. He saw again the expression of puzzlement and deep sadness before the young eyes faded and died. Briefly he thought he heard the far-off cry of his name on the wind. Thought he heard it and then it was gone.

'But you can't have seen him. Grandpa's been dead for years. Don't be silly now. Go to sleep.' But he had. His mother didn't believe him, but he had. Just as plain as she was standing at the end of his bed. That's where Grandpa had been standing. There. 'You must have been having a dream. There, I'll get you some aspirin.' Watched as she went, leaving him alone in the dark. He had slipped out of bed and turned the light on. The room was empty except for all his own familiar things. The posters on the door, scattered clothes and comics.

All his. Nobody else was there and yet he knew that his grandpa had been there. Knew it.

'Max is my guardian. Well, I call him that. He looks after me, gives me everything I need.' Everything? 'No, not that.' Laughing. It didn't seem that funny to him. 'Come on. I mean it. He needs looking after. He gets very worried, gets very upset. He'll be devastated to hear about the accident. Sometimes he gets so ill.' He didn't want to hear all this. Wanted to hear about her, not Max. 'There's not much to tell. Max looks after me. I've nobody else.'

The wind streamed the hair behind her head as they drove. She shook it so it flowed, silken, billowing. He noticed how fair her skin was and the hint of freckles. There seemed nothing evil or menacing about her presence. Pure honesty radiated from her. Something he'd never known before. Whereas he and anyone else he'd ever known would blame Max, she didn't. Maybe it was blind faith. He didn't think so, not with this woman. She seemed incapable of any dislike or hatred. But there was that little deceit over the visit to the hollow. He dismissed it as normal under the circumstances.

The dogs growled, snarled, and snapped their jaws together. Hint of froth at the mouths. They stood at the top of the steps barring the way.

'Come on now, silly animals. What's all the noise about.' Lisa walking past him and patting their heads. They wagged their tails. He wasn't sure about them. Keeping his distance. The castle was strangely quiet. None of the bustle and movement normally associated with big houses. 'It's like this a lot of the time.' Still, strange. He thought he caught a movement in the shadows over by the shrubbery to the left against the wall by the west tower. There was nothing that he could see. He turned back and again that movement.

Lisa moved past the dogs and went inside the castle. He followed, the dogs letting him past reluctantly. Inside the gloom prevented him seeing until his eyes grew accustomed to the light.

'Max? Are you here Max?' Lisa stood in the doorway at the far end of the hall. There was no reply. Her voice echoing through the halls and up into the high ceilings. There was a noise to his left, but no sign of anything when he swung round to see. A scurrying sound. Rats? No, too large a sound for rats. The wind? He shivered involuntarily. Then shrugged. Probably the wind stirring the drapes and tapestries.

'There doesn't seem to be anybody here. Very strange. Unless they've gone into town. Max does that sometimes.' Lisa moving slowly towards him brushing her hair back, tucking it behind her ears.

'They've gone away, shooting and fishing.' The voice made them both jump. The butler stood in the shadows by the door. 'There was no message.' Indeed. It pointed to Max running from him. Max knowing precisely what he had done. Where the hell was Max? 'I can't be precise because they are moving all the time. They do this every year at this time.' Very convenient.

'I'm not playing any more. You never play fair.' Roger walked round in circles then sat down near where he was hiding. It was difficult to suppress the giggles that wanted to burst out. Roger looked tired and fed up. A little scared too. This old house wasn't the friendliest of places. 'David, please. I don't know where you are. Please.' He'd leapt out of the cupboard then and Roger nearly had a heart attack. That was fun. Roger didn't think so.

'Well, we'll just have to wait for him to get back. He couldn't have known about the boy and the dog.'

'The what, Miss?' So quaint. So precise. So fake. Pretending he didn't know what had happened. 'No Sir. No idea.' That your master has killed a young boy and his dog. 'No Sir. Not possible.' Rubbish. Somebody else trying to protect Max. Was there no end to it? Everyone seemed to be on Max's side. The evidence was here. Here in the deserted ludicrous castle. Ostentation on a grand scale. But then Max was like that. When he'd first seen it, he was numbed by the splendour, now it was just absurd. The gradual decay showing now in the

116

light of day, dust, dirty windows, damp on the walls. Again the scurry. The butler flickered his eyes to the noise, hastily looked back at Lisa who turned away. A shared secret? Suddenly he was wary of Lisa. Frightened that he'd become so, angry with himself at the thought. He wondered if he trusted anybody, thought that he could trust Lisa, drove the doubt out of his mind and concentrated on the reason for being here in the castle. He went over to the staircase and took the steps two at a time, wandering the corridors. The place was empty.

As he wandered he was aware of some other presence. A strange, unseen, curious, probing presence. It was unnerving, but his desire to find Max was overwhelming. Especially now that he was becoming more certain of Max's deliberate killing. Yes, deliberate. Max had killed the boy as a method of getting him, getting to him because he'd taken Lisa – was going to take Lisa away from him. Suddenly it seemed very clear. It wasn't that he was afraid of Max or that he was jealous of Max. No, it was the other way around. Max was the frightened one. The realization bolstered his resolve and he went back down and out to the car. Lisa followed. He would take her back to the hollow and plan there. Leave her there when he went after Max.

'You're not leaving me anywhere.' Lisa, adamant.

She dipped her toes into the water, sending bright ripples across to rebound from the far bank and collide in the middle. Bob Marley sounds vibrantly filled the hollow. *No Woman, No Cry*. No Lisa, no Tears. He watched her intoxicated, drunk. Inebriated by her image. Kaleidoscopic images in collision with his emotion. Constant collisions. Crashing feelings confused in the sunlight. He could feel the want rise up and threaten to choke him, could feel the pain of the want.

'He'll be OK. He can cope.' She spoke softly, whispering against the water, the ripples catching the words and taking them away. He heard but didn't listen. Wasn't going to. Didn't want to hear. She turned to him, smiling shyly, eyelids lowered. 'I'd like to swim.' That's fine. The water's warm. 'I don't have a swimsuit.' He felt the shyness. Was amazed that he was concerned for her sensibilities. Wouldn't look. Would like to join her. Did when he heard the splash as she dived into the pool.

He slipped out of his clothes quickly, trying to hide his erection, now very obvious. She had not seen, was turned away from him. Blonde hair now dark and wet. Floating mass on the water, following her every move. Pale, white shoulders, slim, thin shoulders, below elegant neck. Shimmering under the surface the illusory promise of her body. Thought he caught a glimpse of her breast weightless and floating. Thought he saw the shadow between her tapering legs. The thoughts raced around his body, electric charges sending the blood pulsing, pumping, expanding him. His erection was painful. Painfully large. Bursting. Pulsating in the water. He thought she must hear, must feel the thump of his heart through the water, sense the lusting rage in his body, sense his tearing hurting want.

She swam slowly. Languorous. Sensually, teasingly, unaware. She swam enjoying the warmth and the wetness, the silky slide of the water over her body. He felt as he had the previous time. More so now. Much more. Felt his whole being fill the pool.

She swam close to him and he saw for the first time. Saw her want too. They kissed then. Wet. Long tongue-searching kiss. Tasting each other. Could feel her nipples hard against his chest. Feel her hips pushing at him, pressing him between them, forcing him up between them. He tasted her skin, tongue searching over the extent of her face. Lips kissing, closed eyes, travelling across smooth cheekbones. Her light licking, tingling. He felt every nerve. Every cell. Every emotion screeching out, gasping at her every touch.

He began to feel strong then, sure for the first time. Totally sure. Complete. Not like his animal lust for Amanda, nor his despising need to painfully enter Jenny. This was different. How many times had that phrase been used? This is different.

118

Used as an excuse, a justification for everything. One of the biggest self-told lies ever. But this *is* different he told himself. This is like nothing he had ever experienced in his life. The joy and the pain at the same time. The need and the realization together and yet apart. Light-years apart.

She, pushing a little away from him, looking up into his eyes. The water in droplets on her skin, shining in the sun. Eyes flashing at him. Dazzling. Voice trembling very slightly.

'I've wanted to do that since the other night. Couldn't wait.' He felt the joy and the power surge through him now. Like a heroin hit. Charging around his body making him smile, laugh. Laughter that carried all the passion and hopes, joys of a thousand years of emotion. All the repressed instincts of centuries flowing out of him. He picked her up out of the water. Light, without weight. Carried her across the grass laying her gentle on the rough bed. Feeling her soft yielding body below him.

'Make love to me. Now.' He bent and curled his tongue around hers, closing his lips with hers, wrapping his legs with hers, letting his hands roam groaning over her body. Feeling the skin quivering beneath his touch. Feeling the soft, smooth, gentle, delicate, strong skin writhe, move, moaning with him. Felt her hands on him. Pulling, gripping, wanting. Felt her pulling him into her. Into her wetness. Into her close, tight, running wetness. Hot. Enveloped. Felt his entire soul wrapped, encased within her. Moving gently. Moving quickly. Moving. Moving. Not aware of space. Time. Just the essence of being. The Id. One time, one space, one body, one entity.

Existence. Complete existence. They moved and yet weren't moving. They were the orgasm. Both together. A continuous recurring orgasm. Neither one nor the other. Just it. Their sex sighs filled the time and the space, echoing through the hollow, naturally, without shame, without care, without thinking.

Then they lay, exhausted, side by side, watching the last rays of the sun run from the advancing shadows. Lay holding one another, each other, themselves.

119

'I feel . . . feel . . . floating. I feel . . . numb. More . . . I feel like I've never felt. I . . .' He stopped her with his mouth. There was no need for the expression of the feeling. They both knew. No need to talk. Just let the experience rebound in the mind and the boy, reminding. Always reminding. Remembered. Remember, never forget. 'Will it fade? Will it always be the same?' Yes. Always the same. Better. Don't voice the fear. Don't bring the darkness in uninvited. Don't let the destroyer enter here.

'No. I won't.' Her voice soft and gentle. Loving. That's what it was. He loved, was loving, in love. For the first time he understood the word. For the first time.

'Are you sure? It's too soon to tell. You can't be sure.' She was kind with him. He was sure. Didn't need time. It didn't exist. Not here and now. Only existed for the practicalities of living, didn't exist for the art of loving. Time and emotion knew not of each other. She smiled an old wise smile and, leaning up on one arm, traced the corners of his mouth with her fingers. Studied his face as if for the first time, finding new wonders there.

'Blue eyes. I love your blue eyes.' Husky words breathed into his mouth. 'Love your body. Your shape. Your penis.' The flutterings in his belly began again as she moved down his chest. Tongue, finding waiting expectant nerves. Touching them, electrifying them. Moving on across the scar-torn skin, down into his rampant maleness. Felt her mouth close over him, tongue yearning, probing, finding, exploring, goading, cajoling him into his mind-blasting body-jerking ejaculation. She moaned in pleasure. Soft puppy murmurs as she drank him.

Nothing existed now. Nothing except her. The hollow expanded into the night. Grew outwards to meet the boundaries of the stars and beyond. Carried them away to hang suspended on the strings of the passion. He was in the centre with her. Together in the centre. They were the centre.

The fire shook the chill from the air and lit the cave. They sat tired but rejuvenated. She held her head to one side, the flame reflections dancing across her face. The smell of her sex was still in the cave and on him. He enjoyed it, savoured it.

'So you and Max were together. Fought together. In the same place.' Yes, the same place. That hell-hole of boredom and back-shooting. Of hatred and bombs. That place where he'd gone as a boy and left as a sub-human.

'No. You're not that. Not the way you make love.' Gentle words. Kind words that were a lie. Not to her. To him. No, he was never a good lover. Never knew what loving was until now. Always, only, sex. Get in, get satisfied, get out. That's all. Never love. There was never a place for love.

'Then how do you explain this? Isn't this love? What we have here? What we've just had?' Questions again. For a second, the questions annoyed him. He fearfully beat the annoyance down. Swept it away into the dusty corner it sprang from. Love was a word that had only just occurred to him as they were making love. Only then. Never before.

'That's sad. Very sad. Why? Surely you must have felt something. You married.' He lay back and closed his eyes momentarily, afraid that if he kept them closed she might fade. 'Surely there must have been some strong feeling in you?' The cave roof moved with the orange glow of the fire. Feelings? Strong feelings? Yes. Feelings of pure lust. Nothing else. Not until now, with her. She giggled, tossed her mane of blonde hair and adjusted the sarong before leaning over, turning the steaks over the fire. They sizzled with the heat, bubbling brown and smelling delicious.

'So why do you and Max dislike each other so much? You've been through the same things, together. Surely there must be a bond between you?' Was a bond. Thought there was a bond. But Max plays games with people. Superior word–mind games that eventually bore, that eventually become childish. That aren't worth playing anymore. Max can go to hell.

'I'll have to see him. Make sure he's OK. Some time.' She saw his look and, stretching, touched his shoulder. 'Not now, sometime, that's all. Don't worry.' Why worry. Max can take care of himself. The only place he can't come is here. Max can't find us here.

'How do you know?' He smiled to himself. A strange, unhappy, dangerous smile. Max just couldn't that's all, because he was better than Max. She turned back to the fire, a bored expression.

'You're both children.' They didn't talk. He watched her cooking. She, concentrating on the steaks. The silence peaceful, calm and enjoyable. The darkness compressed the hollow into the tiny area of light from the fire. The cave further squashed the area, making it warm and secure. He lay back at peace. A peace he hadn't known before, watching Lisa. Bob Marley had given way to Dire Straits. Love songs in a hollow. Love songs held in a cave. He lay back drugged with the pleasure of it, letting it wash over him. Waves of sound, smells and feelings. Letting go for ever, floating away without constraints.

For now the obsession had receded. The images of the dead boy beginning to float away. Away in the distance he thought he heard the voice calling his name once. Then it was close. So close he jumped.

'We should have stayed together you and me. Not let anyone else in. Just you and me.' He looked around, his heart pounding, but there was nobody there. Just Lisa lit by the fire, a small, beautiful, figure in the soft glow. She was lost in thought, not noticing his alarm. He'd almost lost his sense of purpose. Almost. But he had to find Max.

'I still believe it was an accident. I want to see him as well, so when you go I'm coming as well.' Well, that was something to be thought about later. Not for the moment. There was planning. He wasn't going after Max unprepared.

'You make it sound like a war between you. You frighten me sometimes. Both of you.' The silence stretched between them. Suddenly she smiled and came over to him. 'Let's just enjoy what we have for a while. He'll be back.'

Twelve

THE OIL gurgled out of the sump, black, thick, organic. Gurgled into the pan lying, spreading, under the car. He lay on his back enjoying the feel between his fingers. The smell, hot, delightfully pungent, sulphur strong in his nostrils. The car breathing with relief as the old worn lubricating liquid disappeared out of its bowels. Gone forever. The engine lying in wait for the amber replacement to trickle down its throat from the top. Trickle through its thin tubes, tiny holes, seep into every metal corner, every dark shiny place. Every clean spotless area where nobody ever saw. Where nobody ever would see. Secret places that could stop the workings if they wanted. Block up and never be found. No instruments to measure performance down here in the depths, the intestines. The car knew this and enjoyed feeling the clean fresh 20/40 slide confidently down inside, gurgling from the top. He also enjoyed knowing what the car would be feeling. It was good and relaxing. Tightening the bolts of the overhead camshafts after checking the bucket tappet gaps. Some would need a shim or two to be perfect. He'd have to check the garage in town for some. He wondered if they would have any to fit the Rover engine. Probably not. The garage had seemed pretty poorly stocked from the glimpses he'd had.

Lisa sat close by watching him work. He liked that. Comfortably aware of her presence. She held a book in her hands. Lying open at an unread page, expectantly waiting for

123

the eyes to scan and devour the words. She watched him and the car. The book got bored and turned pages at will. She not noticing, it flicked a few more. She absently brushed a hand across a page, smoothing. The book waited until the hand moved on, then quietly flicked more pages. It would enjoy the confusion and the annoyance when she came to read again. She was blissfully ignorant of the book's conspiracy.

'This is very domestic, isn't it.' He looked out from under the car, trying to see if there was any sarcasm in the comment. It didn't seem so. He smiled. There was nothing domestic about tending to the car. This was his pride. Creative pride. He and the car were both part of each other, both had the same soul. Part of the same soul. Without him, the car wouldn't have existed. Without the car, he wouldn't be here now. Wouldn't have found her. Or so he thought. Quaint thoughts. Romanticized wanderings, without form. Like a baby's dummy he felt for the car. She knew. He knew and didn't care that she saw straight through him.

He turned the engine over, listened to it cough and catch, then, concentrating, finely adjusted the fuel balance, then the ignition timing.

'It's lovely to look at.' He suddenly, chillingly, aware he'd heard that before. Quick panic, controlled. Sent back. Heard it before but not in the same way. Justify. Alter the meaning. The emphasis. That was it. The emphasis was different. That word again. Different. Justify. The word justifies the similarities. He didn't care. It didn't matter. That was past, forgotten now. A life left behind amid the ruins of his unfeeling thoughts, now changed.

He relaxed and listened once more to the engine. Yes, it was lovely to look at. Lovely to drive, too.

'Can I drive it? I'd love to. Really love to. Please?' Her eyes were mischievously pleading. Knowing they would get their own way. Sure he thought, keeping her waiting. Playing the game also. Another game. A pleasant game, this, though, a teasing, sexual, sensual game. They both played it through as they should. He finally agreeing, she giving the expected squeal of delight, trying to hug him under the car. The car, not too keen on these games, ensuring there was a fender in the way. Getting in the way, separating them. She catching her shirt on the wing mirror and tearing it. The car rumbling happily. The book crushed against body and body. Metal and flesh. Not happy. Game finished for it.

He closed the bonnet and watched as she climbed into the driving seat, seriously adjusting the position. Feeling for the pedals. The gear stick. The steering wheel. Seat belt buckled. She was in first and away even before he'd had a chance to settle.

The wheels spun furiously. The smell of fresh cut grass filled the air sweetly for a moment, before being left behind drenched in exhaust fumes. The car lurched onto the road and charged down it, showing the girl who was in control. She paled and then grimly hung on. Then gradually felt the car. Found out its movements. Gently wooed the surging beast, bringing it into order, into control. He sat at first wondering, then relieved and then happy. Watching with admiration as she finally won the animal over, then had it purring gently down the road like a small Mini with an old lady at the wheel.

She turned and grinned. A grin of triumph. Another conquest.

'They only need a bit of persuasion then it's OK.' Voice raised above the crackle of the exhausts and the whine of the wind. 'It's great. Really fantastic – and you built it yourself?' The car gave a hiccup in disgust. He refrained from being too smug, just nodded and smiled to himself and the shaped hunk of metal, rubber and fibreglass, that now ran smoothly down the road towards the town.

The disco music rocked, raged, bounced and pulsated through the room, through them, through every jerking writhing form that moved on the floor. They sweated and looked at each other, letting the music mix with the booze and the erotic signals, letting themselves be carried away, letting themselves be totally absorbed with each other, completely oblivious to

125

anything, anyone else. There, framed in his vision, she was. The music carried him along on waves of emotional yearning. He saw it. Saw it coming. Welcomed it in. Held it close, treasured it. The place was packed. Hot. Sweaty. Mind-drenching sound, vibrating through every tissue in the body, lights flashing so the eyes wondered if they'd wandered into the wrong place. Wandered into a mad time-slip. A strobe-lit planet of electronically-controlled zombies from another futuristic place.

Still they danced, facing each other. Now the sweat plastering the hair and the clothes. Still they danced. Others danced. Everyone danced to the exuberant rhythms of the disco beat. Coloured hair mixed with coloured lights and coloured clothes mingled in flashing gyrating static poses. Wine-filled air, intoxicated brains, separate bodies fed on beat and the driving, screeching voices of wild guitars.

They danced, numbing any thoughts, wildly letting the adrenalin pump the animal instincts into full joyous fury. He leapt, screamed, shouted at the sky, howling freedom songs from the depths. She watched, breathing hard, nipple-hard expectation, nostrils flared, tiny beads of crystal perspiration clinging to her upper lip, clinging to the unseen fine hairs. Mouth, lips apart. Both lips wet. She watched him, eyes closed, allowing the music to drive him, take him over, wrap around with the alcohol and drug the brain. Drug the tired brain. Ease the exploding sensations and free his emotions.

He led her with shaky legs to a corner table, sitting, holding hands, in the darkness, staring into each other's unseen eyes. Knowing the touch and the smell. The animal smell. The safety smell. Clinking thick-rimmed glasses full of sharp cheap wine that tasted like nectar. That didn't taste at all. He was aware that the music had slowed and changed. The room lighted and the people had gone. They were alone. Dressed in white in a white room. Two golden-haired lovers in the purity of their emotions. The fine thin-stemmed wine glasses sparkled in the light. Deep red, blood-red claret. His eyes wide

126

and wild, still feeling the rhythms. Still moving. His urge tight within the confines of the jeans.

'The young lovers. How quaint. How very old fashioned.' Max from nowhere sitting in white as well. Long hair flowing about his shoulders. Black-haired girls at his knees. Staring. He smiling the Max smile. 'You play your game very well David. Very well.' Max raised his glass in salute. He stood and walked the distance between them in cold killing steps. Lisa behind tugging, holding, pleading.

'No David. It's not worth it. Leave him. Don't do it. Don't try.' He shrugged her off, saw Max shake his head and purse his lips, gently reproving. A girl stood up to bar his way. He drove the stem of the glass into her face. She fell. Max had gone.

'Behind you, David. Always behind you. Always a step ahead, David.' Max stood lightly balanced on the balls of his feet waiting. He went for Max. Missed and felt the pain, felt the punch, catch him behind the ear. Felt the brain explode in stars of brief agony. Felt himself falling. Falling. Fell.

'David! David!' Lisa's voice from the past. Music driving, throbbing with the pulse of his head. Faces staring down at him. Faces laughing. Curious. Lisa, concerned, cradling his head.

They sat in the corner holding the glasses. She looking at him. He unsure. The darkness hiding the confusion. The collision of images. He looked around for Max. Felt his head. Felt it clear. Felt no pain. Felt her look.

'You OK? You were out then, somewhere else. I don't know where. I was talking to you and you were out.' Lisa rambling, he thought. What the hell was she talking about? Suddenly he wanted out of here. He stood and, grabbing her hand, ran from the disco, ran outside into the cool night air. Into the deserted street, into the freshness and the silence. Just feeling the thump of the disco through the street. Moved down the road to the car, away from the beat. Moved quickly, terrified. She followed silently, warily. Wondering. He slowed and, breathing deeply, lay against the wall, the rough stone cool and solid. Felt the safety of it. The security. Lisa moved close to him, putting her arms around his waist.

'You've been drinking all night. I thought you'd fall over. Do you feel any better?' No, he didn't. The alcohol swam around in his head, casually flicking nauseous nerves. Blasting balance, obscuring his vision. No, he wasn't better. Wouldn't be until his body had at last driven the noxious fluid away.

He bent to upturned face and kissed her slowly, tasted the wine still on her lips, smelt it on her breath. Kissed her slowly, gently firm. Held her close. Closed his eyes and felt the road spin sideways. Opened his eyes to fight the bile surging in his stomach. Fight it down. Pulled his mouth away from hers and stumbled down the road into a dark corner to retch and puke.

'Come on, let's get you back.' She helping him to the car, pouring him into the passenger seat. He feeling his guts, shredded by the booze. His mind tormented by her and Max. Alcohol confusing the issue. What was the issue? Where did all this nonsense come from? What the hell was he doing? More questions. Max had started that. Started the questions. Begun the cycle. Now the questions came unasked. Sneaked in from a side entrance and sprang before he had time to block them. Questions, always the questions.

'What are you burbling about?' Lisa asking questions, looking at him standing in the road. Looking at him sitting, slumped. Questions.

'Well what's the answer?' Max's words. They are Max's words. He felt the fury rise. The alcohol-induced anger. Max's words. She moved back a pace or two, suddenly frightened by his snarling face, paling under the weak street light.

'What did I say? I just wondered what you were saying.' He suddenly saw himself. Saw the reflection in her eyes. Saw his destructiveness and felt the panic of loss. Didn't want to lose her. Sensed the future. He held out his hands to her, apologized. Didn't mean the way it came out. Didn't want to frighten or to hurt. Certainly not her, never her. She moved

128

forward, mistrusting, carefully touching his hands and then firmly gripping them with confidence as she saw his sorrow.

'It's OK. You just startled me. It's the booze talking. Let's go. I'll drive.' She moved round the car. He relaxed. Felt the danger pass. Enjoyed her once more.

He watched her from his vantage point lying in the cave, watched her flowing movements. The way she brushed the golden hair from her face, the way her hips swayed easily. Listened to her happy hum. Gentle in the sunlight. He soaked her image into his very soul. Wondered if he had one. Watched as her breasts, firmly heavy, moved with her, separate movement, part of the same. She stepped over the grass without seeming to touch, simply floating over the surface without bending a blade, without damaging. She saw him and glided over, sun shimmering, sitting beside him, a little way from him so that she could look at him.

'You slept well. Did you good.' Yes. He slept well. Felt pleasant faint hangover love sensations. He looked past her. The water of the pool lay flat, mirror-calm, black. He wanted to talk. To tell her. Wanted to explain. Didn't know how. A sudden urge to spill the bile out. Verbal vomit.

'Go on. I'll listen.' She sat comfortably silent. Waiting. He looked past her again. Into the hollow. Two of his men were bringing the body in. Half was missing. He got up and went over. Looking down at the bloodied remains.

'Booby trap Boss. Nothing anyone could do. Very clever. Poor little bastard never had a chance. Blew his head right off. We found it fifty metres away. Some of the local dogs were eating the brain. Shot the bastards.' He watched and then bent to help slide the red slimy flesh into the black bag. It made a slurping sound as the gut slid out wriggling onto the ground. He dug his hands into the still warm mass. It slipped through his fingers, plopping onto the ground again. It took him two attempts to get it in the bag. The head was placed in gently by one of the men. They stood dispassionately looking as the bag was zipped up. He turned and walked over to the other procession. His friend lay on the ground. Slowly the life seeping baffled from his eyes until they glazed over and the last gasping rattling sound escaped from the battered body. It seemed to shrink and then lay still.

'They cut his balls off Boss. Sewed them into his mouth. Then rammed a stake up his arse. He died slow Boss. But we'll find the bastards.' No consolation to the dead. They didn't care now anyway. He stood looking at the meat. The already decaying bodies. The past people.

Over in the corner a group of women were jeering. He went past them. There in the centre, young, terrified, was a soldier. A boy. The women old enough to be his mother. They'd taken his rifle. Blood spurted from his shattered mouth. Tears poured down his face. Sobs sprayed the blood down his smock and flak jacket. He tried to duck the blows, but they broke his arms with clubs. He fell senseless, face being mashed to a bloody pulp. A young man came through the crowd of women. They fell silent, revering him. He shot the soldier through the back of the head. The women savouring the sight of the brains splattering the grass. They watched fascinated by the stiff straightening of the already dead limbs. Final nerve tingles in the lifeless body. They waited a moment longer then faded away, uninterested now.

He turned and walked back through the carnage. Back through the torn limbs, shattered bodies, blown minds. Back to where Lisa sat, wet eyes. Pale translucent skin in the day. Back to sit still, looking at the fading soldiers carrying the corpses away.

'I didn't know. Max never told me. Never said anything.' She spoke quietly. The thing was that Max never said anything. Just played with the memories. Max was there as well. They both were. Both saw it, smelt it, felt it. At first he thought that Max might help. Might be of help. Might know. But Max was too interested in Max. So the hell with Max from now on.

She turned her head away, troubled. He knew. Felt helpless. Knew she liked Max, cared for him. He couldn't understand

130

why. Wanted to break the relationship, yes, wanted to destroy it, wanted to get away from Max's sphere of influence. Away. Out of it. Wipe the memory, erase it. Have Lisa with him and live without the ghost of Max haunting them. Wanted to know how to accomplish this.

'Hey. Come on. Enough of this. Come on.' Her voice softly insistent. Hands gently calming. 'It's past. Gone. There's no need to carry on. No need.' He was beginning to believe her. Would believe anything she said. Fell into the pool of her eyes, down into the depths, all the images fading dead away. The memories gone, the pain easing, seeping out, dissipating.

Tomorrow he would start the search. Find Max and destroy the image in her mind. Destroy completely. Wipe the memory from her mind. Tomorrow he would do that.

Thirteen

HIS NOSE hurt terribly and the blood streaked down his upper lip and around the corners of his mouth. Fearfully he came quietly in through the back door. Tears stained his cheeks and the bruise under his eyes was beginning to turn strange colours. There was nobody in the kitchen. He heard voices from the sitting-room. His parents relaxed on a Sunday with the papers. Mother sewing, father with the papers. He crept into the room keeping his battle scars away from prying eyes. Mother didn't say anything, just shot a concerned look in Father's direction. He knocked against the table and rattled the cups. Father looked up annoyed.

'What have you been doing?' Getting beaten up by the boy down the road. He's much bigger. Father buried his face back in the papers. 'Get out and don't come back until you've given him what he gave you. No pansies in this house.' End of conversation. Mother said nothing, just looked slightly ashamed. He slid out of the room. Twenty minutes later he was back with another black eye and a grin. This time he was sent upstairs for tearing his best shorts and rendering his Sunday shirt fit only for a rag.

The blue-black metal glinted with oily menace in the pre-dawn light. He wiped the oil away from the barrel, the shine disappeared, the metal dulling and blending with the dark ground. He gently eased the working parts, feeling the breech-block slide smoothly backwards and forwards. Perfect engineering fit. Precision instrument. A beautiful object until the trigger was depressed and the pin struck the cap on the base of a live round that exploded sending the small bullet at more than 2000 ft/sec twisting to its target. Max's face splintered and fell apart before his eyes. Bone, brain and blood spraying in a fine slow-motion mist back onto the grey granite rocks. The body slumped, final jerk and twist to lie a motionless broken heap. Another round fired into the back to sever the spinal cord. Just to make sure. The *coup de grâce* on an already lifeless body. He smiled at the thought and the image faded.

Lisa lay sleeping peacefully, the duvet pulled up under her chin, looking childlike in her sleep. Innocent unaware naïve child dreams flitting across her body in tiny twitches and little mewing sounds. He watched absently stroking the barrel of the Armalite.

'David.' Mother standing in the doorway. He turned his tear-streaked cheeks away from her, wiping his hand roughly over his eyes, wincing as the bruises reacted to the pressure. She moved into the room and sat down on his bed. 'David. Fighting is silly. Your father didn't really mean what he said. I'm sure he really meant for you to sort things out by making up. That's all.' She was trying to be kind, trying to explain the unsubtleties of the grown-up mind to his uncomplicated child logic. Trying and failing, just confusing him even more.

'No, David, that's unfair.' She stood in front of him. Looking reproachfully at the rifle in his hands. 'That's unfair. Perhaps you are right but I always tried.' Yes, she did. But father didn't. She was silent, the look of sadness more intense. She turned and walked away through the rockface. His father watched her go and said nothing. Stood uncomfortably not knowing what to do and then he too faded, leaving him on his own once more. He sat staring at the empty hollow. The wind moaned softly down the walls and around him. Traces of rain fell and stuck to his bare arms, gently clinging, to be joined by more. Soft warm rain that turned into a downpour. The wind died and the rain fell, vertical streams over him. He sat letting the water wash over him, plastering his hair flat,

133

running around the contours of his face and body into a pool at his feet. The insistent patter on the ground seeming comforting and reliable. The drops ran over the rifle, slipping off the oily surface, leaving the weapon dry. His mother's hand tightened on his. He could feel her tension through the bony flesh. He looked up and could just make out her eyes in the gloom of the sampan. The noise of the rain on the curved bamboo and canvas cover all but drowned out the wailing of terrified Chinese as the over-full boat rocked its way across the harbour. Sometimes a wave would break just over the side and the owner would hurriedly bail out while trying to steer. The diesel engine thumped its way unconcernedly towards the next oil-change. He was an observer strangely detached from all the drama. Apart from one other European family, they were the only whites on board. He watched interested as the fat middle-aged Chinese opposite jabbered away and quivered with fear. At each lurch his eyes would roll upwards, just the whites showing, the fat lips moving frantically in the ashen face. Another man was laughing at him and pointing. An hysterical laugh. The boat rocked and rolled its way tiredly onwards. Resigned to the three-times-daily trip.

The rain eased and the sky lightened as the cloud passed. Dawn crept slowly in behind. Sheepishly. He let the rain evaporate from his body, leaving his trousers and T-shirt wet. He stripped them off and stood naked in the dawn. The grey clouds scudded across the lightening sky, breaking in patchy cumulus. He found another, dry pair of jeans and a T-shirt, then, lifting the rifle and magazines, quietly went to the car. Stowed the weapon and rounds behind the seat and returned to tidy up. Lisa lay awake watching him.

'Going without me?' Her voice startled him. He didn't intend to leave her behind. No. Just preparing. Getting everything ready. Why had she woken? Was it that sixth sense that women seemed to have? That something that warned them without their conscious mind being even awake. Built-in defence mechanism, instinctive survival aid. 'I see. Then you were going to wake me with a cup of tea. How thoughtful.' Her eyes quietly and gently mocked him. Made him shrink to thumb-size and surprisingly he didn't seem to mind. Felt foolish and guilty but warmed through by her presence. Was glad she was awake and, suddenly, he wanted her company, wanted her beside him when he confronted Max. For two reasons, both selfish. One because of his insecurity and the other because of his cruelty.

'How do you think you are going to find Max anyway?' Now there's a thought. 'Isn't it?' She eyed him with, he thought, slight contempt. No, only Jenny had that sort of feeling for him. Not Lisa. Thank God. She was far removed from Jenny's unfeeling, unthinking, selfish attitudes. Jenny stood at Lisa's shoulder smirking at him. He blocked his thoughts and she went. Lisa lay looking up at him enquiringly, waiting for an answer. He walked out into the hollow now bathed in early-morning wet sunlight.

The path was slippery, he thought, as he failed to maintain contact with the mud and slid onto his side for the third time. Lisa floated along effortlessly in front of him. How did she manage to stay upright on this surface? His chauvinism was beginning to show. He picked himself up, slid, but managed to stay on his feet this time. Lisa turned and smiled at him. She was everything he had ever wanted. He shrank from the thought, then welcomed it. Slipped again and Lisa laughed loudly.

The river ran happily in the bottom of the gorge. The grass banks were erratically carved by the river as if some water creature had bitten large chunks out of the earth. Trees of strange prehistoric shapes hung tired, moss-covered, boughs out over the bouncing water. He reached the bottom and sat back against a tortured trunk letting the warm sunshine soak into his body. Lisa bent over the river scooping up a handful of the clear liquid and splashing it over her face. The second handful she drank, delicately wiping the drops from her chin. She stood and joined him. He moved the Armalite into the other hand and then laid it close beside him, checking the

135

safety catch, eyes sweeping the immediate area and the rim of the gorge. He could feel her beside him like a power surge. The energy jumping across the narrow gap stabbing into him. Making his skin tingle and jump.

'This is the place he normally fishes. I don't know much about it, but it's supposed to be good here.' He looked at the shape of the river, the speed of the flow, the waves caused by submerged rocks and, a little further down, a short waterfall. This was salmon country. By the time the returning salmon reached here, they would be sufficiently tired but not too much. Just enough. After all Max didn't want too much competition. But now was the wrong time. There were no salmon here now. Another month and they would be leaping, but not now. Now they were far out to sea, feeling the call to return but not committed. Not yet. He relaxed.

'Oh. I'm sorry. I didn't know. Max never taught me anything about fishing. About anything like that.' He loved the way her eyes looked at him with sadness and apology. Couldn't find any anger or resentment in himself. Leaned over and touched her hand. 'Still, it is pretty here. I love it.' She stood and walked into the small clearing, the sunlit emerald-green grass reflecting off her white shorts and T-shirt, golden hair flowing out over her shoulders. She turned around. Spinning, hair spreading fan-like, rising up catching the sun and flashing jewelled lights at him. She spun and moved effortlessly, unselfconsciously, then walked back and sank to the ground beside him, eyes heavy with thoughts beyond the present. He felt the pain and jealousy of not being a part of those thoughts.

'Right, let's try somewhere else.' She stood again, standing deep in thought. He picked up the rifle and adjusted his belt. She pretended to ignore the presence of the rifle and ammunition pouches. 'I know where he might be. But it's quite a way further.' The look suggested they turn back. He moved forward, waiting for the directions. She laid a hand on his arm and the look of sorrow etched deep into his mind. It was so intense he nearly buckled but forced himself to ignore her

136

unsaid plea. How could Max have such a hold over people? The man was a manipulator and killer. He'd seen it with his own eyes. Couldn't she see it?

'No. He's not. You've got it wrong.' She moved away from him as if the closeness and physical contact were abhorrent. He didn't want that. Needed her with him. 'Need me to find Max.' No. Needed her as she was. Needed her to make him feel alive. Living. She walked off ahead of him leading the way. He watched her, bewildered, shoved the feeling away and hefted the familiar weight of the rifle, the comforting silent friend. Followed carrying his resolve. Belief. Purpose, like a pack. Shifting the weight when it became uncomfortable. He believed that solved the immediate problem. Lisa strode ahead without looking back.

His father fell into step beside him. Puffing away on his pipe. Eyes studiously, purposefully staring straight ahead. Not saying a word. They walked together, speeding up. Father easily kept pace without trying. Just sauntered along whilst his little legs earnestly pounded out the steps. He didn't know where he was going. Hadn't a clue. It hadn't seemed to matter when he packed the little case and sat on the doorstep. It was only when he was on his way that the fear gradually penetrated. An awful heavy dread that sat in his stomach and then spread through his small thin frame. It was when his resolve was just about at breaking-point that his father had joined him. The dread had lifted and the resolve returned but it was gradually being eroded again by the silence. His pride kept him going.

They headed down. The ground sloping away, the river meandering, growing stronger and more confident. Slowing down. Widening. Lisa never slackened her pace. He was impressed. 'I like walking. Always have. Sometimes I just set off. All day, just walking. Anywhere, wherever I feel. I like the hills and the mountains. It's very peaceful.' She stood waiting, not a hair out of place. She turned and pointed to a small farmhouse tucked away under the lee of a hill. More a croft than a farmhouse. 'He sometimes stays there. It's good shooting here. Grouse up on the moor. Wildfowl down near

137

the lake. See over there.' Pointing as a pair of duck rose and
streaked low over the land swinging round before landing on
the water again. He sat and looked at the countryside,
enjoying the natural sights before bringing his mind back to
the moment. 'Come on, let's go down.' She leading the way
once more. He sat a little while longer then headed off to the
right, keeping in the cover of the dead ground leading up to
the farmhouse. He should come out above and just behind.
Able to see any movement. Any sign of a reception commit-
tee. Lisa stayed in his sight as she walked on. He slithered over
the grass, feeling the solid earth in well-remembered contours
beneath his knees and elbows. Lisa approached the door,
opened it and went inside. He scrambled down into a steep
gully and struggled up the other side, lying panting just above
and slightly to the side of the house. Lisa came back out
looking puzzled, obviously wondering where he was. There
was no sign of anyone else with her. She looked annoyed. The
feeling furrowing her brow in lines he hadn't seen before. He
stood up and went down.

'There's nobody here. We must have just missed them. It's a
bit late to follow now.' Very convenient. 'See for yourself.' She
looked bored and moved away from him,. He went into the
house. It was clean, tidy, dark and empty. Freshly cleaned and
tidied. He made to go into the other room. Lisa touched his arm
and he stopped, surprised at the contact. 'There's nothing there.
I've checked.' She pulled him gently, away from the doorway.
'They use that room for hanging the game. It stinks.' He caught
the smell before she closed the door. Caught the cavernous
interior. 'It goes back into the side of the hill. They can keep the
game cool there. No electricity here.' She stood leaning back
against the door, hands behind her resting on the handle. She
smiled. 'We should spend the night here. There's no point in
going on. Not till the morning.' Her eyes bored into his soul.
Outside the day was drawing into early evening.

The malt whisky rolled around his mouth and slid warming
down his throat, deliciously smooth. Lisa, sitting on the floor

138

at his knee, reached up and took the glass from his hand. The log fire crackled and threw yellow light out and around the walls of the farmhouse. He rested his hand on her hair, gently stroking the fine soft fibres.

'I really don't know where to look now. I thought he would be here . . .' Her voice trailed off as if she were speaking to herself. He felt tired and drowsy. A pleasant sensation creeping up behind his eyes, making them heavy, wanting to close. Mind still awake, eyes sleepy. The alcohol sensation. It didn't seem to matter at the moment. Probably wouldn't matter for a few hours. Not worth bothering about until he had a definite fix on Max. Today had been chasing shadows. Pointless. Healthy, but pointless.

He could hear the wind growling round the house and snuggled closer into the soft armchair, listening to Grandmother reading about Mole's experiences, her quavering voice imbuing the words with ancient and mysterious magic; magic that conjured up the images of the weasels and stoats, of the battles, and of Toad shaking in his boots. He shivered with glee, staring into the shadows of the room, expecting at any moment weasels to bound forth screeching, their teeth glistening in the firelight. He shivered, woke, wondered where he was for a split second and saw Lisa had gone. He sat up, suddenly afraid. There was the sound of gentle humming from the small kitchen. He sat back relieved and feeling slightly stupid.

'You're awake.' Standing over him, handing him a cup of coffee. Framed against the light of the kitchen. Moving to one side, features suddenly visible. Smiling. Kneeling down. 'Why don't we move in here? I've always liked it.' She stretched cat-like, staring round the room. Flame-reflected happiness. She'd been here with Max and he didn't want that. Wanted her in his own place without Max. Without the possibilities of the reminiscences conjuring up Max's ghost. She looked disappointed, a gentle sigh barely moving her breasts, the sound a merest hint in the air, then gone, to leave a vague feeling of sadness. 'It's such a lovely spot and Max

will come back here again before they return to the castle.'
Half-hearted attempt to convince him to stay. It wouldn't do
any good. He'd decided. For the moment, it was a welcome
rest from the hard day's hike. He was surprised Lisa was
looking so fresh. She shrugged. 'I'm used to the terrain. I told
you. I've spent many days wandering these hills and valleys. I
love the whole place. There's a lot of peace here. The beauty,
the atmosphere.' She was warming to her subject. Eyes filled
with secret excitement. Opaque windows hiding the varied
colourful images flashing kaleidoscopic through her mind in
mixed remembrances. He watched her, absorbed. Entranced.
'I love to walk by myself and then to sit and watch the wildlife.
Foxes sneaking about, always suspicious. Moles blindly
stuggling through the ground, coming up to sniff the air
before diving back underground. The birds – all sorts of birds.
Birds of prey. Huge magnificent creatures right the way down
to the tiny jenny-wren.' She stopped and looked up at him
self-consciously, shyly. Looked down again and picked at a
hidden thread on her shorts. 'I never talk about it. Max never
wanted to listen. So I never talk about it. It's nice to be able to
talk with someone who appreciates things.' Him appreciate
things! He never thought about anything like this. Used to
centuries ago, but not now. Not until now. Never had time.
Never could be bothered with all that soft sloppy nonsense.
He felt stupid, uneducated, felt he'd missed a whole part of his
life as he sat here listening to her talk. 'I've always loved
wildlife. Loved nature. It can be cruel and hard but never
without purpose. Not like man.' She looked at him, he
thought, accusingly, and he felt uncomfortable under her
scrutiny. Was glad when she turned away, got up, and moved
around the room, touching the furniture. Gently, as if, with
each touch, she gathered something from the object. Something she could store, hold deep within herself to bring out and
remember later. When reality became too hurtful and sanity
lay in the full soft colours of remembered feelings.

'You appreciate anything soft and gentle. Don't make me
laugh!' Jenny appearing scornfully in front of him. Hands on

140

hips, fair hair flung back, her face bitter and hateful. 'You can't feel anything for anybody. You're a fraud. Always have been.' Mother looked at Jenny reproachfully but nodded her head in agreement. Turning her sad look to him. Shaking her head. Jenny triumphant, sneering at him. 'Appreciate indeed. Don't even consider the feeling. There's no point in your case. Fraud.' She took her hands off her hips and extended her fingers to him. Nails growing talon-like, pointing at him, face shrinking, twisting, wrinkling, hag-like. Her voice rising to a banshee wail. He blocked the image, wiped out the sight of her. He stood up and brushed past Lisa, opened the door and stepped out into the warm moonlight night. Lisa followed him quietly closing the door behind her and led the way.

The path was slippery. He felt lightheaded from tiredness. From too much thinking. Too many confusing feelings beginning to implant themselves unwanted into his mind, becoming unsafe. Before, without feeling, he was safe. He could hide behind his barrier of callous indifference. Lisa was hammering with gentle ferocity at the barrier, breaking it down. Part of him welcomed it: part was frightened and apprehensive.

'You're too hard on yourself. There's more to you than you allow.' Her voice floating back to him as they walked on. No there was nothing else. Nothing at all. Had been once but not anymore. 'Nonsense. You are silly sometimes. The way you talk.' Gentle scoffing. Mocking words spoken kindly, lightly, without offence. They moved relentlessly on, never stopping.

'We'll need to rest soon Boss. The lads are knackered. The terrain's messing up their ankles. Some of them.' Yes, his sergeant was right. He was pushing too hard. Wanting desperately to get there ahead of the other Platoons. Striving to win. What was the prize? To initiate the attack. To be the first on top of the mountain. He'd never considered that they might not be able to take the position by themselves. Didn't allow the thought to enter his head. He sank onto the ground and watched the others move into cover positions as they'd been trained. Except for the breathing and the soft sound of

equipment and boots on soggy ground, the night was quiet.
Another ten miles of this to go. Ten miles of slippery,
muscle-wrenching, tendon-tearing struggle before the real
test even began. But they were used to it. He told himself. His
sergeant crawled over and lay close by. Whispering, 'If we can
rest for an hour, they'll be fine Boss. Just ease the old blisters.
A couple are swinging the lead, but I've got them sussed. We'll
be there first. Don't worry.' They lapsed into alert silence.

'There's something wonderful about walking in the middle
of the night. Especially on a night like tonight.' Lisa's voice
again disconnected, floating back. She kept on walking. A
flowing motion up the hillside, over the rocks, between the
scrubby trees like ghostly skeletons in the diffused moonlight.
'Tell me more. I like to hear your voice.' How could she? He
hated the sound now. Thought it thin, boring. A monotonal
dirge. 'Please.'

They came to the top of the hill and he could walk beside
her. She smiled, her teeth catching the moon and shining, a
startling sparkle in the grey monochrome night. At least it
would take his mind off Max. Off Jenny. Off all the things he
despised. All the things he wanted rid of. Here, in this still
night.

Fourteen

THEY'D TALKED for hours, days it seemed. He'd talked and Lisa had listened to his ramblings. Listened attentively to his sorrowful out-pourings without ever a hint of boredom. Now she slept, tired. Exhausted by him. She slept against his shoulder, nestling her chin into the join of arm and neck, her arm spread across his chest slim and light. When he bent his head to brush his lips gently over her skin, he could smell the freshness of her, breathed her in. Sometimes she made little sleep noises, her body twitching slightly, breathing shallow butterfly wings against his chest.

He watched her and loved her. Ached with his feeling, a pain-filled, hopeless ache that he fought, yet wanted. Hated the pain, but loved the fact of it, the fact that he could feel. Did feel. Loved. Was loved. A feeling he'd never experienced. Could have, but had pushed it aside in the interests of his own selfish survival. Now he wanted Lisa with an aggressive passion he could not understand and didn't want to. Just wanted to know that it existed.

The hollow was silent and peaceful, the dying embers of the fire casting red glows over the cave, darting every now and then over the grass with the spitting flare of a piece of unburnt log. Quiet, peaceful and empty. Without anyone or anything else to spoil the night. Despite this, and the fact that Lisa lay asleep on his shoulder, he couldn't rest. His mind still awake, still acutely aware of any sound, any odd movement. The occasional scurry of the field mice made his heart speed until, in the flash of a microsecond, he'd analysed the sound and placed it. Then he relaxed, checking that he hadn't disturbed Lisa. She slept soundly. Quietly oblivious.

Gently he moved her head onto the pillow and, careful not to wake her, got up and went out into the night. The air was cool, with the hint of wind puffing soft breaths against his face. He walked naked out into the middle of the hollow, then across to his place by the pool. The silence and smell of the night were familiar from the past, old friends remembered with fondness and without sentimentality. He sat down by the water's edge and lifted his gaze to the clear starlit sky. Bright dots littered the inky blackness.

'Sometimes, when you lie back and look, you become a part of the sky. It seems to wrap itself right around you. It's the time I like best of all.' His mother's observation had startled him as he sat looking up unhappy and young. 'Isn't it amazing that all that is out there and we don't know what it is. Look at the moon.' He'd looked and suddenly saw the craters, even with the naked eye. Saw the strange shapes the moon passed through on its passage across the sky. Saw the clouds hurry across the face of the moon as if not wanting to heed the progress. He'd loved the moon from then on.

'Going to be a bit tricky with the moon, Boss.' His sergeant was right. The moon was no good for night operations. He wanted pitch-black. He hated the moon then. The moon had no place in his life then.

He looked and looked. Enjoyed the sight. Felt the feelings of youth return. Felt whole and unviolated for the first time ever.

'There's nothing quite like the sky at night. Nothing you'll ever see.' She was right, he thought. His mother was always right. His father had been sitting there too. He nodded in agreement.

'In the southern hemisphere the air is much clearer. Seems to make the sky much brighter and larger too.' His father spoke knowledgeably. He had not listened. Had listened but

144

ignored him. Now he wondered what it would be like in the southern hemisphere. Now he thought perhaps he should have listened. Should have given his father the chance. Not ignored him. Now, looking up at the sky, too late.

He crossed his legs into the full lotus. Half-Indian, half-eternal, now. Sitting in the position of his youth, watching his Indian nanny opposite. Pretty, relaxed and eighteen. Watched her with the intentness of youth. The concentration for something outlandishly new and difficult. Watched, copied, and finally did it. Then sat youthfully arrogant and clever. Here in the hollow he sat. Naked lotus. Peaceful quiet lotus. His Indian nanny nodding in assent, naked assent. Sitting there opposite him her small breasts sharply defined in the moonlight. Her heels hid her womanhood. Hid her from him. She sat, full lotus in the hollow. The sound of the mantra rose insistent in the background until it swelled, filling the air, vibrating through the ground, totally surrounding, building to a crescendo, then dying slowly with the breath. Cleared the mind. Emptied the head of thought. Opened the brain to the infinity of the black sky. Let it swarm in, take over, fill the vision with bright white lights in the blackness. In the eternal blackness.

He sat for a long time, then slowly became aware that his ankles were aching. Unwinding, feeling the creaking pain, seeing the smile from her opposite. Not showing the pain. Feeling the glow of her acknowledgement. He stood, the pain in the ankles diminishing, allowing him to walk over to where she sat, eyes on him; walked through her to the far end of the hollow. He closed his eyes, pacing to the far end. Counting the steps, allowing his senses to tell him where he was.

'You can feel and see everything if you want. If you let yourself. Without need of eyes or ears, you can see.' Her incongruously perfect English. He'd tried it and the first few times walked into the walls surrounding the garden, her tinkling Indian laugh soft amongst the flowers. Eventually he found the trick, but only succeeded now and then, mostly meeting the hard stone walls or dropping onto the sunken pathways. Now, as he moved, he could feel the confidence returning. The mind expanding, becoming a screen whereon the parameters of the hollow played. He walked up to the granite cliff, stopped a few feet away, and turned, followed the contours round. A constant distance from the rock. Avoiding stones and dips on the way, every detail clear in his mind. He became aware of his nanny walking beside him. Smiling, eyes closed, gliding along, her breasts bobbed slightly as she moved. The dot on her forehead bright, leading on. They both walked in their heads. He felt relaxed and peaceful, his body fragmented and yet whole. He came to the pool again and sat down in the same place as before. Opened his eyes and saw the Indian girl sitting motionless opposite. She faded into the pool, down and away, smiling contentedly. He smiled at the memory of her body. The first time he'd seen a naked woman. The first time he'd understood the meaning of sexuality. The first time he'd touched a woman. The first time his child's penis had grown. Unexpectedly. Frighteningly. Thrillingly. The first of many times.

'The body is the pathway to the soul. The senses, the signposts. Follow the signpost along the body and eternal soulful pleasure awaits the traveller,' she had whispered into his mind, into his young uncomprehending mind. Then she'd followed his pathways. She lay there now, next to him, her hands wandering. Touching, finding the signposts, she showed him where and how to follow hers, to follow woman's. Lightly licking her nipples, not knowing what he was doing. Tongue creeping with her insistent persuasive urgings. Telling him. Showing him. Responding when he found the right place.

He stood up, wiping the image from his mind, watching the Indian girl disappear reproachfully, stood feeling guilty of his thoughts, of his memories, casting an anxious glance over to Lisa lying asleep.

'Remember the signposts.' The Indian voice huskily in the echo chamber of his mind. 'Remember.' Then the laugh. The sexual sound of pleasure. Lisa breathed lightly in the dying glow of the fire. He went back to the cave, stepping silently, kneeling noiselessly beside her, his still erect penis lightly brushing her arm. He looked at its pulsating maleness red-blue against her pale slim arm. It appalled him that this crude, obvious phallus should tear and bury itself so easily inside her, could possibly give her pleasure. He decided it was the last resort. That this thing throbbing painfully between his legs would stay out of the way until she begged for him to use it. He wanted her pleasure to be his pleasure. Suddenly he moved away, back into the night, as if the mere touch of her body had scalded him.

The Indian girl sat just inside the pool of light. There, with her, a youth naked and absorbed by her. He watched the two. Watched from his vantage point. The youth moved closer. The Indian girl looked over his shoulder at him, then back at the youth. She slowly manipulated the young body. He turned and wiped the image from his eyes. From his mind. Ran to the far end of the hollow and climbed. Climbed, feeling the skin scratch on the rock.

The night cooled, tightening his flesh, raising the goose-bumps. He felt them and remained still, enjoyed the sensation, let the cold seep into his body, into the bones. Watching over the countryside asleep in the night. He the only watcher, the dark sentinel on the lonely mountain. Here it was quiet and numb. Here the Indian girl could not reach. Here he could sit nakedly alone with himself, without interruption. The wind blew down into his lungs. Fresh tasting in his mouth and nose. Gradually his body tightened into the strength of his being. He was aware of her sitting beside him. An echo of the castle wall. She, as he was, naked. They both sat quietly. She went as silently as she'd arrived.

'You don't need anybody but me, David.' He heard Amanda's voice but refused to turn, refused to acknowledge her. He waited, but the only sound was the soft moan of the wind over the mountains.

Gradually as he sat, the sun slowly lifted above the horizon.

It was odd the way it suddenly, yet slowly seemed to arrive, the landscape growing colours out of the grey, the shapes solidifying. The sky less threatening with the calm blues and the soft white. The dawn, ever present. He sat as the observer for everyone. For everyone who lay asleep, oblivious to the wonder. Sat privileged as he had been before. Before, when he'd considered the dawn the death. The real glaring terror of death then when the dawn had meant naked fear.

Now, sitting here, the fear was gone, hardly remembered. A shadow passing into the disappearing darkness. Now he sat heralding the dawn, welcoming the warm morning light. The goosebumps went, leaving the tight-centred body, the living statue sitting on the bare rock. He looked down into the hollow and saw it move away until it was a small insignificant spot on the mountain – *in* the mountain – then drew closer until it surrounded him. Then he was on the mountain looking down again. Down into the green of the grass and the dark of the seemingly lifeless mirror pool, the cave a shadowed gap in the light grey granite wall. He sat and let the image etch itself onto his memory.

He stood stiffly and climbed back down, entered the cave like an escaped prisoner returning to his cell. That was unfair, he thought. Capable of thinking again now, that was not how he felt. Not a prisoner. Maybe . . . maybe a prisoner of his feelings, his new-found feelings. Lisa still lay asleep. Now the soft light of the dawn slid off her hair and skin. Shimmered in the cave. He touched her, just. To see if she was still there and not a mirage, not a hologram. Getting carried away now with Max's devices.

She stirred and opened a sleepy eye. An eye that focused then glazed and focused again. The eye told the mouth that smiled. She stretched and pulled his mouth down to hers. They kissed lightly. He could feel himself again, self-consciously aware, childishly concerned. She felt for him and pulled him down toward her. He calmed and gently but firmly laid her back against the pillows.

Her nipples were hard and roughly textured against his lips.

148

The end of his tongue traced abstract pattern around her swelling breasts. She moaned and he knew that he'd found a signpost. He followed the path. Down slowly over her body. Over her soft yielding flesh. Over the millions of waiting nerve endings, waiting hidden, for the right touch, given in love, to send tiny explosive charges to the centre of her sex. Down to her wet core. Tongue leading the way, firmly gentle. Naïvely exploratory. Wholly meant. He smelt her femininity. Tasted her femininity and heard her pleasure. Heard her cry with enjoyment and, for the first time, felt joy himself. Felt total, unselfish joy. Forgot himself in the completeness of her.

Without entering her, he felt for the first time in his life he'd made love. Made true love. Not the phrase that provided the excuse for any form of sexual act, but had completely subordinated himself to the true meaning of love. Her body, her mind, her soul, whatever it was, it was her. Neither one small part nor two, but the whole, inseparable. The completeness, abstractly felt, indefinable.

They lay quietly, side by side, holding each other, watching the dawn turn to day, neither wanting to speak and risk spoiling the magical feeling, the extended moment, not wanting it to end. The need for oral communication secondary to the present mutual knowledge.

He tried to explore the sensations, tried to pin them down. Old habits from a different time.

'It's something very special.' His father quietly uncomfortable, explaining. He had laughed to himself. Scorned his father, silently to himself. Now he knew what he meant, too late. Now, when he felt the hopelessness of his feelings. Couldn't understand that. The hopelessness. What the hell. His stupid mental ramblings. Lisa was all that mattered, go with it until it finished. If it did. The hell with any future. Maybe Max was right. Existence was all that mattered. No past, no future. Just now. Here. No age. Ageless. Timeless. Existence without any form. With form. There was no need for concern because that implied future.

149

Christ, he thought that his brain was cracking up. Slowly disintegrating into a grey dusty heap in his head, pouring like fine sand out of his ears, nose, mouth, and eyes, piling into heaps of non-thought. A jumbled mass of nonsense that a slight breeze would scatter in sunbeams across the hollow. Some particles to lie dustlike on the water, others to be caught and rushed away in the stream. The rest to lie sterile and abandoned on the ground. He walked over and kicked the pile and felt no pain. Felt a stirring of thought, the abstraction of his thoughts, lift and float and settle. Dry particles of no value drifting back onto the ground. Lisa drifted off to sleep again on his arm. A strange ethereal creature from nowhere. No past, no future. The past with Max. That's where her past was and again he felt the stirrings of unease. Wondered what Max was to her, what she was to Max. Uncomfortable thoughts blown into a small dust whirlwind, swirling up and out of sight.

'It's something that only happens once in your life.' Puffing the pipe trying to keep the embarrassment in control. He'd watched his father's struggle and enjoyed it. 'Should only happen once.' The pipe puffing caused another pause. 'The first time with a virgin.' Followed by a cough and clouds of the pungent smoke. But Jenny wasn't a virgin when he met her. When they married. There was silence. His father too stunned to speak. Not knowing what to say. He'd enjoyed that moment even more. Now it was a tacky, grubby little enjoyment. With no meaning. A pathetic gesture of defiance at nothing. It embarrassed him now when he thought about it. Another little pile that stirred, touched by the toe of his remembrance.

'Well you've probably missed something then.' By way of compensation for losing parental control. Face-saving in front of uncaring offspring. Perhaps at that moment he'd felt a touch of shame, of caring for his father. Then, when he saw the expression. A mixture of confusion and sorrow, of frustration and unhappiness. For an instant, then gone. Buried as he'd buried everything ever since. The little pile of dust thoughts caught frozen in the sunlight, then gone. The silence between them had lasted from that moment. Lasted for ever. Basic communication for simple practical purposes only.

'Why don't you talk to your father. You never talk. Never say anything to each other. Why don't you.' He'd tried once at his mother's request, but the conversation had slowed and drifted to a halt in the mud of total misunderstanding. He hadn't tried any more after that.

'You should have done.' She stood at the entrance to the cave, looking from him to Lisa. Reprovingly. 'Just to talk. That's all.' Still eyeing Lisa with suspicion.

She lay sleeping, quietly unaware of his thoughts. Suddenly, it didn't matter to him either. He went over to the pool and dived in, a clean knifing dive that barely rippled the surface, and swam fast under water. The first of the day and a refreshing invigorating way to dispel the child fears, water the dust pile of thoughts down to a manageable solid lump, then shovel them away into a hole, bury them for good. He dived down deep into the pool, feeling the pressure build up on his ears. Blew through his pinched nostrils to balance. Continued going down, the light dimming with the depth, the sides of the pool pushing in. He felt weightless now. Rolled over onto his back. Back? Which side is which when weightless? Bubble laughs rippled upwards, towards the distant surface. The mirror high above him. The sky mirror. He rolled around, knowing there were no ripples down here. Nothing to show what he was doing. He could drown and sink and still there would be no evidence. No sound to escape the watery expanse. No movement. Nothing. His lungs told him it was time for air and he allowed himself to drift slowly upwards, the granite passing in front of his eyes like the walls of a lift-shaft.

'The water's for sailing on. Not swimming in.' Sure it was. Of course. He'd not seen the wry smile on his father's face, simply because he didn't want to. Ignored the comment because he'd heard it before, many boring repetitious times before. Repeated supposedly for his friend's benefit. One of the many ignored comments.

'Why are you so disparaging?' She stood at the edge of the pool waiting with a mother's look. Questioningly reproving. 'Why?' Always the questions and there were no answers. No answers to that question anyway. 'Think about it.' Always what she said. Always the same way. And was she right? Possibly. Here now in this watery thought-paradise, possibly. Anything was possible right now. Anything at all. There was no problem. Hell, he'd even speak to the old man now. Really try. Talk to him and see, try and find out, now, here, this moment. He was drugged drunk on love and he'd do anything now.

'Not good enough.' Well. It won't get any better, that's for sure. She faded away, sad figure in the sun-filled hollow. The granite paradise. Sorry, but that's the way it is, he thought. Another of those grey dust thoughts. One that escaped from the water.

Fifteen

HE WATCHED the Jeeps from across the valley. Tiny specks
to the naked eye, brought into sharp relief by the powerful
binoculars. They moved in and out of the forest fire-breaks.
Occasionally the sound of a high-powered rifle could be heard
cracking over the hills. Ahead of the drive, deer leapt, startled
and frightened, diving into the next area of deep cover to be
flushed out again. The shooting seemed to be indiscriminate.
Does, bucks, adults and fawns all falling to the shots. He could
hear the distant cheers and whoops of delight. What was it that
Max had said? Only shoot for the pot.

He leaned behind the seat and took out the rifle, clipped the
magazine into place and cocked the weapon, watching them
all the time. The Jeeps moved in a pincer fashion, driving the
frightened animals into the centre, where, a short distance
behind the pincers, the main killing group were moving
inexorably forward, stopping momentarily to fell another
leaping deer. A stag with a full set of antlers reared backwards
and fell, a kicking heap, into the undergrowth. More cheers
sounded across the valley, a thin sound in the still air. He laid
the binoculars down. He would have to get a lot closer in order
to get the chance. He needed telescopic sights at this range.
Didn't have them. He watched a little longer then, checking
the car was hidden from sight, set off along his side of the
valley, paralleling the hunters, keeping out of sight.

It was easy going through the fire-breaks and the thin young

153

pine forest. Occasionally he would lose sight of the hunters and, when he saw them again, they were closer. Distinguishable figures now. So far he hadn't see Max. His two women were there, following the hunt without expression. Mindlessly moving forward. The crack of the gunfire louder with each step, the revving engines of the Jeeps very near. He moved away and ran through the trees to get ahead of the hunt. He wanted to have plenty of time to set up before they arrived, wanted time to scan for possible ambush positions. Difficult in this close country because he wanted Max out in the open with nowhere to go and his men without room to outflank him. He was starting to tire. Legs feeling stiff and heavy. Breath forced into the lungs.

'What do you think you are? A man or a pathetic specimen of a girl? My daughter could do better than you and she's only four.' The sergeant instructor's voice searing into his semiconscious mind as he struggled up the hill, the fifty-pound pack biting into his shoulders, sweat dripping into his eyes, stinging. Ahead was the top of the hill. Just there. There he could rest for a short while before running down the other side and up the next. Got to keep going. All the pain and abuse of the months of training endured. Wasn't going to throw it away now. Dug deep into his reserves and forced the body against its own better judgement. Reached the top.

'Stand to attention. Don't droop, you're a man not a flower. Or are you?'

Stood upright, the blurred vision gradually clearing. The screeching lungs and pounding heart slowing to manageable proportions. Then off again to the next hill and a repeat. The position was the best he could find. A natural bowl at the end of the valley where the hunt would naturally stop, where the cornered deer would be slaughtered. He lay still waiting and watching. In the distance, the Jeep engines and the baying of the hunters could be heard along with the drumming of hooves on the earth. He waited coolly, calculating the distances to each extremity of the clearing. Didn't want to miss when the time came. The first deer came hurtling into the

154

clearing and slid to a frightened and confused halt below him, brought up short by the sheer face of the cliff. Some, in their terror, tried to climb, slipping backwards on their haunches. The Jeeps stopped on the edge and waited for the main party to arrive. There was no sign of Max. The girls arrived with the main group. Still no sign of Max. The girls took rifles from the Jeeps and stepped forward. The men remained where they were. Apart from the terrified stampeding of the frightened animals, there was no sound. The firing lasted for what seemed a long time, the girls dispassionately emptying magazine after magazine into the pain-wracked dying bodies. No sign of emotion at all. When it was over, the echoes faded away across the valley. The carcasses piled high below him. The girls waited, checking for any movement, and then turned, replaced the weapons, and walked away back down the track and out of sight. There was still no sign of Max. The men in the Jeeps reversed, turned and went away too, leaving the clearing with its mound of death.

A movement from the shadows caught his eye. A small stunted figure darted out and ran amongst the dead deer, stopped, grinned, and then vanished back into the shadows. There was no more movement.

He lay shaken by what he'd just witnessed and then moved, following in the tracks of the Jeeps. Max had to be close. Had to be. He wondered briefly if Lisa had woken and missed him yet. Brushed aside any feeling of guilt. He was after Max and she was a hindrance. Possibly doing it on purpose. No, that was a Jenny trick. Lisa wasn't into that. Or was she? It was disturbing. She liked Max, thought a lot of him. Respected him greatly.

More so than she loved him probably. The thought irritated, angered. He slipped quietly along through the forest. The noise of the Jeeps driving slowly up ahead, keeping him in the right direction, the direction in which he thought he would find Max. Sometimes he thought he heard strange mumblings, voices murmuring in the trees. He stopped, crouching to listen. The murmurings ceased. Maybe just a brief breath of

155

wind or a dead branch dropping onto the soft cushion of pine needles and leaves. He moved on again, eyes scanning ahead and to the side. Feet stepping in the tyre tracks. The track wound up and through the forest. Up to the head of the valley way above where he'd been waiting for Max. At every fire-break, he stopped and checked. Sat quietly, ears tuning in to every minute sound. Once satisfied, moved onwards.

The camp lay before him in the gathering dusk. Laughter, lights and the smell of venison cooking over an open fire. A large fire, the tall wide flames licking around the carcass, sizzling, spitting, succulent, fat dripping around the meat and down onto the white-red-black logs. A stooping figure strangely wrapped turned the spit mechanically. Round and round. Slowly cooking all sides of the animal, what once had been an animal. Antlers lay stacked near one of the trailers, an obscene aluminium oblong, reflecting images of the laughing, dancing people. Music resounded around the rocky clearing. Tall pine sentinels, well back from the flames, stood silent observers to the revelry. He moved beside one of them, the branches stirring with his passage, swinging gently back, still again. The Jeeps sat close to the two trailers. Tents were pitched forming a circle, a wide circle, the walls of the tents tucked up close under the pines. He stayed high above the camp, moving carefully on the steep slope, the treacherously unstable slope. The loose ground shifted beneath his boots. He moved a few careful feet then stopped as the soil slipped. The loamy surface sliding very quietly, secretly, down a couple of metres, to rest uneasily in the dark.

The noise from the camp seemed to stop at the edge of the trees, intruded a short distance, and then was blocked to a muted sound by the unyielding pines. He felt the sound of his own movements were the loudest. Crashing, gut-wrenching, heart-trembling dead-branch cracks that made him stop and nervously listen. Gradually the revelry subsided, the exertion of the day's hunt taking its toll. The carcass had been reduced to bone and odd-shaped hunks of meat, some hanging in

156

threads, being eaten by the flames. Occasionally the spit-turner stretched out an arm and grabbed a piece, hurriedly shoving it into his mouth before anyone noticed. There was still no sign of Max.

He waited until the camp was quiet, until it seemed that everyone was asleep in their tents or trailers, until the spit man had gorged himself and left the rest of the carcass to blacken and burn in the dying embers of the fire. The man left. A strange disappearing silhouette among the trees. He waited longer.

'Allow time. Don't expect just because things seem right, that they are. Bad mistake that. Has cost many people their lives.' The class was silent. Mainly because most thoughts lay in reminiscences of the past weekend, some pleasant, others not so. He split up with Katherine. Shame, that. Still, as John said, plenty more fish and all that. He stretched lazily, caught himself just in time, and looked interested when the Captain fixed his one eye on him. 'Bear that in mind Trowse. Don't consider the obvious is necessarily the obvious. That includes this lecture.' He waited in the trees, shivering in the darkness. Shivering as the sweat cooled on his body and a slight wind blew through the thin material of his T-shirt. Mistake, that. He should have catered for the fact that he might be out for a few days. His stomach watched the burning carcass and tempted him down. He stayed in the trees.

A figure came out of one of the trailers. He tensed, then relaxed as the overweight man belched, stood legs apart, and relieved himself in a noisy stream into the fire, spraying the carcass with hissing boredom. The feeling in his stomach subsided. The man belched once more and went back into the trailer. The camp returned to silence. Just the final hiss of the carcass, now ignored.

It took five minutes to move carefully down the slope to the edge of the camp. Stopping, listening. Feeling all the time. Senses acutely aware. Once on the edge, by a tent, he stood very still, listening to the slow breathing of the occupant. Somebody snored in the tent beside. He waited, then moved

157

silently towards the trailers. Max would be in one of those if anywhere. With the girls. As always. Yet he wasn't with the girls during the day. They had been on their own. Where the hell had Max been? Following him perhaps. He shrank into a shadow and peered into the gloom of where he'd just come from, ears stretched to maximum. Any freak out-of-place sound latched on to and examined. He stayed there for what seemed like hours. Waiting. Waiting for the possibility of Max following him. Eventually it became an absurd thought. He was either here or . . . or where? No point in thinking about it. Check this place first. Check it thoroughly. He stepped forward once more. The first trailer felt cool to the touch, the glistening aluminium almost organic in the slight moonlight. The window was open. He carefully pulled himself up and looking in saw the fat man lying spread across one of the girls. One of Max's girls. He slipped back onto the ground, puzzled. Went to the door and, quietly opening it, stepped inside, keeping low. There was only the sound of sleep. Back outside, he checked the other trailer. The same. One of Max's girls with a gross man, lying slobbering in sleep. No sign of Max. The tents received a cursory examination and then he left.

Once outside the perimeter of the camp, he sat leaning back against a tree, Armalite cradled in his arms. Useless and silent. Dead weight to carry without purpose. Where was Max? Back at the castle? At the farmhouse? Wherever he was there was one thing for certain. Max was avoiding any contact with him. Guilty. No need for a trial. A Judge or Jury. Guilty. The boy's puzzled face appeared against the pines and faded.

'You can't judge people like that, David. You really can't.' Elderly mother standing in the sitting-room. Elderly father standing by the window, defeated look on his lined face framed by grey hair. He, standing in the centre of the room, teenage accusations flying around, bouncing carelessly off the walls. Barbed cruel comments lancing in deep. Destroying his father. No, not destroying, trying to. Hoping to. More vitriol poured out in the safety of his own articulate educated grasp of the already-paid-for words. Paid for by his father. Now

158

standing listening, taking the punishment. Mother close to tears. 'Please David that's enough. We've done our best for you. Always done our best. This is the way you repay.' Repay what? The old clichés. What reason to repay anything. They made him what he was. They and their attitudes. Their need for him to be educated. Their need, not his. What to repay? Saw the pain his words inflicted. Wanted them to. His father turned and looked at him. The look stopped the tirade. The look that spanned centuries. The look Father didn't know anything about. The look that bore all the pain ever meted out by ungrateful offspring. He had turned and walked from the room then, hearing his mother collapse into heartbroken tears. For the first time in his life he had seen the consequences of his actions to them and didn't care.

He shuddered, the rifle rattling against the tree. Shuddered again, shaking the thoughts away, stood up and climbed, slow going in the darkness of the forest.

It was just before dawn when he reached the car. Daybreak, by the time he switched the engine off and listened to the familiar comforting, cooling tick of the engine. Sat watching the sun and hearing the birds begin the day with tentative song, growing louder with the passage of the sun up the sky. Got out of the car and wearily went into the hollow. Back to the safety. Back to sanity. Back to a bed and his woman.

'You have to be kidding of course? Who the hell do you think you are?' He swung around, rifle held clenched tight, hand working the cocking-handle, thumb releasing the safety catch. Jenny, standing close to the entrance sneering at him. Standing nakedly sneering at him. Amanda moved beside her. 'You think anybody's going to wait for you?' He relaxed and brushed their images away. Delighted in seeing their concern as they shrank, then fizzled out, leaving nothing to mark their existence. Walked past the spot now forgotten and into the hollow.

There was nothing. No sign of Lisa. She had gone. Left. He stood shocked. Head reeling momentarily. Hadn't thought

159

that she might leave. Thought that she would understand and wait for him. Know why he had to go on his own. Surely she understood that? She wasn't like the others that didn't. Surely? He sank to his knees, feeling the fatigue suddenly twice as heavily, hanging like a shroud around his shoulders, dragging him down. Suddenly feeling the filth of his exertions like a close skin, drying on him, changing him, changing him into a broken man. Feeling the pain of her absence dragging his emotions down. Felt the tears start for the first time ever. Felt the wet flow on his cheeks, felt the pain of his loss. Cried, the sobs welling. Stopped it before it took control. Pulled his discipline back, staunched the weakness, pushed the emotions back into the recesses, never to emerge again. Stood and let anger take its place. Hurled the belt and pouches to the ground, screamed with anger at the sky, hearing the strange alien sound hurtle back and swamp him.

'Peace can only come from total inner control. Total knowledge. Physical control over emotion. Over pain. Over living. Life itself. Only then will you find peace.' The Old Man's thin voice strangely resonant in the air. Thin sing-song tones from the fleshy cupid's-bow mouth hidden amongst the white beard. The Indian girl standing, eyes closed, slim and sari-clad beside him. He looking up, trying to understand, his young legs moving restlessly. Eyes wide. He wanted to play. Not like this but with the boys his own age. He was getting bored. He wanted to play. The Old Man seemed to sense this. 'The young are so full of impatience. It is they that have the energy to do great things. To channel that energy into great things and yet they squander it in mindless pursuits.' He laughed happily, sighed, and shrugged. 'Well, it doesn't matter. Just try and remember. Some day it might help.' Hand placed on his head. He didn't like that. Moved away. The Old Man went. The Indian girl took his hand and led him away.

He placed the Armalite on the ground and stood watching the Indian girl; she smiled and unravelled the sari, allowing the brightly-coloured fine cloth to fall in soft folds on the grass until she was naked, her firm olive body shining sleekly in the

160

early morning sunshine. He did likewise, letting his clothes lie neatly at his feet, not making a move until she did. She stood smiling enigmatically at him then, crossing her feet, gracefully dropped into a sitting position. She pulled her feet onto her thighs into the Lotus and closed her eyes, hands held lightly on her knees, forefinger and thumb touching. He copied, closing his eyes. Emptying his mind. She remained in front of a frozen image. Gradually her image faded and there was nothing. No pictures, no images. Just a grey expanse. An unmoving grey expanse. The colour gradually dissipating until he was in a colourless expanse. A limbo land.

'Do you believe all those things?' Roger's voice in the darkness. He didn't reply. 'Really. Do you believe it all? All that stuff about being able to leave your body?' Shaky voice. He still didn't reply. There was a pause. 'Come on, David. I know you're awake. Don't mess around.' He still didn't reply. Lying in the dark waiting for the time to be right. He could hear Roger breathing. Hear the breathing growing quicker. Could almost see his little face, eyes wide in fear. He waited, and then let out a groan. A deep moan of despair. As horrible as he could. As his young larynx would let him. 'I know it's you, David. I know it is. I'm not having you to stay ever again.' Tremulous voice. Making him laugh inwardly. Suddenly he felt he was floating, felt he was rising. Thought he could see the room stretched out beneath him, see Roger lying in the bed next to him. Next to him! To his body, lying, eyes closed, smile on his face. Screamed in terror then and sat bolt upright in bed. He had done it without wanting to. Without believing. Roger, sitting in the pool of light, wide eyes gradually turning to disbelief. No, it's true, he had, he had seen them both lying there in their bed. He had seen it. Tears starting to form with fear and frustration at not being believed. Roger's triumph was obvious in his face.

He started at the touch. Shook the vacuum clear and allowed the world to flood back in. The sun was high in the sky. Burning high. Burning his bare shoulders. Lisa stood looking down at him. Perfect in every way. A strange sight

161

against the hard rock background. She looked down at him with curiosity. He untangled his legs and stood. She let her eyes drift down his body, scorching, He dressed quickly.

'You're back. I see.' Expressionlessly. Back! He was back! Just where had she been? She walked to the pool and sat down at the edge, letting the water lap around her bare feet. 'You didn't find Max.' It was a statement. It annoyed him. He grabbed her shoulder, wished he hadn't when he saw her face. Backed off. She turned back to the pool. Silence. He wandered aimlessly before returning and sitting down, his temper controlled, placed a hand on her shoulder. She remained looking at the pool. 'Max had no idea the boy was in his way. Had no idea he'd hit the boy. He's utterly distraught. That's why he wasn't with the hunt.' He reeled. Tried to grasp what she was saying. Grew angry again. She'd seen Max and yet, for two days, she'd led him everywhere except where Max was. She looked at him as if he'd just crawled out of a sewer. 'I told you that with me you'd find him. But you had to go on your own. Don't you trust anybody?' No. That was the answer. Who the hell was there to trust? Certainly nobody here. 'What do you expect when you disappear without a word? Just what do you expect?' Her eyes blue orbs of accusation. He didn't like the look, felt the pain in his soul, didn't want her hate. Didn't know how to apologize. Tried. She kept her eyes averted from him, letting him sweat a little. When she turned back there was a deep hurt. A pain he didn't understand. 'You have to trust, David.' Thought he heard his mother's voice out of her mouth.

He knelt beside her and took hold of her shoulders, wanting to crush her to him. Knew that he had to be gentle. Knew that now of all times he had to back off. Be gentle. Be understanding himself. She looked at him again.

'Max is devastated by the accident. Completely devastated.' He was not convinced but didn't say. Decided to let her believe he had had a change of heart. Whatever happened, he just knew, deep inside, that Max was to blame for the boy's death. Knew it just as sure as he was here beside Lisa. He saw

162

the belief in her eyes. Saw the relief and the tears of joy start from those blue eyes. Wiped the tears away with his thumbs and kissed the wet eyes. Suddenly she moved back and looked deep into his eyes. Searching.

'You don't believe it do you?' A quietly spoken question. How did he answer it? No, he didn't believe it, but he was prepared to accept it and call a truce. Max was still the enemy in his eyes. Always would be. The boy was dead because of Max and that couldn't be forgiven. Never. She studied him a moment longer. Her eyes seemed to glaze over and she turned. He felt a loss without knowing why, felt she'd gone from him. Reached out but didn't touch, held his hand away, fearing the touch.

'Max wants us to go down into the town tomorrow. There's a pub. An end-of-hunt drinks thing. It happens every year. He wants us to go.' Monotone voice, mechanical words with the emphasis removed on purpose. So as not to give any idea as to the thoughts or wants of the speaker, and yet trying to convey in those short sentences a plea, a longing. OK, so he'd go. He'd play along for now. Try to find a way to keep Lisa without Max always being there. Without Max.

Sixteen

HER EYES kept straying over. He saw them out of the corner of his. Constantly vigilant, continously worried, she seemed in another world in her look. In a material world beyond his grasp. Somewhere not here with him, now. He sipped more of the scotch, allowing the single malt to slip easily down his throat, unnoticed as he checked on her. She turned back to him with a smile from thousands of miles. Unfocused happiness falsely portrayed in the reflections of her eyes.

Max sat at the far end of the bar, girls on either arm. Through the window behind him, his latest toy, a Porsche Turbo, black, sinister, low on the tarmac. Max saw his look and raised a glass, toasting the exchange from a distance. From next to him. He felt the competition across the room like a hand–slap. His passions stung by the arrogance. Pride meeting in the middle of the room, two protagonists in the arena circling warily. Max turned away smiling, playing on his temper now, playing with him as he played with the hair of the girl on his right, tangled the black threads between his fingers, pulled hard, the girl wincing through a smile, hand gentle on Max's cheek.

Lisa touched his arm, moving out into the sunshine, sitting on the grass beside the road. The clamour from inside the bar lessened to a diminutive roar of background musak. He could still see and feel the faces inside. The faces staring at him. Contorted faces. Faces cheerily red and maniacally grinning.

164

Purple-veined noses, large white teeth. Red smeared teeth in crimson gashed faces. Fluttering bat wings above hard bitter eyes. Leering faces. Jeering faces.

He watched as a cripple sat helplessly, the butt of jokes from his uncaring spouse. Hat on the floor. Crutches knocked over. 'Pick that up then.' Laughter. Booze-filled fun. Hand diving into defenceless pocket for the ever-full wallet. He'd watched as Max watched, enjoying the scene as the referee who sat on the sidelines. He looked over to the car sat, claustrophobic, between glistening machinery. Hard uncompromising money machinery. Mass-produced, boxed-electronically, ventilated, depreciating, junk. Gold-leafed junk. Max's black turbo-charged menacing beast slouched ground-hugging, close by. Threatening. The car quietly shrank into the background of glitter.

Lisa sat, eyes latched onto the black car. Fascinated. Drawn to the drop-headed, whale-tailed, power of it. Drunk on the fantasy.

The faces were clamouring at the windows. Hanging, pushing, shoving from the door, spilling over into the garden and road, moving in on their territory with their loud forced happy non-talk. Alcohol-induced nonsensical rabbit.

'That's not fair. They're not all like that. Not when you get them on their own.' Aye, there's the rub. So what's the purpose of all this then? If they're different people elsewhere? She half smiled at him.

'Come on, for Christ's sake. Cheer up. Have some fun. Max thought it would be good to meet here. Talk. Enjoy.' Always Max. Everything was Max. He didn't want anything to do with Max.

'Well you're here. With me. And Max asked me. So . . .' The sentence trailing off into the spilt beer and glisten of broken glasses. Max was sitting inside, aware through the window, enjoying his discomfort. He could feel the eyes on him. Boring into him. He refused to look. Max wouldn't have the satisfaction.

The cripple struggled out of the door, tripping on the step

amid laughter and comments, smiled ruefully and step-slid over to the silver Rolls Royce. The following wife grin-signalled to a surrogate gigolo and climbed into the driver's seat, impatiently revving the engine, while the cripple pain-crawled his way past the door into the leather prison.

Lisa sat an avid spectator to the show. The weekly theatre. She licked away saliva from the corner of her mouth. He thought she did. Her eyes glinted in the sun, staring at him. Not at the spectacle. What was it that he saw? Thought he saw? Perhaps imagined.

'David, don't stare. They can't help it. Don't stare.' The lepers crawling past on his mother's calf-length skirts in the dust of the Indian fifties. One-eyed, torsoed, shuffling figures on the filthy sidewalk. Passed-over humanity in the gutter of existence. He continued to stare at the silvered stump ends of has-been limbs. Soaked in the sight, etched deep into the memory of his child-mind. Childhood reality come to life in the tyre-screeching, engine-growling noise of the silver-wheeled cripple cart. Resigned, fixed grin-wave, from the passenger seat. Sickening.

'Not that. It's not like that.' Really. 'Really.' He was not convinced. Never would be. Now didn't care.

The leper peered up into his face with sightless eyes. Glazed orbs in a scarred, haired, scab-featured caricature. He felt no revulsion, only a strange, cloying, skin-crawling fascination. The stumpy, black-and-white bandaged hands waveringly stretched out to the sound of his breathing. He stopped. The stumps moving now without sight or sound. Lost in the blackness. Going on to the next. He observed the parade, the continuing parade. The eternal parade.

Lisa was transfixed. The leper crawled over to her, hearing the sound of her breathing. Visibly decaying limbs reaching out, pulling at her dress. Silver slime covering her feet. She moved. Stepped through the leper who fell into disappearing dust.

'I could do with another drink.' Taking his glass and going back inside the bar. Inside, where Max stood. Where Max

166

kissed her whilst he watched. Stroked her hair, hand drifting down her back. He started forward and the crowd of mindless manic faces blocked his way. Crowded in, suffocating. The stifling heat and the stench of the breath. Decaying, dying, death breath like a hand over his nose and mouth. Mouths working close to his. Green, orange, hot, flashing vapours leaping at him, forcing their way into him. Crawling hands, shaking his. Pumping his arm. Pulling. Trying to rip him apart.

'Here you are.' The glass offered to him through the squirming, garishly-dressed, Italian-shod bodies. Lisa, moving through the sea of painted flesh, handing him the glass. He drank long and deep. Erasing the taste of the stench of platitudes from his mouth. Washing it through his system. Lisa was talking to some of the faces. Beautiful easy-flowing talk amongst the baying pack of half-beasts clawing, growling, screaming hyena laughs, watching the carcasses being dismembered by the bigger beasts. Waiting their turn. Knowing it would come, so they could leap and grovel on the already-insensible ripped-up being. Lisa floated amongst the filth of the back-stabbing with ease. Seemingly unaware of the viciousness, the destruction all around her. He stood riveted to the ground, unable to move. Unable to take his eyes off her. Glass mechanically lifted to mouth, to his grinning mouth, not feeling the forced smiles. Using the drink as an excuse to hide. Seeing the mass through the distorted uneven bottom, through the liquid, distorted from beasts into a semblance of human beings by the glass.

The party was in full flight. Balloons descending from the ceiling whilst drunk parents and others grabbed each other in the half dark. Quick passionate gropings to the tune of *Auld Lang Syne* and laughter. Old gnarled hands squeezing drooping breasts through the wheezing gasp of tired lust. He stood at the back of the room with Roger, his friend. Diminutive figures on the ballroom landscape, surrounded by unintelligible sights and sounds, close to one another in the shadows, hiding from the noise and the terrifying clamour of the adults at play.

A dyed blonde came up and stood in front of them, red-blue eyes drooling over them. She moved a red-clawed hand up over her breasts and over to rest it on his shoulder.

'Come with me, David. I want to show you something.' He followed, fifteen, confused and dutiful. Not wanting to be rude to his parents' friends. The dyed blonde carefully slipped with him out of sight into the dark tall echoing hall and up the marbled staircase. The desert night crept in silently through the open windows. Peculiar food smells mixed with the dust and carnations. Geraniums and bougainvillaea. Dry heat smells that he knew and loved. Mingled now with excessive perfume and drink. He nearly fell as the dyed blonde stumbled on the steps, giggled and continued up, finding an empty bedroom. The moon shone shyly through the part-shuttered tall windows, shone partially onto the bed. The dyed blonde grunted in satisfaction, dragged him into the room and shut the door. He heard the lock turn.

Panic and dread sat like a dead dog in his belly. He could taste the stench of death creeping up his throat. The blonde moved over to him. Talons reaching for his body.

'Come over here, David. Look what I have to show you.' She pulled him again. He could feel the finger nails insist in his arm. The shoulder straps fell over the puffy floppy flesh whilst drunken fingers fiddled with straps and reluctant clasps. Finally, the white nylon fell away and the droopy white blue-veined breasts settled lower. Large aureoles and over-sized feeding nipples pointed disillusioned at the floor, helped upward by the red-taloned hand. The dead dog in his stomach turned over. The rest of her clothes fell around swollen ankles and cracked toenails. White whale belly against the sheets as her hand fumbled around inside herself.

'Watch David.' Drunken slurred lust sounds deep in the throat. 'Come over here.' Commanded, dutifully, well-trained, Pavlov's dog, beaten into obedience. The hand took his hair, painfully forcing his head between her heavy thighs.

168

He could smell her. Thought of the Indian girl. Smelt her strong in his nose. Hair tickling his nose. Wet silky skin. A surprise.

'That's it, David. Go on. That's it.' Voice half-heard as the thighs opened and closed over his ears. He felt he was going to disappear into that silky wetness, as it opened in orgasm drenching him. Felt himself rise unexpectedly. Saw himself strip and climb all over her, suddenly assured and powerful. Felt her close around him, saw the sudden panic in her drunken eyes.

'No. I didn't want that, No . . .' The last words cut off by his demanding movement. All too soon finished. He lay back whilst listening to the quiet sobs of recriminations from the dyed blonde. Now defeated and flaccid on the bed. The moon having moved to show her misery in romantic silver-white light.

Lisa lay crying quietly. He beside her not knowing what to do. Divided by his emotions. Wanting her to feel his hurt. Wanting her to love him. Wanting to destroy and create at the same time.

The blonde stood and dressed, subdued in the vast-ceilinged bedroom. Wine-filled fantasies banished by reality. Dressed and went from the room. A moment and Roger crept in past the edge of the door, quietly closing it wary of any noise.

'Christ. What was all that?' Excited stage whisper in the half dark. 'You didn't, did you?' Incredulous in the room. Roger sat on the end of the bed. He could see Roger lift his chin. And sniff. Delicately as if testing wine. 'That's what it smells like.' Eyes filled with teenage wonder.

He laughed. It started as a giggle escaping from tight lips, moved to his mouth and nose. Snorted between breaths, finally to explode in belly laughter. Both of them. The fear gone now, only the delight of the impossible filling them both.

'I'm sorry, I didn't realize you felt like that.' Dragging him back into the cave and Lisa. The sigh drifted out of him like a silently deflating hot-air balloon. He'd watched them out in the fields as they went past in the sky. The sigh still moving out of him to mix with the other particles in the atmosphere of the cave. Feeling contented that he'd brought the matter to a successful conclusion. Successful? Conclusion? He was sounding like Max now. The one thing he wanted to avoid. Lisa wouldn't know a feeling if it leapt up and bit her.

'That's not fair. You know it's not. Why do you do this?' Unanswerable question. Another question. Everyone was asking him questions. 'Because some of us want answers.' And what if there are no answers?

Lisa turned away and faced the wall. Gothic tapestries wove themselves into the pattern of the rock, slipping backwards into prehistoric paintings. She drew the patterns with her unhappy fingers. What was she to Max anyway? Why this strange obsession?

'You're the one with the obsession. I knew Max before you. Have known him for some time. So why shouldn't I see him?' There's seeing and there's seeing. There's touching and touching. Lisa grunted and an angry flush appeared up her neck and onto her cheeks. 'You're pathetic sometimes. Really pathetic.' He knew that. Had known it for a long time, but that wasn't what was in question. Again. 'We've been happy haven't we?' She was getting pretty repetitive with these questions. 'Why not just let things be?' Rhetorical this time. He let the silence extend itself away into the night. It came back later. Not that much later. Just later. It had never gone.

'So what was it like then? Go on, you've got to tell. I've never done it.' He enjoyed Roger's eager inquisitiveness. Enjoyed the agony that he knew Roger would be suffering waiting for the detailed account. Roger squirmed in anticipation at the imminent disclosure of hitherto undisclosed facts. From the source this time. Not second-hand imaginings. He let Roger sweat for a while. Then told him in languid casual tones that added to the interest and the enjoyment.

'And then you did what?' The voice rising to an incredulous howl of excited, believing disbelief. He lay smiling as Roger walked around the room shaking his head and laughing.

170

Imagining all sorts of things that didn't exist. Imaginings that would leave his first time a confused disappointment. He didn't care about that. Didn't even think about it. Was then completely incapable of thinking beyond his own little world. His own desires.

So what had changed?

He leaned over and traced the line of her arm to the elbow. She remained facing the wall, still. The feelings of triumph had dimmed into a dull, fading, grubby thought that got worse as he stared at it. Felt dirty now, felt he'd stepped back into the slime of his treatment of Jenny and Amanda. Had thought he'd finished with that, and now to see it rising again to claw and destroy what he'd long hoped for.

'Then why destroy if you don't want to?' He didn't know the answer. Truthfully had no idea, perhaps hadn't bothered to find out. Too late now. Now was what mattered, Lisa here, with him. Love. That's all that mattered now. Here.

It was the lack of warmth and sound that confirmed to him that she'd gone. He knew it before he opened his eyes. Before he was fully aware of any normal waking sensation. It was a strange feeling. The knowledge. Comforting in one respect. The fact that he knew. Disturbing in that he felt the loss rising up his throat and belching out of his mouth in the sudden call of her name. He fought the panic down as he saw the empty bed, cave and hollow.

'I'm not going to live like this.' Said in the darkness. Half-asleep quiet words without meaning, he'd thought. Wrong again. The brain messing things up with too much thought. If he'd stopped for one moment to consider what she said. Then maybe . . .

'Messed up again?'

'Can't get it right can you?'

He threw a rock at the two images. Jenny and Amanda vanished laughing, hand-in-hand.

He went over to the stream and sank his head into the cool water, gasping at the first shock of the cold on his face. He felt a hand on his back and swung up, rolling sideways, defensive, ready. The Indian girl stood sari-clad, sad smile, and went, leaving the faint smell of oriental musk hanging in the air.

Lisa. That's who he wanted. Now. Not any of the others. Lisa. The name called over and over again in pain at the unforgiving rocks and the unconcerned water.

They were right, those harridan images from the past. They were right. He'd messed up, allowed his crazy jealous thoughts to creep around and insinuate themselves between him and his love.

'She's at the castle, David. Lisa's with me now. Not you, David. She's back with me now. In my bed, David.' The voice drifted down out of the sky and reverberated around the hollow. No figure. No outline. No body. Just Max's voice from the air. From where? 'Outside, David. You were right, David, I can't get in. But then it doesn't matter now does it? I don't need to.' The laughter, loud and sure, pierced through his head, became background. Went away, leaving him alone, more alone than he'd ever been in his life. Suddenly the hollow became oppressive. The walls once bright, now dirty, creeping slime closing in.

He stood calm now. Ice-cold in the centre of the arena. They would be waiting for him. He knew that. But it didn't matter. That's what he wanted. That was the way he was going to get Max. He turned and the walls halted their advance.

'Grenade-launchers are already packed Boss. Plenty of grenades, both hand and for the M79s. Four magazines each. Full. Hundred rounds spare per man plus a futher five thousand rounds in the vehicle. Flares in the boxes. Schermuly hand held. An extra two thousand rounds for the gun. Should have enough.' He watched as the guns and ammunition were laid out, each man collecting his own. Quietly, conscious of the impending mission. Quietly thrilled and terrified at the same time.

He sat in the cave then collected his equipment and went out to the car. It sat as he had left it. Patiently waiting as always. He carefully checked the oil and water, tyres and brakes.

Checked the Armalite rifle clipped behind the seats and the curved magazines in the glove-box. Hand-grenades in their own box in the passenger footwell.

He bent down, tightened the boot laces and got into the car.

'Don't be rash son. There are other ways of settling arguments.' Not this time, Mother. Max wants to play games. Well, he's going to have to play this one. And Max is not as good. No. Max wasn't as good at this as he was. Max never was as good.

He unclipped the Armalite and felt the cool oily surface of the weapon. Friendly touch. Firm gentle touch, like being home. The rounded ends, the sharp edges, the balance and feel of the weapon. He reached for a magazine and slid it with a firm solid comforting click into place. Right forefinger and thumb slid back the cocking-handle and let it go. A round picked up and slotted into the chamber. Air-tight.

The burst splattered against the rock. Chips of dusty grey spraying upwards, arching over and down. The hammering noise reverberating over the countryside, with the buzz and whizz of richocheting rounds. The gun worked perfectly and he smiled. A wintry smile.

'When you smile like that, Boss, I get the feeling you're in a killing mood. So did the last suspect. He pissed himself when you smiled.' Max would find out about that soon.

'The point of a gun is to kill, not maim. None of this cowboy flesh wounds. Please sir, can I have a small shoulder injury? This weapon is designed to extinguish human life. Quickly. So the aim is to shoot to kill. Kill.' The weapons instructor paused to let the words sink in. 'The best way to kill is to aim for the centre of the biggest target area. The body. The torso. Not the head. But the main chest – abdomen area. The impact of a round here will cause maximum injury. Will be bound to hit vital organs so, if the man doesn't die straight away, it will only be a question of time. And his screams should deter the others.' The hard eyes glinted with the knowledge of the screams.

He slipped out of the car carrying the Armalite and climbed

to the top of the cliff to his right. His scan quartered the ground expertly, noticing everything that moved, looking for the tell-tale glint or odd shape, the give-away shift of position. The countryside lay quiet. Birds singing contentedly in the trees, wavering softly with the wind. Dotted shadows of moving clouds against the grey-green-brown of the earth. He grinned to himself behind cover. Slid backwards and climbed back down to the car. They weren't going to go for him too close. They were going to suck him in to them. Well, that was OK as well. That was fine. 'Hope you know what you're doing Boss. Scares the hell out of me.' He looked down the road towards the bomb. To where the bomb was supposed to be. One thousand pounds of home-made 'co-op mix'. Yes, he did know what he was doing. Provided the other platoon was in the ambush position. They'd better be, he'd planned this little operation carefully. Any mistakes and there would be little tiny pieces of soldiers spread over a very large distance. His stomach squirmed at the thought. He felt light-headed and doomed. Dead already. He just nodded to his corporal and headed the group of four down onto the bomb. Smelling the marzipan strong against the sweat and barely controllable guts.

He had been through all this before. There was no problem now, because he'd learned and now didn't care. Had no feeling about himself anymore. He would get Lisa and destroy Max.

Seventeen

THE CAR'S ENGINE overran a couple of times and reluctantly stopped. Its familiar cooling tick quietly disturbing the sounds of the forest. He sat listening for a moment before getting out of the car and collecting his equipment. The car nestled easily between the pine trees, hot in the forest. Pine needles sticking to the tacky rubber of the hard-pressed tyres.

He moved carefully into the trees. Bending under the branches, sometimes having to crawl on his belly in the ditch between the rows of pine. It was dark in there. Dank darkness without a sound. Only the struggle for breath and the scraping, sliding-forward movement of his progress. Now and then he stopped and lay still for many minutes. Statue-still. Even his chest moving barely. Listening for other sounds. Concentrating carefully. Every sense channelled into his ears. Then he moved forward again. It was a long way before he would be able to see the castle. A long way but a safe way.

'I think we've found them, Boss. The last patrol caught sight of a glint of binos up on the ridge. They're in a position that can be reached, but only by crawling from about a mile away. They won't be moving so we'll be OK. Have plenty of time.' He watched his sergeant's earnest excited face. So the bastards were pinned down. Compromised, as the manual says. Good. A night assault. Strike at first light, quietly. Catch them quietly.

'OK, Boss.'

They crawled away from each other. Two yards and lost in the darkness and the foliage. Crawling, touching, finding the rest of the patrol.

He crawled forward alone in the forest, gripping the Armalite tightly, keeping it zealously clear of the mud and the dirt, checking that nothing had found its way into the barrel. He needn't have feared. The condom he had attached over the flash hider saw to that, kept the water and the dirt out. It was a nervous instinctive reaction. Check and double check. Always check everything, over and over. Life-saving checks. The rifle pointed purposefully forward, ignoring his paranoia.

It started to rain. Persistent drops percolating through the branches and down into the ground. Leaving a soggy spongy surface to crawl over. The drips fell, hit, sat and soaked into his clothing, one after the other, gradually filling the fibres and eventually saturating material, giving up its load onto flesh. With the rain came the cold. The gentle wind that breathed into the clothes turning the water to ice particles that lanced into the skin. Shivering crawl. Teeth chattering. Keep them quiet. Bones felt iced inside the frozen envelope. Brain starting to seize with the cold. He remembered the training. 'Mind over matter.' That's what they said. Of course. But it depends whose mind and what matter. He shook the dangerous thoughts out of his ice-blocked head. The rain gradually eased. Just the soft patter of water falling off laden branches, the shower caused by a brush against a branch.

'I love the forest.' Jenny on a good day. It was a good day. The sun sent solid shafts of light into the glade, hitting the ground in sudden spotlit detail. Heat haze amongst the green-brown straight sentinels, guarding their privacy. Guarding their glade. The grass tall, off-green, in the heat. Shaggy heads sending seeds billowing away on the breeze to descend upon another open patch. For somebody in the future to rest their head on and gaze at the sun through the tree tops. The dog snuffling in the dead branches of long-fallen trees, too far in to recover. Now moss-covered and overgrown with grass. Peaceful Sunday in the summer. One day of peace from many battles. But it was peaceful.

He crawled further and stopped at the sound of footsteps on a path. Uncaring footsteps. Unprofessional footsteps. Footsteps that didn't know he was close. Footsteps that idly sauntered past not two feet from his face. Brown-booted footsteps that didn't break step. That continued down the wet path, bored, unseeing. The footsteps squelched away to silence. He was left alone with the occasional drop from the sky into a rapidly-disappearing puddle for company. He crouched at the edge of the path and stared after the soundless feet. The evidence was there in the oozing mud. Treaded-sole bootmarks slowly being covered, the ground now relieved of the weight of the passing foot, but there long enough for him to see the direction and the type of sole. The military sole. The direction towards the castle. Homeward-bound feet, careless in the anticipation of the warmth and the relaxation. He smiled to himself. It didn't touch his eyes.

'You can see the way they came in, Boss.' Whispered in the dawn. Staring at the bent grass and the half-obscured bootprint. Fresh. They were amateurs this lot. Soon find out what it was all about. 'I reckon about another two hundred metres and we've got them.' He was probably right. Usually was.

The trip-wire was carefully disguised. Cleverly disguised in the ditch at crawl-height, its green tone blending perfectly with the grass. It was only the hanging drops of rain along its length that gave it away at the last possible moment. He looked at it from a distance of one inch. Nose almost over the taut steel wire. He froze for a brain-numbing minute until the heart started again and his training took over. He searched to the left and right, finding the Claymore. Plastic green curved death sitting on neat scissor legs. Pull switch detonator with micro-second fuse. Enough time to know that there was no time. He left the device alone and stepped over the wire, feeling for the back-up trip on the other side, stepping close to the Claymore to avoid the pressure-pad booby trap.

177

'Very good, David. Very good indeed. My congratulations.' The voice boomed out from the treetops. He was half-way through throwing himself to the ground when he checked and froze again. The ground was a strange texture just in front of him. Careful scrutiny and he saw the outline of the hole. The image of the sharpened stakes at the bottom of the pit shone through the woven grass and matted sticks.

He stayed where he was, analysing the next move. Animal cunning now. The human being subordinated to the need for survival. He threw himself backwards over the trip wire just as the sprung bough whipped through its sideways arc, the staked board missing him by inches. He landed heavily. Blackness hammered into his skull with the totality of an eclipse.

The singing was soft, sensual, easy in the background, coming closer. Closer with his returning consciousness. Singing in the sunlight. His head ached. Fingers finding the bump, tenderly stroking the raised skin in the hair. The sun was in his eyes. Fiercely burning down through . . . ? Through what? Vision blurring. Was blurred. Still blurred. Clearing slowly into shapes and forms. Solid forms, surreal shapes. He was lying on his back in a small clearing. The singing stopped. Didn't stop. Changed. Wasn't singing any more. Was the foreign sound of a bird. Maybe a bird. God, how his head ached. A shake to clear the fuzziness and the ache proved wrong. He had done it before a lifetime ago and should have known what the outcome would be. The whirling, reeling clearing steadied and stopped. The pines had given way to tropical vegetation. Lush green succulent leaves, thick juicy leaves and the constant chitter of monkeys in the top branches of tall canopied trees.

He lay still, trying to get the brain functioning again. If it ever had been. He thought of the sound of Max's voice jeeringly ringing in his ears. Thought that this was one of Max's electronic illusions. Felt the bite of a mosquito and wasn't sure anymore. The smell was real enough. The heat.

178

The oppressive suffocating tropical heat. It was all too confusing. Too unreal. He closed his eyes and lay back, listening to the birds and other wildlife. The loud constant noise without end.

'I didn't see you there. Are you OK?' The voice startled him out of the stupor. Startled him into reaction, searching for the Armalite. He found it, gripped it tight and locked on to the source of the voice. The girl was Polynesian, he assumed, standing looking down at him quizzically, half-naked in the sunshine, speaking perfect English.

Max! Shouted to the forest. Get your Goddamned box of tricks out of here. Commanded against a sponge soaking the sound, deadening all responses. The girl looked around questioningly.

'You lost a friend? I haven't seen anyone else. You're the only one. Perhaps he's lost. Or is it you?' The smile turned into a grimace and the body into a screeching gargoyle filling the clearing. The hammer of the Armalite in his hands was only drowned out by the wailing howl of the beast and the crashing, thundering change of the scenery.

The rifle clicked to a halt in the silence of the pine forest. In the distance, the splatter of falling leaves and branches, scythed through by the rounds. So, that was the way Max wanted to play. Illusion and disillusion. Fine. The rules were becoming plainer. The rules were: there weren't any. Amazing discovery while the jungle images faded and the echo of the Armalite rattled away into the gathering mist.

He crawled back into the undergrowth. Back under the lowest pine boughs. Burrowed into the thick bed of decaying pine needles, wedging himself into the earth walls of the shallow ditch, lying on his back able to move his head to the direction of any odd sound. Here, in the total blackness of the oncoming night, anyone searching for him in here would be coming out of the comparative brightness into the dark. They would be at a disadvantage, and they knew it. He knew they wouldn't try. Felt safe while he thought through the predicament.

'What's the matter, David? Don't you like the game?' The voice some way off. He didn't answer. The dripping forest waited with him. 'Oh come on, David. Your game, remember. Your rules. You wanted to play this way. Come on then, I'm waiting.' Again, the silence, and a long way-off faint laughter, harsh on the air. He stayed tight and quiet. Not rising to the bait. Waiting for Max to make the next move. Trying to calculate what Max would do next. Use his electronics again? Well that was OK too. This time he'd be up to it.

It looked like a face hanging at the window. Another on the door. He cried eight-year-old tears into the eiderdown. Wide terrified eyes piercing the night. At the bottom of the bed, a seething mass of scorpions writhed and flicked their tails. They started crawling up the bed towards him and he screamed the high-pitched terror of youth. His mother came sleepily running.

'It's alright darling. There. It's only a bad dream. There's nothing there.'

But there was. Was before. Not now. Only the dressing-gown on the door and the model hanging by a thread from the ceiling near the window. But there was. He knew there had been.

'No nothing. Look.'

Gesturing to the empty room. His wide-staring unfocused eyes gradually seeing the reality. Knew that reality. Still unsure.

A branch shifted its weight and let a cascade of water patter down around his head. A welcome cooling draught. He opened his mouth and tasted the clean fresh rain-water. Filled his mouth to overflowing, drinking greedily from the brief torrent. The bump on the side of his head ached intolerably. Pounded right through. He carefully felt inside one of the side pouches and pulled out the first-aid pack. There was just enough light still for him to make out the contents. He slipped four paracetamol tablets into his mouth and washed them down with rain-water.

'That'll make you go to sleep. No more silly imaginings. Sleep now.'

And the light was turned out once more. This time the dressing-gown and the model looked just that. He slept half-awake. Half-aware.

A piece of tablet stuck and dissolved behind his teeth and he tasted the bitter granules, pulling a face at the once green, now black canopy of branches above his head. There would be no sleep now. From now on. The night was the time to move, to be wide awake; every sense tuned in to the sounds and smells, eyes taking a back seat, pupils wide open trying to see. Guessing at shapes in the dark. Guessing right. Instinctive guessing. But now it was wait. Wait while the night closed around and all the old fears came flooding back, painting images against the black backcloth. Childhood images that were welcomed as friends and despised as enemies at one and the same time. Well-remembered images that stayed for ever.

The darkness closed softly in, bringing the cold with it, bringing the scurry of nocturnal creatures, the curious, scuttling, unseen sounds of the night – the soundless flight of an owl dipping easily through the branches. Bats fluttered like large fast butterflies awaiting unheard, high-pitched signals into the constant clamour of the quiet night. He lay and listened to the busy nightly routine. The routine that was aware and cautious of his presence. The routine that had to go on even though a threat was there, in his form. Survival. The same as he was. Surviving in a hostile environment. He felt a strange affinity with the invisible creatures. Imagining the small furry bodies with the large night eyes and quivering noses. Warm in the cold night, out of warm cosy burrows into the dangerous nightly forage for food. Owls feeding on mice feeding on insects and grain, feeding on the plants and the land, the air. He breathing the air, feeding on the plants. The cycle continuing with or without him. The cycle not dependent on humans at all. Humans, the useless destroyers of the land and polluters of the air. Killing plants and animals. Changing evolution. Killing evolution. A contradiction, he thought to himself. Darwin theories crumbling into nothing through ignorance and mistrust. Through greed and the need to survive. He tried to think for what purpose the human was here on the land. Couldn't. Shoved the ridiculous age-old thoughts away into the library of his mind. The unopened unread library.

It was difficult crawling through the forest during the day. At night it was virtually impossible. Impossible, that is, to make constructive headway. There was no way of knowing how far he'd travelled. It felt like miles, but was probably only a hundred metres. He followed the moon, being careful to check the stages on his watch. Sometimes able to catch the north star through the trees. Not wanting to hit the clearings and fire-breaks. Avoiding the booby traps and the trip wires. Circuitous route in the interests of safety. The sharp low branches of the pines, without the covering of needles, were dry lances that dug into his flesh when he didn't keep low enough. The blood trickled and congealed on his cheeks and forehead. Necks and hands already a bloody, muddy, mess. Right hand holding tight to the Armalite still with intact condom on barrel. Every now and then he checked the magazine, ensuring that it was still attached. The rifle still didn't care. An impartial partner in this game. Would play for both sides.

'You can't do that, it's not fair. You're dead. I saw you from miles away. You're dead.' Roger on the verge of tears, in his mock cowboy outfit. Roger was wrong. He had crept up on Roger and caught him easily, because Roger's first shot had missed. 'That's not fair. It didn't miss. You're not playing fair.' Oh yes he was. Because he wasn't going to lose. Never lost. The Indians always won in this game. 'No they don't. The Indians never win. They always lose. You never play fair. I'm not playing with you anymore.' They would play again tomorrow. They always did. He watched Roger walk off, head bowed. He whistled tunelessly and dirt-kicked his way home.

The paracetamols had helped, but the exhaustion from the crawl started the thumping grind again. The last two hours had been uphill all the way, the soft wet ground making him slide back every few metres. Then he fell over the edge, fell crashing into the stubborn roots of an oak tree that refused to be shifted by the land erosion. The tree saved him from toppling over the escarpment. He clung on looking straight down at the rocky bottom where the cliff had slipped its way down to the road. The recognizable road. Now he knew where he was. In the distance the castle towers plainly visible against the moon sky.

Back on top of the cliff. Shaking with cold exhaustion and the narrow escape. He lay like a wounded animal plotting the next move. The carbine rounds dug chunks of chalk out of the ground at his elbow. Threw dust up into his face. He felt the thudding impact and spun over and back into the shattering pines. The arm felt numb, felt broken. He felt for the entry hole and found none. Just a bruise where the chunk of rock had hit him. The firing stopped as suddenly as it began.

'That's not the way, David. You'll have to do better than that. I thought you were better. What's happened to you?' Again the laugh and again the silence. Just the settling of the broken branches and the smell of the chalk dust in his nose.

'The Mission is the most important factor. That's what all the preparation is for. Therefore the Mission must be clear and unambiguous. Simple, straightforward, with no room for interpretation. The Mission is to destroy. Or the Mission is to observe. Or the Mission is to capture. The Mission is positive.' Said with an aggressive thump on the table. He listened to the Instructor. Face eager, mind in neutral, thinking far-away thoughts in the summer. 'Everything else that comes into Orders is to ensure the success of the Mission.'

What was the Mission? Was it to find Lisa? Or Max? Destroy Max? Questions again but no answers. Maybe the Mission was unimportant? If that was the case, then he might as well go back. He pushed himself into a sitting position leaning back against a tree. Shaking the defeatist thoughts out

183

of his mind. Lisa was what it was all about. He wanted her back. Loved her. But there was still Max. He sighed and moved into a better position to see. There were no more shots. No movement from the valley floor. Just a peaceful country night scene.

He crawled back to the escarpment and, keeping low, peered over the edge. They wouldn't expect him to come this way now. He crawled over the edge and slid-climbed his way down the crumbling surface keeping to the narrow water-coursing gully. Chalk-covered, soaked from head to foot, he crouched by a boulder at the bottom, catching his breath and his tattered wits. Fear pumping blood rapidly round his body. Excessive adrenalin making him shake although he was hot from the climb. He unslung the Armalite and checked it. Replaced the torn condom with another and moved, under cover of the rocks, to the other side of the road. Moving in a crouching, low, crablike run. Hairs standing like antennae all over his body. Feeling for the unfeeling. For the unknown. For anything.

He crouched in a ditch and looked towards the horizon. Even now, the sky was beginning, imperceptibly, to lighten. The warning of dawn. He calculated another two hours before he'd have to go to ground again. By then he should be fairly close to the castle. Close enough for the final assault on the following night. He was just about to move when a slight sound brought everything to an abrupt halt. The clink of a rifle against rock. There again. Just the faintest tell-tale sound. He waited and heard the scrape of a boot. Another. Then a sigh. Almost inaudible. He checked the wind. None. Distance, then, anything up to twenty metres. Sound travels at night, he thought. Calculate. Must be right. The direction. Which direction? Another sound. He wanted another sound. Something distinctive. He waited. Then patience rewarded. The cough was clear and pinpointed the man. Hidden behind a rock just fifteen metres from where he crouched.

He moved forward slowly, inch by inch, stopping to listen every few feet. Eyes concentrated on the rock. Ears open to every sound. He risked a look around. Nothing moved in the countryside. Nature held its breath with him. Another cough from the rock made him stop and wait. Then move carefully, parting each blade of grass. Shifting his body forwards without sound. He worried about the time it was taking. It seemed like hours here in the open ground between his rock and the other.

The flare lit the sky with a popping noise of brilliant white light. He froze, listening to the sizzle of the flare and the scramble of the man behind the rock. Eyes fixed on the rock. The head appeared and the body, confused and unsure in the lights. Fright on a young face before a burst from his Armalite caught the teenager in the chest, flinging him back against the rock, shock and bewilderment on his face. A face that disappeared with the next burst. He got up, sprinted over in the last dying seconds of the glow from the flare, and checked the dead, still-warm, sticky body. Then ran tripping and stumbling in the dark into the cover of the rocks and trees of the rough marshy land. Shouts and the sound of engines approaching told him he was in the middle of them. The middle of the forward troops waiting for him. Max wasn't taking any chances. He grinned to himself. So Max was afraid then. Must be, to go to all this trouble. Max knew who was the better and, therefore, was using everything. But Max wouldn't win. Wasn't going to. Not this time, not ever. He sat hard against a boulder, smelling the blood of the boy on his hands as he rubbed his face.

'I've killed men with my bare hands. Did you know that?' Hard cold fatherly proud eyes boring into his innocent unblemished face. He shook his head, unsure of what to say. 'Yes. Not a pleasant business with a knife. It's when you're that close that you really know you've killed someone. The lad I killed had photographs in his hand. Must have been looking at them. Cost him his life, his fiancée did.' Unwitting callous statements in the evening sitting on the stoep. He looked at his father's profile, noting the proud jut of the jaw. 'Still, that was war. Have to do these things in war. It's all part of the job.

185

Them or us.' He didn't understand then. Didn't think about it much now. Hadn't thought about it until he smelt the blood on his hands. Dismissed the thought. Agreed with his father and scanned the ground and the horizon. He couldn't see the castle now, but knew the direction. The dawn was catching him and the voices were getting closer.

'Very good, David. Very good indeed. I'm glad to see you haven't lost your touch. We'll have to see if we can make things a little harder for you. Wouldn't like you to get bored with the game.'

He noted there was no laugh this time. Did he detect a slight tone of unease in Max's voice? Maybe. It just might be that Max was really rattled now. Now that his gadgets and trickery weren't working. Now that his troops proved to be fallible. Perhaps now it was time for a show of strength. It was a nice thought, but was it practical?

'Never underestimate your enemy. He's been trained as well. A first success doesn't make you invincible. Only a victory gives you that luxury. And there are precious few of those.' The Instructor waved his hook in the air, the metal gleaming in the strip-lit room. 'Never think that your enemy is a fool.' Spoken quietly. 'For he may be thinking the things you should be thinking, and if he is, then you're dead.' Pause for effect. It worked. There wasn't a sound in the room. The Instructor turned his burn-scarred face back to the class. The glass eye stared sightlessly away from them, disconcertingly. 'If there's one lesson you take away from here, let it be that.' OK. Lesson learned but what to do about these? The voices almost on him.

He jumped up from behind the rock and emptied the magazine into the approaching group. The four men staggered and fell bleeding and dying onto the soggy ground, blood mixing with the rain and the mud. He turned and ran again. Ran faster this time. There would be reinforcements soon. He wouldn't be allowed to get away with this one so easily. Never underestimate your enemy. They'd underestimated him. But they wouldn't from now on.

186

The dawn was growing in the sky. Light happily waking the birds and other day creatures. Light that was his enemy now. The light he loved and enjoyed now combined with Max's men to be the enemy.

Up ahead, the ground became rougher and harder to negotiate. Boulders from the Ice Age strewn in haphazard sculptural abandon, slippery, moss-covered, soggy marsh trees, others draped and weird in the half-light of dawn. He slipped, fell, crawled, scrambled into the middle of the maze where the boulders became denser. Deep crevices between the rocks down to water-logged ground. He found a hole and crawled into it. Discovered it wound its way through, between the giant boulders, sometimes the tunnel open to the sky, sometimes covered and dark. In the middle, what might be the middle, opening out into a cave. Dry and tomb-like. Sometime home for an animal. The smell still lingering in the air. The floor covered with dried grass, moss and droppings. He lay down. Got up and crawled to the end, looking out across the fields to the castle, plain in the distance. He lay digesting every way of approach. Then went back to the other end of the cave-tunnel. There was no sign of anybody following. Satisfied and relaxed, he crawled wearily to the bed of dried grass and moss. There were sticks and dead branches scattered around. He built a fire and hung the soaked clothes close to it to dry. Broke open a tin of cold minced beef and ate in the flicker of the fire. He spread a lightweight groundsheet over the grass and moss, and sat crossing his legs in the full Lotus, allowing the tension to seep out of his bones as he watched the Indian girl, following her breathing. Coming back into himself. Reorganizing, recharging. Letting the silence and stillness in the cave block out all thought. Letting the abstract whirlwind of images spiral into nothing.

He stirred some time later, unhooked his legs and threw another branch onto the fire. The smoke billowed up to the top of the cave, dissipated and vanished, out through the many small holes leading up to the surface of the boulders.

'Stillness is probably one of the most important lessons to

learn. And when learnt at a young age, becomes easier in old age.' Tiresome talk to an impatient six-year-old. But the Old Man's quiet, understanding face did command a stillness. When the wise eyes turned onto him, he felt the calm in his body. Felt it then, but didn't realize what it was. 'From stillness you can see the whole world. You can see everything in that moment of stillness. That everlasting moment.' So they tried the stillness. Tried the everlasting moment. It lasted just under a minute before he grew weary of the game. Didn't realize that that minute was the everlasting moment, that at that moment, no other moment existed. 'That is the first of many lessons. Learn it well.'

The Old Man's face wrinkled in a smile in the fire, grinned all the way to the roof, and went out through the holes into the sky beyond. Only the presence of his stillness remained in the cave-tunnel. Stayed with the image of the Indian girl sitting still in front of the fire. In the fire, drifting through the fire unharmed. How do they walk over the coals? Lie on the bed of nails? How do they do it? She turned expressionless to him. 'Because they transcend the simple feelings of the physical. Can control their bodies. Are in spiritual control of them-selves. The body does not belong, is merely a vessel.' Yes, but why don't they get hurt? Answered only by a smile and a wise shake of the head.

He brushed the image aside with another branch and lay down. Exhaustion closing over him in waves, lapping at the core of his consciousness.

Eighteen

THE FIRE WAS OUT and he shivered awake, listening to the whispering of the night. Groaned inwardly at the stiff bones and aching muscles, packed his kit and moved to the mouth of the cave-tunnel. There, way beyond, dancing lights in the distance, the castle beckoned. Warm welcoming lights. He thought of the room with its gallery and log fire, tray of malt whiskies and brandies, remembered the comfort of it and felt the need rise. Wanted the restful peace of that room – thought of Max in that room and forgot the notion. He strapped the pouch-belt on and moved out into the night.

He moved quickly and openly now. Close to the objective, the need to find good cover inside the confines of the building. It would be easier, he thought, within the building itself. Less chance for locating exact positions in a building that size.

'Caution should be tempered with the need to complete the Mission as quickly as time permits. Delays can lose the battle. Possibly the war.' So that justifies taking risks? 'On occasion. That is up to every leader. That is the purpose of leadership. To calculate the risk factor. Get it wrong and you're dead. Get it right and you win. A fine balance.' Indeed. 'Rely on the instincts.' At the moment he thought they were calm, that he was doing it right. Therefore he'd win.

The castle was drawing closer. Once over the surrounding wall then it was a matter of negotiating the grounds. He stopped and, lying down on the still damp ground, listened once more. For the thousandth time. Nothing. Not even the sound of an engine. There was something, though. In the distance. Probably from the castle. Probably another of Max's feasts. He wondered what sucker had been conned into attending this one. Wondered, and then rose and continued his rapid approach.

The wall was substantial. Eighteen feet high and a good two feet thick. He thought there was the possibility of intruder alarm systems. What would they be? Remote cameras: one? Infra-red system: two? No. Too basic, and prone to accidental triggering. Ultrasonic? No, probably not, out here. Inside, yes, but not here. What then? He sat away from the wall looking at it. Wondering. It was just possible that the top layer was pressure-sensitive. Sensitive to the weight of a man. Even less. To the weight of a small boy. That would allow birds and small animals like cats to roam at will without triggering the device. So what happens then? Climb on top and trigger the alarm. A soundless alarm. Had to be. So, link the device with the cameras and what do you have? Alarm sounds in the control room, directs the camera onto the spot, and alerts the guard. The guard follows the intruder's progress through the grounds and to capture. Fine. That's one method. Were there anymore?

He sat thinking. Digging back through the memory of half-forgotten lectures. Lectures given on hot sunny days, when the eyes and the mind were out by the river or in a hayfield with a girl. He thought hard, trying to recall.

'The purpose of an alarm system is to warn of approaching danger, not to discourage the intruder. The intruder should be unaware of his compromise until you, the defender are ready for him.' Ergo, an intruder should expect to enter by the least defended most circuitous route. Therefore that is where the defender should be expected to place his systems. But the intruder also plays the game and therefore knows that. So he plans an attack from the most obvious quarter. No. Not obvious. The most difficult and dangerous quarter. No. It still didn't work out. He'd have to think through again. He was

190

dealing with Max here, Max with the tricks, Max who had been trained as he had. Knew the same things, thought the same way. Had been through the same hoops when he designed the defences. So what was the answer?

The answer was – it didn't matter. The answer was to get to the main building as quickly as possible, in and out while they were rushing around trying to figure out where he was. The chances were that Max didn't have any intruder alarm systems here on the wall. It was too obvious a place for them. Max was devious, he'd have them in a ridiculous place. Where you'd never think. He moved to the wall, tossed the grapple and tested the hold. The other side of the wall was quiet. He wouldn't know if he was right until he got into the castle itself. But his instincts told him he was.

'Learn to feel the air around you. Feel the very essence of every living thing that moves. That breathes. That exists. When you feel that you will become one with them. Be a part of the very essence itself and you will know what is around you without ever looking.' The Old Man's wise smile never changed. The peace that surrounded his old frail body never changed. Even the slow walk never changed. He would sit in peace, walk in peace, eat in peace. Sometimes he would have liked to have disturbed that peace, but later he understood it – no, didn't understand it, appreciated that he could never have shaken that peace. Saw that as he watched the monk die in silent flames in the street.

So he applied that experience to that for which it was never intended. Applied the principle of awareness to the art of killing. Instead of living. Honed it, practised it, until he could do it, could feel the air around him. That was how he had stayed alive so long.

'What is it Boss?' Fearful question in the road. No time to answer just to run, yelling, for cover, just in time before the bomb took half the road away in a ear-blasting, roaring, ripping, splintering explosion, leaving the patrol dazed but otherwise unhurt. Nearly hadn't been aware that time. Had nearly allowed fatigue and boredom to submerge the awareness.

It wasn't going to happen again. Especially not now, when he was so close. When he could almost hear Lisa's breath against his cheek. Smell her next to him. The thought was so strong he turned and expected to see her beside him, knew she wouldn't be, but was disappointed when she wasn't. Just the tree next to the wall sneering at him. Skeletal jeering in the night.

He looked out over the meadow land towards the castle. Innocent, peaceful grassland, a white colour in the dark. Trees, black shadowy guards dotting the route. He took a deep breath and blew out his cheeks before kneeling and feeling carefully in front with his knife. Prodding the surface, knife at an angle. Gently feeling for the mines. The small anti-personnel mines with fairy-tale names from children's books: 'Jumping Jacks', 'Dingbats'. Designed to maim, to blow off a foot or part of a leg. Leave the unlucky fool screaming on the ground among a garden of mines waiting for the next idiot to come through. He felt his way forward very carefully. Sliding the knife in, taking it out, moving over an inch, and sliding it in again. Tedious, mind-sapping, exhausting work. Twice he found mines. Dingbats. Lying on the surface. Scrap of material attached to the top of the oval-shaped device that melted into the grass. Just scatter them like seeds in the early summer. Watch and wait. No sprouting with these seeds. Just a garden of mutilated human beings.

As he crawled forward, he trailed a piece of green para-cord after him, hoping it would be long enough, wondering where the end of the minefield would be. The question was answered as he saw the sheep grazing ten metres ahead and to the right. To the right. He was about to move that way when he froze. Max would do that. Max would lure him into a trap. Just when he was most tired. Just when the resolve was ebbing. Just when he needed the end to arrive. He carried on straight ahead and knew he was right. It was another fifty metres before he knew he was clear. He was shaking. Sitting in the shadow of a tree and shaking.

After a moment, he looked down at his shaking hands and saw his fingers gripping the end of the para-cord, gripping it

192

with the ferocity of life itself. He relaxed, drew a small peg out of his pouch, and tied the end of the cord to it. Pushed the peg into the ground by the tree and then very carefully examined the area, fixing the details in his mind for the return journey. The trees became denser just up ahead and he recognized the particular shape of the cedar, fixing his position close to the main entrance. He moved quietly into the shelter and cover of the trees and bushes. Pushing through until he had the castle firmly in sight. Waited a moment then ran quickly into the cover of the castle walls.

The lights blinded him, the lights and the wail of the siren. He dived to the ground as the first of the rounds cut across the granite above his head.

'No chance, David. No chance. You're a dead man now. Fool!' Followed by the familiar laugh. He scrambled to his feet and zigzagged back to the trees, firing a burst into them as he ran. The screams told him he'd hit. He crashed into the branches ignoring the tearing skin. Dived into a dark shadow, rolled, fetched up against a trunk and looked around. Instinct now.

'The best form of defence is attack. You have to go for it. He's not expecting you to lay into him. Surprise him. You've got to, otherwise you'll lose.'

He saw his trainer through a haze. His face and body hurt from the beating he was taking. One eye half-closed. He breathed in huge lungfuls of air, and even that hurt. Everything hurt.

'Come on, son. You win and we've won the championship. Lose and we lose. Think of the school. Think attack. You can do it. Attack.'

It was the last thing on his mind. He wanted the final bell to go. Wanted the next bell to be the last. Then he could stop the nightmare. The bell went and he was on his feet walking into the blitz again. Lost his temper. Refused to accept the beating and was unaware of what was going on until they dragged him off the unconscious figure on the canvas. He'd been disqualified.

Not this time. There were no rules here. Only his rules. He saw three guards run across his field of fire. They ceased to

193

exist. He ran for the entrance to the minefield then. Ran, feeling the passing shots, hearing the crack as the small objects spun past him. Hit the ground near the tree and felt for the peg. Panicked when he couldn't find it. Calmed down, felt again, fingers closing around the cool metal. Holding the thin cord tight, he crawled forward, out into the open. A shout from behind and the searchlight swung across the open ground, stabbing the night, blindly looking for him. It wouldn't be long. He moved carefully, the area between his shoulder-blades crawling, the hairs at the back of his neck standing up. Terror, sheer terror stalking him. Calm down. Concentrate.

Rounds marched towards him from behind. Regimented lines of kicked-up dirt. Some hitting mines that exploded with small sounds. Surprisingly small sounds. Knew it was an illusion. Firecrackers that tore flesh apart, leaving the red, raw, bloody stumps littering the battlefield. He felt his nerve going; they hadn't spotted him yet, but when they did, he'd be a dead man, felt it go, got to his feet and ran, terrified eyes glued to the path of the green cord. Holding tight on to his lifeline. Hearing the scream tear out of his throat as he sensed that the end of the minefield was receding, drawing away from him. Sobbed in relief as he hit the perimeter wall and scrambled up it, tearing at the brickwork to get over the top and into comparative safety, get away from the murderous gunfire. Fled into the open country, away towards the hills. Away from the car. Something told him to stay away from the car. Head for the farmhouse. They wouldn't expect him there. Unless Lisa had told Max. Prayed she hadn't told Max. Prayed. Trusted her now, had to, had no option. Now the greatest trust of all. Trusted her with his life.

He clung onto the rifle and stumbled onwards over the rough country. The beckoning rise of the hills ahead firmly fixed in his sight, never taking his eyes off them in case they disappeared.

The first Jeeps passed close by the hole he lay in. Passed so close the wheels nearly slid down on to him as the edge crumbled. Passed on in the opposite direction. He watched their lights gradually diminish and vanish from sight, got up, moved across the track and up the rocky bank on the other side, hoping he remembered the way to the farmhouse. Twice he'd thought himself lost, then saw a feature. A recognizable feature.

'Know where we are Boss?' Doubt in the corporal's voice. Doubt and hope. The mist restricting vision to nothing. He strode confidently along the path. To the left, open mountainside and safety. To the right, a sheer cliff dropping a thousand feet to the valley floor. They couldn't see it. Only the corporal and he knew it was there. They were disciplined to stay on the path, he argued, therefore that's what they should do. Blindly follow. In this case it would be the difference between a boring tiring march and a scary death. It wouldn't do to let them know. Just keep on marching. 'OK Boss. Scares the shit out of me not being able to see the bloody cliff.' Echoing his sentiments.

He peered down towards the river. Was this it? The place Lisa and he had rested? It looked different in the dark. Closer. Squashed in. The trees were the only things that convinced him. Moss hanging from the spiky boughs. He slid down the hillside and fell exhausted, face in the cool stream, letting the water run over his head, then taking large mouthfuls.

'Not too much. Get stomach cramps if you do.' The Instructor had gone before he could lift his head out of the water.

He sat back, resting. There was an ache in his side to add to the other injuries. A bullet had passed just that much too close, gouging a chunk of flesh out, the heat cauterizing as it went. The wound just suppurating a little. The body's defences and rebuilding schemes trying to come to his aid, trying to cope with the ravages meted out in such a short space of time. He had to continue. There was nothing left to do now, no turning back. He was totally committed. It was a battle to the death. Max or him. One of them had to go. The boy, that he could have lived with grudgingly for Lisa's sake. But not Lisa. No,

Max. Not Lisa. That was the nail that would pin Max to the floor. No excuses. Not even Lisa could persuade him otherwise now.

The fury eased the pain of his wounds, gave him another dose of energy to continue. The resolve now hardened to an indestructible degree. No going back. He stood, winced and groaned, and forced the stiffening legs to carry him on. Onwards. He could rest at the farmhouse. It wasn't far, if his memory served him right. A few miles. But he had to be careful. Watch the approaches. Max was devious and cunning.

'It's in a beautiful spot. Really lovely. Pity it doesn't have any electricity. Presumably there is running water?' Jenny, looking at the small cottage nestling against the Welsh hillside. It did look beautiful there in the summer sun. He picked her up and carried her down and into the house. Searched for the bedroom. She scowled. 'No. Not now. It's still the middle of the day.' He dumped her on the bed and felt the anger rising. Tried to control it, not wanting to spoil the first holiday they'd taken. Couldn't afford anywhere exotic. He went back outside and walked up the hill slightly and sat down looking back at the little cottage. Jenny came out and stood searching for him, gave up and went back inside.

He watched the farmhouse. Dawn wasn't far off. The tell-tale lightening of the sky hastening his actions. He wanted to be hidden by sun-up. Maybe in the loft. No. An obvious place to look. He'd wait until he got down there, then decide.

There was no movement, no sign of life, so he used the same route as before, coming out above and to the side of the farm building. He lay watching the house and the surrounding area. Especially the surrounding area. They were good, Max's men. Good, but they could be spotted because he was better. Better trained. Had better instincts, had a killer's instincts. Needed them when he came face to face with Max. It was the only thing that was going to keep him alive.

Jenny stood by the front door looking up at him. 'Playing cowboys and Indians. At your age. Jesus!' Stared at him silently, laughing, and then walked through the wall and out of sight. He went down, keeping close in to the wall, feeling the rough stone surface. Rifle ready. Dirty, but still functioning well. Checked his pouches for the grenades. Moved crablike along the wall, sliding up to the window, pausing before sneaking a look inside. Couldn't see anything. Ducked down and moved along to the corner. Waited and then moved quickly round, rifle ready. Nothing. The entire valley empty, hearing only the sounds of his breathing and the wildfowl in the air flying down to the lake.

The front room was empty. Nobody had been there since Lisa and he had spent the few hours. How long ago was that? He couldn't remember. The fatigue was catching up. Fatigue and the after-effects of an overdose of adrenalin. Light was beginning to brighten the interior. He didn't have much time before dawn caught him out.

Outside, he checked that he'd covered his tracks, covered any scuff-marks on the rocks and loose stones. Satisfied, went back inside to find a place to hide. The kitchen held no possibilities. There was the storeroom Lisa had talked about. He opened the door and went in. It was pitch black inside. No windows, the only light coming from the door and he was blocking that. He moved sideways but it didn't help. Went back into the main room and searched for a torch. Found one and went back to the store room. There was nothing special about it. It went back a long way and, at the back, was piled high with boxes, wooden crates and some old barrels. He tapped them. They were empty.

The movement at the door dropped him to one knee, the rifle coming up and his finger closing on the trigger, the rounds accurately fired to catch a man in the upper chest. There was a giggle and more scuffling. Nobody fired back at him. He doused the torch and stayed where he was, without moving. The scuffle again. Another short burst and another giggle.

'Enough. No more firing. Please.' The voice was high-pitched and sounded good-humoured. He couldn't trust anybody. 'Please. No more. I can help you.' Then where are you? Shouted so the sound reverberated around the stone walls, confusing anyone trying to pinpoint him.

The laugh. 'Only if you won't fire.' OK. Not meaning it. 'Lay your rifle down then.' It's down. The movement closer. He snatched up the rifle and fired at the figure suddenly illuminated. The rounds bounced harmlessly away. The laugh was right behind him. Close. He swung and fired again. 'I'm right here.' The voice came from beneath him. A strong arm wrenched the gun from his hand and he looked down staring into the eyes of the small dwarf he'd seen in the clearing after the deer massacre. 'No, I'm not one of the entourage. But I know who you're after. Everyone knows who you're after.' The little man paused. 'I can show you where he is.' How could he trust the man. 'You can't trust anyone else. Can you? Here.' The rifle was handed back. He brought it up and placed the muzzle against the dwarf's head. 'Go ahead. You won't find him if you do that. Never find him. But he'll find you and kill you.' He took the rifle away and let it hang by his side. The dwarf breathed a sigh of relief, gave a nervous laugh, and sat down. 'Do you want to find him?' Of course. The dwarf stood up, waved for him to follow.

Nineteen

THE DRAIN was a tight fit. He pushed the rifle ahead of him, pulling himself forward with his fingers, pushing with his toes. Inching along the pipe. Ahead the dwarf scuttled, turning to urge him on. 'Come on. This is the way. Not far now.' High-pitched excited voice in the gloom. 'She told me you'd be coming.' Lisa guiding him in, so perhaps Max was holding her against her will. Maybe Max had kidnapped her from the hollow, enticed her out? Whatever, it didn't matter now because he'd found a way in. That was what mattered.

The crawl was tearing his skin to pieces. The dwarf had offered to take the rifle, but he'd refused. The gun was his lifeline. Now he almost wished he'd given it to the misshapen creature. Ahead a light shone, a yellow spot in front. Dull yellow from a weak dusty bulb hanging in the middle of a damp forbidding grey stone-walled room. More like a dungeon. He struggled out of the pipe and stood feeble and stiff, exhausted from the crawl, his mind recovering from the near-panic of claustrophobia. The dwarf was by the door. A heavy oak wrought-iron strapped door.

'Come on. No time.' The dwarf slipped round the door. He followed into a narrow dingy passage. Rats scuttled and shrieked around the floor. He shivered, skin crawling at the sight of the thick reptile tails and the sleek grey-furred bodies. Pink eyes and noses wriggled at him. Some stood on their hind legs to sniff him as he went by. He shuddered. The little man

199

disappeared into another small hole. He followed again, crawling down this time, down the tunnel. The slope eased and they both fell out onto a bed of soft hay. Roger's head poked out through the straw bales, eyes wide. 'There's funny sounds in here.' It's the rats, he'd taunted, pulling an evil face. A large grey one shot out of the other side of the bale, stopped, looked and raced away again. Roger squealed and wriggled rapidly out, standing and running to the door. Stopped, turned and looked. He looked back at Roger, then deliberately crawled into the tunnel through the haystack. The straw scratched his face and soon the light was gone. He could only feel the way, hear the scurrying of the rats and mice, his imagination working at breakneck speed. 'David. Come out. Please.' Enjoying Roger's discomfort as always. Crawling further and then feeling the haystack cave in, sealing him in. Panic grew. Terror froze him solid, saving his life. Roger watched in glee as his father beat him, the rescuers standing by.

He was aware of a large cavernous enclosure. Slime-covered sewer-reeking walls and the filth and squalor met his eyes. The cavern stretched out of sight into the gloom. What he could see with blurring vision was lit by stakes burning in holders on the walls and by individual fires and some lanterns. The multi-layered floor, divided like steps, provided room for a couple of dwellings. He could feel his head throbbing, and closed his eyes. The vision remained. Plastic and metal shanty shacks perched precariously on the edge. Water, probably sewerage judging by the smell, was everywhere. He thought he was going to throw up, felt the nausea rising. Opened his eyes and still the vision remained, revolving slowly, settling on the dwarf. People milled around the little man beckoning for him to follow. Hardly people. Legless, armless, sightless, moaning, groaning, has-been people, now just travesties of their former selves, appearing and disappearing in waves with the nausea. 'Come on. We've got a long way to go.' The dwarf leading on, stumpy legs rapidly covering the ground. Eels dropped from an outlet drain, falling down the wall at his back onto the floor to squirm away and into the main sewer. He half suppressed a cry of horror. The creatures appeared again, giggling at his discomfort.

The dwarf stopped and turned impatiently, seemed to grow huge, shrank back again, turned as he stumbled after the figure, brushing aside the creatures pawing at him from all sides. They moved away leaving the stench behind, their decaying bodies falling in flakes of dead skin onto the floor of the cavern, their moaning and mumbling dying away as the effort was expended. They stood, squatted, sat, waited to see what he would do. He stumbled forward trying to refocus on the dwarf. 'Follow me.' He did. Followed behind the strange little man, through further ranks of foetid stinking degenerating bodies, climbed the sewer-wet steps to a small ledge, feeling his leaden feet slow and stop. 'Come on David. Don't be a drag. Keep up.' Mother looking back down the path at him impatiently. He didn't want to go on the hike. Disliked the idea intensely. 'Please hurry up. Not far to go and we can picnic.' He scuffed along, head down and sulking, thinking of his new bike and the fun he could be having with his friends. 'You'll get left behind and lost if you don't keep up. And then anything can happen.' Father threatening, angry furrowed brow, sweating with the exertion of carrying the rucksack.

He felt the clawing tearing grasp of a thousand hands dragging at him from behind. Screamed and staggered up the steps, past the dwarf and on. Stopped, exhausted, swaying and falling, the cavern spinning around. Tried to refocus his mind, to drag it back from lightheaded exhaustion. The dwarf appeared beside him, offering a water canteen.

'Here, drink. We must keep moving. There's a long way to go.' He drank the liquid greedily, dwarf watching, slowly smiling. He felt the water enter every part of his body, rejuvenating. Looking back down the steps at the swelling mass of obscenely crippled human life, forcing the image away, forcing them back with his power. The dwarf looked past him intently and grasped his arm. 'We must keep moving. Not this way. We'll have to backtrack. Ignore the creatures. I'll deal with that.' He followed again. Lightfooted. Surer than before. Facing the horrors, brushing them aside. They screamed, pushed, glared, howled. A one-eyed, rag-covered excuse for a man, shouted at him. 'You are supposed to rescue us. She said you would.' The dwarf moved him gently aside.

'He will. He is. Let us through.' Moving past One-Eye who fell into step beside him, single eye piercing into him, filling his vision with a great bloodshot eye. All around the scuttling sound grew, accompanied by an excited chattering, hoarse whispering that resounded around his head. The dwarf turned to him again, noticing he was slipping behind, slowing down. The little man retraced his steps, pushed the one-eyed man aside, stood as the rest melted away into the shadows. The whispering remaining. The dwarf reached into his bag and handed him bread and cheese, signalling him to eat. He suddenly felt the hunger pangs lancing into his belly and ate ravenously.

'I'll show you the way. The route into the castle.' The dwarf was joined by the one-eyed man. They talked running, occasionally glancing in his direction. Sometimes, it seemed they were right beside him. At other times a great distance away. He felt his head swelling and contracting. Swelling and contracting. Waves of sleep and nausea washed over him. Down on the floor of the cavern through the flickering gloom there was lots of movement. Shouts, screams and some laughter. He finished the bread and cheese and drank from a flagon the dwarf had handed him. The beer tasted strong and good.

'Let's go. Come on.' The dwarf shaking him awake. How long had he been asleep? 'Not long.' He stared around. The cavern was brighter. Lighter. Lit by thousands of torches, noise of hundreds of voices all talking, arguing at once. The dwarf still leading the way, downwards this time. Down into the mass of pushing, yelling, stinking, decaying flesh. Music came from somewhere bubblegum music that whined from tinny speakers crackling away in competition to the huge fire on the floor of the cavern and the screaming, laughing, cackling demented crowd.

He hated shopping. The noise. The heat. The smell. Especially the bazaar. That was the worst. Just pushing, shoving and the constant stream of shouted Arabic. Mother grasping him firmly, ensuring he didn't get loose and go back to the car. That's where he'd rather be. Reading a comic by himself. He knew that the only reason he was brought along on the shopping trips was to carry the bags. A chore to end all chores. Hateful duty. He thought of the delights of the comic superheroes waiting for him and cheered up a little. Idly turning his attention to the haggling stall-owners and the pushing shoving chadar-clad woman. Past fish stalls with whole shark, tuna, sting-rays, squid and octopus lying bloody and oozing. Next to fresh fruit, dates, figs, melons, grapes and myriad other exotica. Superhero flying to his rescue and sharks coming alive and wriggling along the ground towards him. Jaws snapping. 'David stop dreaming and carry the bag properly.' Pulling faces and walking along behind.

The dwarf stopped suddenly at the edge of a small arena. Stopped, then continued along around the edge. In the centre by the fire a girl stood, her face and head covered with a white wispy veil, her features impossible to make out. Her body was covered in a long multi-coloured, multi-layered sari. It covered her from head to toe. Next to her stood a slavering hunchback, half-naked, body hairy and glistening with oil. The music swelled, talking ceased and he felt himself drawn into the centre of the arena, the only observer. Slowly the girl started to move her hips, then her body to the music, slowly running her hands up and down her body then taking off one of the layers of clothing. A shoulder appeared and the crowd moaned with pleasure and anticipation. The hunchback took the garment, draping it with care over his arm.

The girl began to move around the arena, taking off layers of cloth, returning to the centre to drape them over the hunchback, who snarled and slavered as she approached, sometimes reaching a hand to paw at her now bare white delicate arm. He stood transfixed, catching her perfume as she passed, inhaling deeply, lightheadedly. Appalled and aroused by the sight. The Dwarf was forgotten. The girl stood slowly, swaying, and removed the last layer. She ran her hands up her thighs and body, over immaculate breasts and into the air, walking back to drape the cloth over the hunchback. Her veil was still intact. He wondered at her perfect body. Wondered how she was here. The hunchback shambled over to a table, placed the discarded clothes and ran back to the centre of the arena. The girl was kneeling now then moved onto all fours. The hunchback stood, head thrown back and howled, arms outstretched towards the roof, then quickly stripped off the loincloth and plunged into the girl, who screamed and writhed. The hunchback clung onto her grunting and snarling whilst the crowd bayed and screeched with pleasure.

'Jesus, look at this David. Look at it. Ever seen anything like this before?' He shook his head, feeling the youthful erection. Embarrassed lest anyone else in the darkened strip club should see. Watching fascinated and disturbed as the girl, inches from his face, slowly exposed herself to him. Pink wet flesh, he catching the odour and feeling sick. Suddenly rushing from the club out into the fresh air amid the laughter.

The hunchback roared and bucked, shouted primeval birth sounds to the air. The girl writhed and moaned against him, stiffened and then fell forward onto her face. The hunchback let her go, stood up, wrapped the loincloth about his body and, stooping, picked her up. The veil slipped and he had to close his eyes to prevent the sudden nausea from boiling over. The girl had no face. Just holes for eyes, nose, mouth and ears. She was completely bald. Quickly the hunchback covered her up again and hurried away.

'What are you waiting for? Come on. There's no time to lose. None at all.' The dwarf tugging at his sleeve. He looked around for the girl. The arena was empty. The fire crackled away and lit the menacing presence of the one-eyed man surrounded by his henchmen. They moved toward him. He felt the comforting weight of the Armalite and shifted it across to the other hand, feeling in his pouches for the grenades. The crowd melted away into the shadows. He looked for the dwarf, now striding away towards the far side of the arena, shouting back at him. 'Hurry up. There's still a way to go and the others are getting impatient.' He forced his feet forward, shaking his head to clear it. Shake the heaviness away, the double vision, telling himself he'd be able to rest soon when the task was finished. When he'd found Max and destroyed him. When he'd found Lisa. Rest then.

Finally the dwarf stopped and indicated a dry area above the floor of the cavern, away from the floating river of sewage. The crowd behind stopped as he turned and showed them the rifle. One-Eye seemed to grow, enlarge, distend and contract again, the single eye never shifting its gaze, even as he talked to the dwarf. 'They don't trust you. Don't think you'll get them out.'

He glanced back around the cavern. The crowds were dispersing, as always back into the shadows, into the slime and the filth. He suddenly wanted to get away, to get out. Lisa wasn't here. He had the growing sense of entrapment. The dwarf had lured him here to help them. What then? What if he did? What would happen to him then? The questions whirled around with the floating vision of the dwarf's face and the reeking hell hole. One-Eye crouched a short distance away, watching. He shifted his Armalite again and laid it across his knees. It felt very heavy. The pouches sat firmly against his hips, the importance of these items now paramount.

'Your rifle is your best friend. Your closest friend. It goes everywhere with. You cosset it. Pamper it. Care for it. Love it. Because it will save your life. All you have is what you carry. Never, never let any of it out of your sight. Is that understood Trowse?' The instructor standing tall and menacing over him. He nodding in eager agreement. Running his ignorant fingers over the unfamiliar metal. Feeling the cold smoothness of the barrel.

'These people need to be back "on top". You are the only one who can destroy Max.' So that they could continue to howl and bray at depraved spectacles, transfer the squalor to the surface and contaminate the rest of the countryside with it. Purposefully infect it so that that disease and deformity were the norm, he thought to himself, convinced now that they would have to die. One-Eye shifted warily. The dwarf looked carefully at him, offering water. He was suddenly suspicious, feeling his head throbbing and struggling to control his vision.

'You will help us won't you? I'll show you the only way out of here. You'll never find it alone.' He nodded, his head like a block of lead, waving almost uncontrollably on his shoulders. A nagging thought bubbled around just beneath the surface of his consciousness. A disturbing thought, if only he could grasp it. Hold onto it. Examine it.

The dwarf produced a map and waved it in front of him, the flickering torchlight throwing strange shadows dancing across the paper. It showed the route out of the cavern complex to the castle through the main drains. Times were pencilled in, showing when it was safe to enter the drains. They led out to the main dining area. He tried hard to concentrate. The dwarf passed him more water for his dry throat. The nagging thought struck him and he stared at the water canteen, then at the dwarf and One-Eye who were bent over the map. He pretended to drink and handed the water back. The dwarf smiled and pointed to the map. Slowly he dragged his eyes down.

'We go in this way. The tunnels are very narrow and long but you'll be fine. Left here and once inside it's up to you.' He was trying to take in the details but the dwarf folded the map and put it away.

There was something crawling over his feet. He looked down with difficulty and saw an old hag, naked, staring up at him, toothless, with bony, taloned fingers and large flat wrinkled breasts. These she held out to him, grinning. He forced her away, blotting out the image. Struggling to retain control of his mind. To fight the insidious chemicals, force them back.

'They'll use all sorts of methods to catch you out. To grind

206

you down. Break you. Destroy your mind. We euphemistically call it tactical questioning. Don't be fooled. Torture goes under many guises, many names. Sometimes you may not be aware that you are being tortured. That's the dangerous time.' He tried to remember the advice. The training. Tried to remember this was only an exercise as for the tenth time the water was poured over the hood, seeping in through the sacking and choking him, drowning him. He tried to remember that these were his friends and colleagues eagerly trying to drown him. Tried to hold out, to fight the terror, to fight them.

Holding on was imperative here. Now. As the underworld people rested, slept and ignored him. Memorized the plan? Hold onto it. Fix it in the mind. Feeling it slip away as the images burst around. Forcing them back. Sweating with the effort. Concentrating on the Armalite and the comforting discomfort of the grenades digging into his hips through the pouches and clothing. Invoking the image of Max and the anger. Above all the anger.

Eyes closing. Forcing them open. Closing again. Head reeling. 'Really David. I hope that teaches you a lesson.' Vomiting into the sink, head held by his mother. Eyes watering, bad taste in the mouth and head pounding from the alcohol, the whisky stolen from his father's bar and drunk as part of a midnight feast. Vowing with each retch never to drink again. Never.

Twenty

'OK, DAVID. The game's over. Your game's over. You've had your fun. Now, it's time to take stock. Now, it's my turn.' Max's voice ringing through the tunnel, ringing out among the corpses and the still-smoking Armalite. The dwarf lay at his feet, a bewildered expression on his dead face. One-Eye gurgled bloody death into the sewer and fell into the thick slime. The howling grew, drowning out the chanting and Max's voice. He turned and tossed a grenade into the crawling mass of sightless slobbering creatures and wriggled into the tunnel. The exploding vibrations banged against his ears off the confined walls. The screams of pain and terror filling the tunnel. He crawled, panting frantically, onwards. Find Lisa. He must find Lisa.

'We'll find you, David. You know we'll find you. There's no escape. You know that.' He ignored the diminishing voice. The sneer. The unsure command. Thought that Max sounded unsure. Had to convince himself for his own survival. Had to believe in himself. Especially now. Had to carry on. Nearly there. Nearly with Lisa. Max wasn't going to win. Which way did the diagram show the route? Come on, think. He shook himself, growling in the dark. Became the animal he destroyed. There was a scuttling behind him and bony fingers closed around his ankles. He cried out and kicked viciously, feeling teeth or bone crunch under the boot, heard the pained whimpering. Kicked again and again, unable to turn in the

208

confines of the tunnel. Grinding, crushing the bone into pulp, until there was only the sound of his own sobbing, gasping for breath. He crawled on, feeling his nails rip and tear back. Lancing pain shooting up his hands and arms. Ignored it. Continued.

He pushed the torch on in front, the flames licking up against the wet sides of the tunnel. Every now and then the squeal of a rat and the stink of burned hair and flesh as he poked the torch into the firm grey body. The squealing stopped as the rat rolled over dead. He crawled over the body. Up ahead the junction of tunnels. What was it the dwarf had said? First tunnel on the left. He had to squeeze his way round the right-angled corner. At one point he thought he was stuck but the next tunnel proved slightly wider. He paused. Took a hand grenade out of his pouch and pulling the pin sent the little object bouncing, hissing back down the tunnel he'd just left. He crawled quickly for three seconds and then lay flat, covering his ears. The sound bashed around him and he could hear the wails of wounded creatures. He carried on. The torch was getting low, so he moved faster. Creeping through the slime on the floor of the tunnel. Hoping that his timing was right. He thought it was, because he'd killed the dwarf at the entrance to the tunnel as they were about to start. Saw the startled look in his face, and nearly got caught by the one-eyed man. Nearly, but he was quicker. Far quicker. And he had a gun.

'David. D-a-v-i-d.'

He lay still. The voice was coming from behind. The sound travelling through the maze of tunnels. Max knew he was in here, but he didn't know where. The sound of his name drifted to nothing, and the drip of the water off the walls was all that was left. He moved on. Afraid now that the torch would give out before he got to the lever on the wall. He hit the end of the tunnel with a thud. The torch extinguishing itself against the wall. The darkness complete. Not one speck of light anywhere. He couldn't even see his hand held up against his nose. The rats started to crawl over his body. He could feel their inquisitive noses and their sharp claws wandering at will over him. He writhed and struggled to get them off. They squealed and dug their teeth into his thrashing limbs. Where was that lever!

He fought his way back down the tunnel, mashing furry bodies against the walls. Screaming, fighting, feeling for the lever. Hands roaming the sides trying to locate it. Where was it? Where had the dwarf said it would be? He hadn't. He just said it was on the side. He didn't say where. Panic was starting to take the place of reason. Walls sheer with slime, rat-covered, scratching, clawing, screaming panic.

It was on the right-hand side. The dwarf had said it was on the right-hand side. He mashed another rat into the rough stone and felt along the right-hand side. Then suddenly there it was. He pulled. Hard. In desperation. The panel slid aside and he tumbled into the dining-hall. The quiet, empty dining-hall. Dark and silent.

He squatted in the corner. Shaking, sobbing, trying to compose himself. Trying to bring his reason back. Think of the Mission. Remember. His whole body shook. His skin crawled and blood ran from the bites and scratches. Bile rose up his throat and he vomited into the corner, the retching racking his body, forcing the blood up into his head with the strain, turning his face red then blue. It stopped and he sat back shivering against the wall. Pale and weak from the terror of the tunnel.

There was no sound in the hall. No sound in the castle. He stood shakily to his feet. Stood still, listening, gripping the Armalite. He checked the magazine. Changed it for a full one, and looked to see if there were any grenades left. Two. The silence was almost as unnerving as the screaming chaos below. He waited for the madness to begin again. He waited but there was nothing. Just the empty hall laughing at him.

He wandered into the centre and looked around. The tables were in position and laid. Everything ready for another banquet. The light night sky sent shafts through the tall windows into the hall, spotlighting him. He moved into the shadows. Moved carefully over to the door, the open door, went through and into the galleried room, still keeping to the shadows. It, too, was empty; the fire laid but not lit, the drinks and glasses waiting patiently for takers. He tested the atmosphere. Let his senses test for any signs of any other presence. Nothing. He poured himself a large Scotch and went back to the shadows, drinking carefully, slowly, eyes constantly flicking round the room.

'Whisky or brandy can have a useful effect. Especially when there is a need to calm down, to slow down the body's responses just that little bit. Stop yourself from jumping out of your skin. The danger is always the dependence on alcohol.' The doctor had toasted him from the hip flask. Washed his hands and stood looking down at the body bag. 'It helps in moments like this. Here.' Passing the flask across. He took it and drank, spluttering on the harsh liquid. The doctor looked disapproving and took the flask back. 'For Christ's sake don't spill any. Sacrilege.'

The doctor was right, the whisky did help. Gradually the trembling eased. He finished the glass, placed it on the floor by the wall and went towards the gallery steps. The wood creaked gently under his foot. Not loudly. He walked close to the edge, carefully testing the steps for creaks before putting his full weight on them.

He stood by the gallery rail looking down into the hall, and thought for a moment that he could see himself standing there that night. There, in the middle of the room, dodging Max's hologram figures. But the shadows from the high windows called him a liar. He looked around the gallery for the control panel. There must be a control panel somewhere. There wasn't. At least not that he could find.

'I know you're here, David, and I'm coming for you now. There's no way you're getting out of here. I'm coming for you, David.' The voice blasted right into his ears from the hidden speakers. He fell back against the wall, covering his ears. The tinny ringing tones banged around inside the room then went, cascading away through the dining-hall and the corridors of the castle. Max probably had speakers everywhere, to terrify the victim into believing that Max could see where he was. But he knew that Max didn't know exactly where he was; if he had, the game would have been over. But it wasn't and he had the upper hand now, because Max wasn't sure anymore. He'd rattled Max by getting this far. Into the very heart of the empire. Now he was going to find Lisa and destroy the empire. Destroy Max.

'You haven't got a chance, David. Give up now. Make it easy on yourself. Why do this?'

No, Max, you aren't going to get me like that, he thought. No way. He edged to the stairs once more and crept down back to the room.

'Lisa doesn't want you, David. Doesn't want you. Do you understand?' Not even that way. There was no way he was going to be suckered into the trap. Back into the dining-hall and through another door into the huge main entrance hall. He took the stairs two at a time, his soft-soled boots barely making a sound on the stone steps. Lisa must be up here somewhere. In one of the rooms in the tower. In one of the towers.

He saw her. Briefly. Saw her in the half-light of the dark corridor. Thought he saw her vanishing round the corner at the end. He ran shouting her name. Ran, sprinted down the endless corridor until finally he fell round the corner.

'D-A-V-I-D. David. D-a-v-i-d.' Whispering from the wall. His name on her lips softly uttered. But where was she? 'D-a-v-i-d. I'm here. Come on. D-a-v-i-d.' He ran on down the next length of seemingly endless corridor. They were waiting for him round the next corner and he was almost too slow. The Armalite bucked and kicked in his hands and the three men fell, gurgling, and disappeared in front of him. No time to figure it out, just onwards. Find Lisa.

'David. You can't get her. She's not for you. I've got her.'

Still trying it on. Couldn't get him any other way. He allowed himself a barking laugh and the spear carved a neat V out of his arm before clanging off the wall and falling away down the corridor. He threw himself to the floor and two more narrowly missed him. Sound-triggered. So that was Max's intruder alarm system.

'D-a-v-i-d. Please. P-l-e-a-s-e. Help me.' Pleading. Her voice, imploring him. He tore a strip of bandage out of his first-aid pouch, wrapped the wound, and crouched by the wall, staring into the gloom of the corridor stretching away. Away to where? The voice still quietly begging him. Was it her voice or was it another of Max's tricks? Could he afford to ignore the plea? Weighing the odds against what he knew Max capable of.

Crouching, then moving slowly forward, careful not to make any sound. Just follow the voice. Allow the voice to lead him. Knowing the possibilities, but having to find out. He had to know. Had to find her. Loved her. Wanted her. Driven on by his unreasoning emotion.

'Fool. Unfeeling fool.' The laugh he knew well. He turned and fired into Jenny. Missed. She'd moved. Laughing still. 'Grow up, David. Grow up. Stop playing child games.' Amanda appeared beside her. They both laughed at him. 'Look at yourself. Take a good look at yourself.' He fired again and the breech-block slammed against an empty chamber. He had no more rounds. He threw the useless weapon away and pulled out the grenades.

'Oh dear! Do we have to go through this nonsense?' Amanda, tired expression. 'Let him find her. He'll know then. Serve him right.' They vanished and he looked around, haunted.

'I know where she is, Mister.' The boy stood there. Where did he come from? Max killed the boy. He saw it. 'No, he just wanted me out of the way. Come.' He followed the little figure. Bewildered. Bemused. Confused. He wanted to stop but found he couldn't. Seemed to be dragged forward. They came to a door and the boy opened it and went in. He could hear the moaning before he saw Lisa. She lay on the bed sighing and groaning with pleasure as the hunchback moved in and out of her. No! Screamed out. The little boy turned to him.

'I told you to stay with me, but you didn't listen. You never listened to me.' He went away, leaving him stuck to the spot. Lisa looked at him, smiled and closed her eyes in ecstasy. He stood, forced to watch.

'Well, what's it like then? Hey. Watching her make love with someone else and loving it. Look. She loves it.' Jenny's taunting tones whispered into his ear. 'You shouldn't be upset. You can't feel anything. You don't care about anything. You and Max together make a great pair. He at least has some understanding. But you have nothing.'

'She's right, son. You don't care for anybody. You never did. Now it's your turn to feel. To be on the receiving end.' His father stepped aside and his mother looked reproachfully, moving aside also. The dwarf strutted to the centre of the room followed by the one-eyed man. The hunchback finished with a grunt and slipped out of Lisa, his huge throbbing purple penis dangling obscenely, dripping. The one-eyed man leapt onto Jenny onto Lisa with a howl of pleasure. Jenny was Lisa. She cried out as he entered her and grasped him to her. Panting and thrusting him deep into her. Lisa was Jenny, both one. The same.

'You shouldn't have done it. We only wanted help. Your help. We helped you and you turned against us for no reason.' The dwarf pulled the girl and the hag into the room and they fell on him. He tried to scream but the sound wouldn't come. He felt the clothes ripped off him and the talons of the hag dig into his testicles, tearing, ripping. The girl took him in her mouth, the featureless face mocking him.

'Enough!' The voice cracked out through the cacophony of groaning and crying. Max stood at the end of the room. Naked. Long hair falling down over his shoulders, beard glistening in the light from the window. The sunlight. Suddenly he was free to move. The girl and the hag shrank back. One-Eye slowly moved to a stop. Lisa writhed and sighed. Max walked slowly down the room towards him, deliberately, antagonizingly slow. 'Well, David. The end of the line, I think. What do you make of it then? Any of your questions been answered? No, I don't think so.' He listened to the soft commanding voice. Was completely frozen by the presence of the man. By his body. Noticed that Max was getting aroused as the distance between them lessened. Felt himself rise. Felt he wanted this man now. Max stopped just in front of him. They faced each other. There was a silence in the room. He could see Jenny watching avidly. Lisa? Which? Amanda, mouth slightly open. On the bed, Lisa watched with tears in her eyes. He didn't know anymore.

'Well, David. What do you think? Shall we make love? You know that's what you want. Don't you? I can tell.' Max let his eyes drop and he could feel the pulsating ache. Max stretched out his hand and he could feel the fingers tighten round him. Max smiled into his eyes. He could see his reflection in Max's eyes. Could see but didn't notice. Max's head disappeared from view and he felt Max's mouth close over him. What was it he'd seen in Max's eyes? Then the realization of what was happening started to catch up with him. He backed away and smashed a fist into Max's face. Max disappeared in a shower of glass.

'Look over there, David.' The dwarf. He turned and saw Max. Saw himself in the mirror. Max and himself. One. 'That's right, David. You're in love with yourself. Love. Hate. Both.' He turned and threw the two remaining hand-grenades into the centre of the room. The room and everyone in it disappeared in the explosion.

He felt himself falling. Plunging, plummeting, falling, falling. Down and down.

The car was where he had left it. He sat, crying into the soft leather. Tears welling up and falling down his cheeks. Huge glistening drops that rolled down his naked flesh. His body shook with sobs. Heartrending sobs. Tears for himself. Poison pouring out of his body, bottled-up emotion. Years of bottled-up emotion spilling out in the howling screaming uncontrollable crying. It came in waves beating at his soul. A soul he knew he had. Now knew he had. He cried for his lost years, for the love and the feeling he'd lost all this time. That never could be replaced.

Gradually the crying eased. He felt empty. Freshened. Drained and yet somehow full. For the first time in his life. The landscape dissolved slowly about him. He welcomed it. Was no longer afraid.

The doctor straightened up and went out into the hall. Jenny sat calm. Expressionless. The doctor paused, watching this woman. He looked back into the patient's room, sighed, and walked over to where she sat. She turned slowly to the sound of the footsteps. The doctor stopped in front of her.
   'You can see him now.' Her face lit up. The doctor placed a hand on her shoulder. 'Please. He's made it through the critical stage, but there's still a long way to go. I don't know if he'll pull through.' Jenny stood up and went into the room. David lay pale, thin, barely breathing, on the bed. She stood, then sat and took his hand. He felt the hand stroking his fingers. Got out of the car and walked towards the feeling. Jenny saw his eyes flicker, close, then open again. He looked at her. Looked for the man opposite, the man with the shaved head. The room was empty except for Jenny.
   'I've been away Jenny. I've been away.'
   'I know, darling. I know.'
   Lisa leaned over smiling and pressed the pillow over his soundlessly screaming face.